The Chieftain's Daughter

The Chieftain's Daughter

THE IRISH WITCH SERIES, BOOK 3

LEIGH ANN EDWARDS

TULE
PUBLISHING

DEDICATION

I am dedicating this book to my four precious grandchildren. To Darien, for your humour and quit wit, to Daniella for your beautiful smile and amazing hugs, to Grayson for your infectious laugh and keeping me entertained, and to Novak for your mischievous grin and affectionate manner.

I hope one day you truly know how amazingly special and wonderfully unique each of you are to me. I have a cherished relationship with all of you and I'm so grateful to be a part of your lives. You bring me great happiness. When you hug me with such obvious love, or when I see the smiles on your beautiful faces when we are together, that is when I feel absolute joy and purpose! Thanks for keeping me young and bringing new magic to my life. You are among my heart's greatest treasures, my four sweeties! Love you forever! <3 <3 <3 <3

Acknowledgements

I would once again like to express my deep gratitude to Danielle Rayner, former Editorial Assistant with Tule, for believing in The Irish Witch Series and recommending my books to Tule Publishing. Thanks for all your help with my many questions and for always being in my corner. I am so thankful to have met you, and I wish you all the very best of luck in your future endeavors.

I would also like to send a huge thanks to Meghan Farrell, Managing Editor at Tule, who has also always been so patient, competent and willing to assist me in numerous ways as well. I truly appreciate it!

Thank you to Lindsey Stover, Marketing and Editorial Manager at Tule, for everything you've done. I am so grateful for all your assistance, your great promotional ideas and your quick responses to my many emails.

Thank to Shae Aremu, Editorial Assistant for all the many ways you have helped with getting The Chieftain's Daughter to print.

I'd like to acknowledge the content and copy editors I have worked with for all their hard work and expertise in refining my manuscripts.

I am continue to very grateful to Ravven for designing the amazingly beautiful and intriguing book covers for my series. I've had so many positive comments about your lovely cover designs.

Thanks to my husband, my two daughters, and to all my wonderful family and friends for the endless ways you have encouraged and supported me and my writing throughout the years. I could not have gotten to this extremely exciting and rewarding point as an author without each of you being there for me.

Many thanks to the valued readers who have been drawn into my novels. I'm so pleased you have become intrigued with Alainn and Killian, their love, and their lives. I hope all of you continue on this wonderful journey with me and that the Irish Witch Series will go on for as long as it brings magic to its readers.

Chapter One

A S JAGGED STREAKS of lightening illuminated her unfamiliar surroundings, Alainn O'Brien swiftly ran to take cover behind a nearby bush. As she crouched low, hoping to remain concealed, a deafening crack of thunder rumbled ominously across the dark sky. She was nearly breathless. Her soggy garments felt heavy and frigid against her skin. She shivered uncontrollably and fought to stem the angry tears brimming in her eyes. The rain continued to pelt down with a new ferocity and soon the raindrops were replaced by ice pellets that bruised her arms as she shielded her head.

"Use your abilities woman!" A mighty voice boomed above her nearly as loud as the thunder. "Protect yourself and show me these great powers I have been assured you possess."

Alainn's fury grew at hearing the demanding arrogance of the male voice.

She had vowed he would not compel her to reveal her abilities. She heard the whizzing, popping sounds before she smelled the unusual scent upon the air. A streak of fire flashed through the black sky and hit the bush beside her. She watched in horror as it burst into flames. The sleeve of her garment sizzled as though a hot iron had just been pressed upon the wet cloth. She flinched as the heat burned her arm and she quickly jumped away from the flaming brambles.

"You are admittedly assigned to be my guardian and protector and this is how you would protect me?" She raged. "Was I taken against my will from my home... from my beloved husband on the very day we were wed, simply so that you might inflict fear and pain upon me?" Her voice shook as she screamed.

"You have forced my hand, woman. It is you who have brought this fate upon yourself...you and your stubborn insistence to keep your alleged abilities hidden... and your constant attempts to escape and hide from me."

"I will not partake in this absurdity simply to amuse or entertain you. Not ever!" she replied in a voice that shrieked with emotion.

"Are you so damnably simple or dull-witted that you will not be driven to protect yourself, woman? Though it is true enough humans are undoubtedly weak and inferior with limited intelligence, I was led to believe you were of a higher breed than most. Perhaps I was misled or Aine was biased in her opinion because of her blood connection to you!"

"You pompous coward!" She stood now holding her arm where the tender skin continued to sting unrelentingly from the deep burn. She stared up at the rumbling clouds and bellowed. "So brave are you to send your thunder and lightning, to create your unfavorable weather, but you remain hidden away. Are you unattractive to view, unappealing to the eye, so hideously disfigured, if a mere human were to witness your deformity the repulsion would cause certain death... is it that you are simply plain and unimpressive, unworthy of the great status given to you? Could it be possible you actually fear me and wouldn't dare to be close enough that I might actually use my powers against you?" She baited.

Her outburst was followed only by silence. However, she did notice the sky had finally begun to lighten, and the wind and rain had abruptly stopped. She hesitantly called upon her own powers and willed her garments to dry, and her damaged skin to heal. Feeling more in control of her disposition and her abilities, she decided to truly put them to use. She created a swirling veiled mist that enshrouded her completely before she wished herself away from the prying eyes of the obstinate and unpredictable god.

ALAINN HAD HOPED to be transported to Aine, the fairy princess and Celtic goddess who was protector of women, the being who had taken her to this realm of the gods. But regrettably she found herself outside the grand castle where she had first wakened when she arrived in this realm. Allowing her anger to abate and her fear to lessen, she glanced around at her foreign surroundings.

This location was not without appeal. In truth it was remarkably lovely and if she allowed herself to feel anything beyond loneliness and resentment, she would grudgingly admit it was stunningly beautiful here. The trees were surely ancient, the trunks massive, twisted, and gnarled in intriguing displays, the branches unbelievably immense. The grass was of the deepest shade of green perhaps akin only to the variety found in the fairy glade. She bent to touch it and found it was unusually soft. She sat down upon it and inhaled deeply, taking in every detail of her unusual surroundings. The ground was dotted with a scattered array of peculiar, yet beautiful, wildflowers in brilliant shades. Their perfume was soft and delicately pleasing to her keen sense of smell. She glanced skyward and noted the most unusual sight of the four suns, one in each direction.

The sky was now a softer shade of blue and huge fluffy clouds appeared to nearly touch the ground. A new peacefulness enveloped her. Though she was hesitant to trust it, she took several deep breaths and warily relaxed.

She was uncertain how long she had been in this realm, and her memories of how she had happened to arrive here were muddled and nearly incomprehensible. Even if she'd known how long she'd been here, she couldn't estimate if time was measured the same in this realm or altered as it was in the fairy glade. She distinctly recalled waking in a large bedchamber. She had been entirely alone and what unnerved her most was the complete absence of sound. As she peered out the open window in the chamber, she could detect not a chirp of a bird or even the rustle of wind upon the grass.

She was no longer clothed in the gown she'd remembered wearing, but in garments that were most unusual. Although there were many flowing layers, they were nearly transparent and most assuredly not of a fabric Alainn had ever seen before.

She recalled the first time she'd heard the now displeasingly familiar male voice speaking to her.

"Ahh, beautiful enchanting woman, you have finally awakened! What a deep slumber you were in! I have taken immense pleasure in watching you sleep for so many days now!"

"Days?" she replied. "That cannot be!"

"I assure you, it is so."

"Who are you? Why do you not show yourself?" She spoke to the emptiness.

The response was a deep and audible sigh. "I have been instructed to remain hidden."

"Instructed by whom? By Aine? Who are you?"

"So many questions, woman; I am the mighty Celtic god, Lugh, god of the sun, a skilled champion of a myriad of endless abilities. For now I am to be your instructor, your guardian, and protector! That is all you need know at this time."

"I do not require lessons or desire your protection. What I do require is to be returned to my world and to my husband. I have much to contend with there!"

Alainn's mind went to her new husband, Killian O'Brien. He was nephew to the Chieftain Hugh O'Brien, ruler of Castle O'Brien and the entire chiefdom. Alainn was healer at the castle and when Killian was but two and ten and she a small child of only seven years, by way of her magical abilities she had healed him from a wound that most certainly should have been fatal.

From that day forward, they had remained close friends and allies, and although it felt like she had been in love with him for as long as she could remember, it was only months ago they had begun a romantic relationship. Because she was merely a commoner and Killian was from a noble family, they had been forced to keep their love hidden. They had each been promised to others; she to a local farmer, and Killian to a dark haired Scottish lass of wealth and position, but they had purposely gone against Hugh O'Brien's orders and recently been wed. The chieftain had yet to learn of their marriage and would undoubtedly strongly disapprove of their union.

Killian and his uncle were already at odds, for Killian had learned of his uncle's misdeeds toward her. Hugh had attempted to rape her in retaliation of Killian alerting him to his intent to end his arrangement of marriage to a noble to be allowed to wed a commoner. When Killian had learned of his uncle's unscrupulous and unforgiving deeds, he had challenged his uncle to a battle to defend Alainn's honor. Her mind went to the upcoming challenge between her young courageous husband and his uncle, the chieftain, and to his uncle's recently discovered madness. The chieftain had been consuming vast quantities and unsafe combinations of herbal potions, which had surely caused his mind to become adversely affected.

But even these many nagging vexations were not as great a cause for worriment as the devastating O'Brien curse! Years earlier, Mara, the glade witch, whom Alainn had recently discovered to be her mother, had placed a harrowing and seeming irreversible curse on the O'Brien line. As a young woman already carrying Alainn, she had been viciously raped and abused, severely mistreated by Hugh's father and she had uttered a vengeful curse in hope of causing the old man to suffer. The curse ensured the O'Brien line would die out. From that day forward, all O'Brien wives either suddenly became barren, their babies were stillborn or lived only hours. Hugh and his wife had lost five babies of their own, and his brothers had lost many newborns as well.

Mara had not been killed for issuing her malevolent curse for she'd assured the old chieftain that if she died before the conditions had been met to undo the curse, then it would truly remain a blight upon his line until the O'Briens lived no more. Instead of putting her to death, the chieftain had banished the glade witch, as Mara was referred by, to live in the caves past the fairy glade and through the stone close.

She dwelled in the lonely and desolate location entirely alone, but for the old farrier's severely disfigured and malformed son whom she had raised as her own as was agreed upon in the arrangement she had made with the farrier and his wife. They were to raise Alainn as their child, but after the farrier's wife's death, and the discovery of Alainn's magical abilities, he had taken her to live with Morag, the old healer.

Now Alainn was in a most unenviable position for she carried Killian's child, an O'Brien child who was surely ill-fated due to her own mother's retaliatory curse. She lightly pressed her hand to her belly and was rewarded with a welcomed movement. She experienced great relief at knowing for now the child within her remained safe.

The boisterous resonant voice of Lugh interrupted her thoughts. "Your unborn child has most certainly not been harmed, woman!" The god assured her in an insulted tone. "You have been brought here to keep protected and to ensure the alleged powers Aine claims you possess, though surely minimal since you are, after all, only human, are tested and honed so they may aid you in times of need."

"I have no time for these irksome trivialities." She ignored his maligning comments. "You must allow me to return to my home straightaway! I am needed there most assuredly."

"There are those with dark associations who have shown

much interest in you and your magical abilities. It is the decision of the gods you will remain here and so therefore it is not to be questioned, it shall be so!" He declared in a voice laced with distinct superiority and conceit.

"I wish to have private audience with Aine, immediately!" Alainn demanded as she struggled to push through the weighty wooden portal that led out of the chamber.

"Aine is not here in this location at this time." The voice grew louder and less patient.

Alainn felt her heart lurch at hearing this and her fears continued to escalate as she stepped out and found herself literally amongst the clouds. She gasped and held tight to the stone archway fearful she would fall through the mist. She heard the condescending chuckle coming from somewhere above her.

"You, the powerful witch, descended from druid, fairy and the line of Aine, quake in fear to step amongst the clouds? Surely your abilities have been greatly exaggerated, perhaps even fabricated."

Alainn's temper began to flare as she placed one foot forward and gingerly stepped, when it held her weight, she attempted to conceal her relief and calm her fury.

"Aye, I have entirely no powers and I know nothing of magic! I possess no abilities whatsoever; surely I am of no interest you. Therefore you must send me back to my world. I demand it!"

"No, that is not a possibility and clearly not my decision

to make, woman! I am only to watch over you."

"So you are but a servant to greater gods then?" She challenged in a haughty tone.

"I am a servant to no one, woman, and there are no gods greater than I!"

"Then allow me to return to my world and be done with me!" she reasoned.

You may be beautiful and perhaps even clever for a human, but I will not fall prey to your enchantment, or your trickery."

Alainn raised her eyebrows and detected the slightest hint of uncertainty in the god's voice. She smiled to herself, closed her eyes, and vanished amongst the clouds.

⌘

APPARENTLY HER DISAPPEARANCE had greatly displeased and infuriated Lugh and from that time forward he'd followed her unrelentingly and though he never allowed himself to be seen, he was unwilling to leave her alone or give her even a moment's peace.

When she had refused over and over to reveal her abilities, she had seen firsthand what consequences resulted from his enragement. He had created the forceful thunder storm accompanied by his perilous fire balls that echoed his violent temper.

Though her arm no longer burned quite so viciously, her skin remained raised and deeply reddened. If she should reveal her abilities to Lugh, surely he would wish for her to remain here so that he might instruct her in the ways of further developing her powers. She knew time was short and she must somehow get back to her world. She would need to be much more cunning in her dealings with this god if she hoped to be allowed to return to Killian any time soon.

Chapter Two

Ireland 1536

KILLIAN GLANCED UNCERTAINLY toward his companion as they neared the churchyard. Although he was not one given to fearfulness or dread upon entering a graveyard after dark, as many people were inclined to be, he had to admit the way the long shadows fell upon the many broken and uneven grave markers this night, left his heart racing. The wind seemed to howl unnaturally through the nearby grove where they'd tethered the horses. The cemetery was overgrown and nearly concealed by the huge oaks. Though he'd lived in the area for over a decade, he'd not even been aware of its existence. As he pushed open what remained of the large, decrepitly twisted gate, it creaked loudly and added to the eeriness of the situation. He attempted to ignore the fact the hairs on his neck were standing on end.

Danhoul appeared unaffected and intent in keeping his eyes focused on the young spirit woman ahead of them. They had lost sight of her may times as she appeared and disappeared at will. At present she was but a hazy specter, barely visible in the limited moonlight. They had been following her for what seemed to be hours. Killian had considered more than once that perhaps she was taking them on a fool's chase, but he clutched tightly to the sprig of thyme within his hand. Old Morag had instructed the spirit to give this to him as a sign of assurance she could be trusted. He needed to believe it to be truth even though he was well aware Morag's body was not buried here in this churchyard.

"Why would she lead us here when Morag does not lie at rest in this location?" he whispered, finally voicing his dubiousness.

"Sure I cannot answer that as of yet, but there is most certainly a reason why she has ensured we are here," Danhoul replied.

"And your abilities of second sight cannot assist you in this?" Killian whispered once more.

"As you may have observed in instances with your wife, clairvoyance is not always precise, especially when dealing with supernatural beings."

Killian smiled and thought how odd it was that they were discussing this subject as though it were as commonplace as speaking of the weather.

Finally they heard a bemused feminine voice before them as the female specter spoke. "Why is it the two of you grown men whisper here within the gravestones, 'tis not as though you'll waken anyone who rests here!"

"Could you explain to us why we are here in this long forgotten churchyard when 'tis not anywhere near Morag's grave?" Killian asked ignoring her humorous comment.

The young woman's silhouette began to take solid form again now that they were not moving. As Killian looked at her, he once more noted her unusual blue eyes and how similar they were to Alainn's distinctly beautiful eyes. His heart felt heavy with concern for his new bride, with not knowing if she was truly being protected after being taken away by the Celtic goddess, Aine.

"My mother would see no harm come to your wife, Killian O'Brien! Sure, it is best she is not here at this time."

Nodding to the spirit woman, his face registered his doubts on that count.

"It would appear I am at a disadvantage, being the only one who does not lay claim to the gift of hearing people's thoughts." Killian's sarcasm was evident.

"Why did you bring us here?" Danhoul asked this time, since the spirit had yet to answer Killian's previous query. "Why are we not at the old healer's grave if she has employed you to take us to her?"

"The portal to the spirit world nearest Morag's grave is watched closely by dark entities. They are preventing her from making contact with Alainn. They will use all methods of evil to make certain Morag is silenced. Anyone, human or spirit, who attempts to assist her will be in grave peril, I fear! 'Tis why I searched for such a lengthy time to find an abandoned churchyard, one no longer remembered or frequented by humans from this world for perhaps two centuries or more."

"Are you not in danger as well, then?" Killian dared to ask the spirit woman.

"Aye, it could be so, but I am not as vulnerable as many for I have carried my magical abilities with me to the beyond. You are a chivalrous sort to fear for me, young O'Brien." She smiled at his concern for her.

"So, we are to enter the spirit world then?" Killian continued without acknowledging her comment.

"Nay, 'tis not advised, but as a last resort it may be so." The spirit spoke on, "Morag has made many attempts to return to the world of the living. She was set upon being present at your recent marriage; she managed to materialize for mere moments, but the dark spirits would not allow her to draw near to Alainn. I will attempt to summon Morag, for perhaps she can make contact with us now that your new wife is no longer in this realm."

The young spirit woman moved to the center of the graveyard, floating wispily just above the ground. Her long flowing skirts skimmed lightly over the toppled grave markers and she stopped before a particular stone. She spoke in a language Killian did not recognize in a voice that unnerved him. His green eyes filled with wonder as the stone began to move. His eyes grew wider and he glanced at Danhoul, again in hopes the other man would offer some explanation of what was transpiring.

" 'Tis the grave of Morag's ancient ancestor, one unknown even to the old healer herself until after her death. Perhaps she will be capable of appearing here or sending her message through another spirit at this location." The spectral woman informed them.

Both men watched on with trepidation as the stone moved, the ground rumbled, and the remnants of what surely was once a wooden coffin were cast aside. They waited to see what form of creature might spring forth from the open grave. Ainna, the spectral woman who was Alainn's maternal grandmother stood watching as well. Killian crossed himself and prayed it would be the old healer who would reveal herself to them. They all appeared taken aback when, instead of the skeletal wraith they might have expected to emerge from the grave, the large imposing figure of the recently murdered Ramla, loomed before them. His life had been ended while attempting to assist Alainn. He now appeared as he did in life, wearing the same garments as when he'd been killed, still stained with his blood.

"The old healer cannot come to you at this time—she is imprisoned by those with dark alliances. She has sent me with a warning for you to stay distanced from all portals to the spirit world, for you would surely meet much harm. You must leave now and make haste!"

"Sure there must be something more we can do!" Killian insisted. "Can Morag not simply inform you of the important message she had hoped to convey to us, regarding the proof of Alainn's paternity?"

"There is no time; you must leave this place at once!" Ramla's voice grew louder and more insistent.

"But..." Killian stopped his protest mid-sentence and stared around him. He saw that Danhoul was doing the same. Soon all the grave markers began to shake and become unturned. Many of the stones and large crosses toppled against others and crumbled as they loudly smashed together. Ainna, the spirit woman's regretful expression was quickly replaced by one of fear as she began to turn to mist.

"If and when I am permitted, I shall return to assist you," she whispered to the two men as she faded away before their eyes.

"Go now!" Ramla warned once more. "Before you are unable."

Danhoul roughly grabbed Killian's arm and pushed him toward the gate as nearby the horses whinnied and reared wildly. Wolf, the Irish wolfhound who was with them, had stopped short and refused to enter the churchyard, but now he howled in a ghastly unnatural tone.

Danhoul's eyes grew wider and filled with unhidden fear as he glanced back at where they'd been standing. The ground had opened up and swallowed the entire graveyard. The grave markers, the earth, grass, bushes, and trees all fell into the depths. Killian and Danhoul made it through the gate just as it was being dragged beneath the ground as well. Wolf barked and snarled, baring his teeth at what Killian could not see. The sounds behind them were clearly not human and likened to the sounds he'd heard when entering the fairy realm when passing through the Unseelie Court. He could only imagine what demons, devils, and unsettled spirits were at their heels.

They reached the horses as the wind grew stronger and the rain began to fall. They mounted looking back. Killian was relieved to see Wolf racing alongside them. He was almost certain he could feel ghostly fingers clawing at his back. By the grimace on Danhoul's face, it appeared he was experiencing the same unearthly sensation. They did not need to coax the horses to plunge forward at an unusual speed for, they, too, seemed well aware they were running for their lives.

Chapter Three

A LAINN SHOOK HER head to dispel the dizzying sensation and opened her eyes. She had yet again attempted to wish herself to Aine's location but, to her dismay, she was now simply back in the bedchamber where she'd first awoken in the realm of the gods. But this time, she was not alone. Standing in the doorway, looking down upon her was an unusually tall, muscular male who wore absolutely nothing, bar a most displeased expression on his face. His arms were crossed, his jaw set and his intense dark eyes glared at her. Finally, she was being permitted to actually look upon Lugh! She quickly turned away and could feel her cheeks grow warm and ruddy. She averted her eyes and instead looked down at the formation of stones beneath her feet.

"Surely you have learned by now, you cannot run from me, woman, nor hide! Now I demand you offer explanation. Do you actually use your powers to vanish or by some treachery are you simply able to hide within the magical clouds for a time to deceive me?"

"You, in all your godly superiority and magnificence, are

not capable of discerning between the two?" She goaded him once more in spite of herself as she looked down at the large blistered burn upon her arm.

"You truly mean to rile me, is that your purposeful intent, woman? Aine warned me you would be a difficult sort but, truly, it is in your best interest to cooperate and not bring forth my temper again. It would not be advisable to do so."

"You might heed your own words and not risk angering me, your godliness!"

"Do not threaten me or address me in such a rueful manner, and look at me when you speak to the likes of me."

"Then clothe yourself!" She uncomfortably kept her eyes from falling upon him.

"I have no need for garments to cover me. They are a human necessity perhaps, but not one I require."

"Aine was most certainly clothed when I saw her, and she possessed weapons. Are you not skilled in weaponry or are you not to be trusted with weapons? Legend tells of a mighty spear you once possessed. Is that simply a falsehood?" She continued to gibe at him.

"Aine is female and prefers to be clothed in the presence of humans. I assure you I am most capable with all manner of weapons, and my spear is indeed a mystical weapon, but I have no need for garments or weapons here in this realm!" With that, he insolently rubbed his hands together and created a large ball of fire, which he hurled toward the open window.

Alainn chose to ignore entirely his display, which was clearly meant to impress her. However, she was finding it exceedingly difficult to maintain a conversation with the male without actually looking at him. Instead she stood and peered out the arched window in the chamber and watched as the fireball sizzled and eventually burned out in the lush grass.

"Why is it you choose to keep your eyes from looking upon my physical grandness and the great endowments I possess? Does your human husband not lay claim to such grand attributes? Are you not attracted to me and my most obvious potency and virility?"

"I am most certainly not attracted to any part of you!" She chided with chin raised and nostrils flared as she inadvertently turned toward him.

"Apart from my husband, the only occasions I have ever looked upon unclothed men is when it has been required in attempting to heal them. And, truly, in my experience, I have found men who actually possess great attributes, physical or otherwise, seldom need to boast of them! Cover yourself or I shall not speak to you again."

The god huffed loudly in exasperation, but apparently decided to appease her for he stepped behind the doorway so that the lower half of his body was concealed.

"Better by far!" She half sneered at him as she spoke.

"Now, you must show me what you are capable of; reveal

these powers you possess so that I might teach you how to better yourself, to perfect your abilities."

"It is as I have told you, I have no further time for this; I must be allowed to return to my husband for I fear he is most certainly in grave danger."

"And do you sense this by premonition or simply intuition?"

When it was apparent she would not reply, he spoke further. "Summon his image then so that you might see what perils your man may face this day."

He glanced down at the floor and simply by looking upon it, created a large pool of water, clearly aware Alainn would be capable of using it to create an image of Killian.

"Why are you so insistent on me showing you what I am capable of?"

"How am I to teach you to develop your skills and abilities if you do not reveal what you are now able to achieve?"

She shrugged and shook her head impatiently. "How long do you intend to keep me imprisoned here?" She posed an inquiry of her own.

"As long as it takes… by human terms, perhaps a month, a year, a decade… a century! Who can say?"

"A century? Surely, you jest? By then, all I hold dear would be gone from earth. I am not immortal; I would be dust by then!"

"Ah, well bones at the very least." He sniped. "Therefore, I suggest you not wait that long to show me your magical powers!" He advised in a voice steeped in superiority. He then purposely stepped before her once more and smiled seductively in a way that made her skin crawl. Then it was his turn to disappear without warning.

Alainn knelt upon the floor and glanced into the pool of water Lugh had created. She longed to envision Killian, to see for herself he was well, for her heart ached with the loneliness of being parted from him. But she was hesitant to use her abilities, knowing full well Lugh had baited her and would be close by, waiting for just this opportunity to witness her powers. She formed a plan within her mind, took a deep breath, and closed her eyes. She used her powers of concentration to be taken to another location distanced from Lugh, but where she would find water to conjure an image.

⌘

As ALWAYS, WHEN she was transported in this supernatural manner, Alainn found herself disoriented. She inhaled several times to abate the dizziness often accompanied by nausea, before she eventually opened her eyes to find herself standing precariously on a narrow ledge overlooking a steep precipice. She leaned back against the stone wall and tried to avert her eyes from the lengthy drop to the ground. There was a magnificent waterfall that appeared to originate above her and the water cascaded down as far as her eyes could see. As lovely as it was to look upon, this form of water would be of no use to her in summoning an image. As she continued to look upward and assess her surroundings, she reasoned she was on the side of an immense mountain with no way up or down. She clearly needed to be more cautious in the future, for she had no way of knowing how her powers would be presented in this realm. Even in her own world, her abilities were oftentimes unpredictable and inconsistent, but here she had no notion what she might be capable of.

She had wished herself to a location with water, and she was certain she could detect the scent of dampness in the air even beyond the waterfall. She slowly and painstakingly made her way along the narrow ledge until she espied an opening not much further along the stone wall. She was relieved to reach the entrance, but also reluctant to actually enter, for she was certain there could be any number of unknown creatures found within the cavern.

As she dared to step closer and glance inside, she saw an unusual glow being emitted from within. Alainn was gladdened in the knowledge this was undisputedly a magical place. As she was about to enter, she sensed more than saw something covered the opening, it was nearly transparent, as if it was a veil, or perhaps a portal to another realm. Her heart raced with combined excitement and nervousness at the prospect of meeting magical beings as she pushed forward surprisingly meeting no resistance.

She felt the coolness upon her skin as she warily made her way inside the cave. She thought she detected the sound of wings flapping and she stopped short. She'd always been repulsed and somewhat frightened by bats and therefore avoided them whenever she could. The flapping seemed unusually loud and Alainn recalled having heard many tales of mystical creatures such as giants that could be found in the realm of the gods. And if there were giants, could there be giant bats as well? She shivered and regrettably turned back toward the entrance, thinking she would need to find another way to learn how Killian fared this day. Perhaps she would need to go back to the castle after all… and yet she was undeniably fascinated to possibly witness magical creatures.

As always, her piqued interest and curiosity won out over her clear intelligent thought and she turned about once more and waited for her eyes to adjust to the dark. She looked up and could see sunlight far above her, which would allow her to see more clearly. She reasoned if something untoward should happen or she should meet with a creature that was not benevolent, then surely she could simply wish herself back to the castle at that time. She wasn't completely confident in this regard, but still she continued.

As she moved deeper within the cave, she noted the walls glowed unnaturally and partially lit the area. Beautifully colored spiked formations could be seen hanging from the ceiling and rising from the floor. She walked slowly and purposefully, careful not to stumble on one of the uneven formations. Guided by the steadily increasing sound, she entered an immense chamber and within the middle was a beautiful round pool surely nearly as large as a lake. She inhaled the pleasant scent that radiated from the effervescent water. It bubbled and churned in a manner, which combined with the mist emanating from the water, nearly lulled her to sleep.

Kneeling down beside the pool she attempted to summon Killian's image, for as lovely and mystical a location as this was, her true purpose for being here was to reassure herself that her husband, Killian, was not in peril. As she knelt closer she noticed sudden reflective movement in the water and she gasped. She heard an unsettling and eerie howling fill the cave. She turned toward the sound and her eyes skirted the area. On a ledge not far above her head stood a beast, the like she'd never witnessed before. Its head was large and shaped like that of a dog, but the animal was immense, surely bigger by far than any wolf Alainn had ever seen. It made no attempt to come near her, but it kept on howling loudly. She *had* wanted to discover what types of animals might be found here, but she wasn't certain she cared to make acquaintance with this clearly unpredictable creature.

Alainn had heard the many myths and legends of hell-hounds. The tales were common and many believed that hellhounds existed in Ireland some centuries ago. Perhaps here in the realm of the gods they continued to do so. She half expected it to leap from its perch, pounce upon her and tear at her throat but, instead, it simply continued to howl and keep its eyes intently staring at her. She wasn't remotely sure what to do next for she felt any sudden movement might cause the animal to become aggressive. She looked up at it careful not to meet its eyes when she saw a shadow on the wall beside her. She glanced toward it and was startled to see another of the canines had jumped on the ledge directly across from the other. It joined in the loud eerie howling which echoed of the walls of the cavern and made the hairs on her neck prickle.

Her knees began to ache with kneeling upon the hard stone, but she continued to sit there barely daring to breathe lest she startle the canines. Always in the past she had been capable of taming the wildest of beasts, but that was back in her world, and with animals she knew much of. These creatures, presumed to be hellhounds, might be completely untamable and most likely capable of supernatural feats. In little time more of the beasts appeared on the overhead ledges and Alainn found herself surrounded by no less than thirteen of the creatures.

A pack of hellhounds.

Chapter Four

THE SOUND OF their loud incessant howling was beginning to gravely affect Alainn's ears and she wondered how long they intended to keep on with their unsettling baying. The disturbing thought crossed her mind that even on the slight chance *they* didn't actually mean her any harm; their noisy howling would surely draw attention to her presence. She could only dare to imagine what other dangerous and frightening creatures might exist in this realm. She was certain she didn't care to dwell upon that notion.

Perhaps she could simply wish herself back to the castle, but with her heart beating wildly and attempting to keep her eyes focused on any movement, she wasn't confident she would be capable. Her arm continued to sting fiercely with the burn that Lugh had caused and slowly she dared to submerge it in the water of the bubbling pool for she was certain it consisted of healing qualities. Each of the creatures turned their eyes upon her even with that slight movement. Alainn attempted to predict what their intentions for her might be and to weigh her options.

She could possibly speak to them in a calm, steady voice

and make them understand she was no threat to them and clearly not even much of a meal for that many of them to share. She could attempt to put a spell upon them or tame them by way of her magic, but if they were mystical beings, would her magic actually have any effect on them? She was contemplating all of this when she felt a slight nudge against her hand that remained dangling in the water. A fish, she questioned? But then she noticed the water had begun to swirl and froth. She ever so inconspicuously pulled her hand back and slowly dared to stand. The entire pool turned a deep blue. For the moment, the hellhounds seemed preoccupied by whatever was present in the water.

Alainn's eyes bulged and her jaw dropped as she hesitantly stepped backward. An enormous creature was emerging from the depths of blue and had huge black eyes on either side of its massive head. Its neck appeared to have no end; it was unbelievably long and thick. Alainn continued to back up until she was trapped against the cold wall of the cave.

Chapter Five

THE WATER BEAST further rose from the depths and its head now nearly touched the roof. Alainn was almost certain she was viewing a mighty sea serpent.

The hellhounds had ceased their infernal howling and a few of them had actually begun to whimper as the immense creature appeared to nearly fill the entire cavern. They each moved from their positions and gathered close to Alainn as if she would be capable of protecting them from this enormous and surely menacing beast. It threw a quick glance at the canines, but focused most of its attention on Alainn. One of hellhounds rubbed its enormous head against her hand and she absentmindedly petted it all the while intently watching the water creature. It made a loud trumpeting sound as though it were in pain and Alainn only then noticed the bloody mark upon its long neck. As she tried to determine what might have caused the gash, she noticed a large object protruding from the wound.

Alainn held her hand out to the creature, attempting to call it to her and immediately it bent its head down toward her so close the water droplets falling from the creature landed on her and thoroughly soaked her garment. The sea serpent seemed strangely docile or perhaps it instinctively trusted Alainn as a healer. It moved closer to her and she gingerly touched its neck in reassurance of her good intentions. The beast did not appear to object so Alainn continued to move her hand closer to the gash. Upon closer inspection, she realized the object stuck in the sea serpent's neck was a massive tooth. Not allowing her mind to dwell upon what creature might lay claim to such a gigantic tooth, Alainn began chanting magical words and sending warmth and healing through her fingertips. She dared to lull and charm the beast and finally, with some difficulty due to its sheer size, she capably removed the tooth from the wound.

She was disturbed to learn in actuality it was only part of a tooth for it had broken off. She sealed the wound with her hands and a magical healing enchantment. The creature opened and closed its eyes in a manner Alainn recognized as an expression of its gratitude. She smiled at the huge creature as it moved backward into the water almost gleefully and it made a sound that was clearly joyful. It splashed about playfully, once more soaking her and the hellhounds in the process. The canines shook the water from their shaggy coats as they, too, playfully nudged Alainn and each other.

Sighing deeply at the most fortunate outcome, Alainn suddenly noticed the ground beneath and around her had begun to quake. The hellhounds terminated their play and once more whined and pushed closer to Alainn for protection.

"Now what?" she whispered aloud as the ground continued to shake and an opening in the wall grew wider as the rocks crumbled and fell. Fearful the entire cavern might fall down upon them, Alainn contemplated wishing herself and the hellhounds to another location. The beast in the water made another sound and this time it was not one of pleasure as it spotted the gargantuan beast that appeared from within the next chamber.

This creature was brownish-green in color and it appeared to be the largest lizard Alainn had ever dared to imagine might exist. She had heard tell of such beasts that apparently lived thousands of years previous. This creature appeared to come forth from the earth and it bellowed loudly at the beast in the water. As it widely opened its mouth, Alainn could see that there was a partial tooth in its mouth and immediately she knew who was the responsible for wounding the sea serpent. The earth lizard lowered its head, scuffed the ground, and fiercely snorted before it began to charge at the water beast. Alainn put her hand up in protest and shrieked.

"Stop that this instant; she is already wounded!"

She was startled to see it obey her command for it stopped in its tracks and turned its attention and its enormous head toward her.

"I didn't intend for you to charge me, at any rate, but you needn't harm the serpent further."

The water creature trumpeted yet again and tossed its long neck forward in protest of the other beast's presence. The earth lizard opened its mouth once more to reveal a damaged tooth, and it moaned loudly, evidently in great pain.

"Oh, now I understand, the two of you have been involved in an ongoing battle then. Well, come here; let me see what I can do."

The earth beast listened to her command and Alainn reluctantly put her hand in the mouth of the enormous creature. She was pleased to find the tooth was partially detached. However when she put both of her hands around the giant tooth and tried to pull it out, it wouldn't budge. She attempted it three times, but to no avail. The beast made such a pathetic, forlorn cry she knew she must give it one more try.

Alainn was stunned when the water beast forcefully nudged her and caused her to be tossed against the earth lizard and then to the ground. The sudden movement knocked the tooth from the beast and, as Alainn stood brushing herself off, the creature appreciatively licked her with its huge, slimy tongue. It left an oozing green substance on her skin and it clung to the burn upon her arm. Strangely enough, the burning seemed to be alleviated by the gooey slime.

"Thank you, I think." She chuckled as she watched the burn on her arm become less red and angry.

The sea serpent bent closer to her once more and she gently rubbed some of the healing substance on the wound on its neck. It allowed her to do so without resistance and within moments the two enormous beasts affectionately nudged each other as if they were friends and not the enemies she had believed them to be.

"Now, if you'll just be still for a moment, water beast, I'd like to do what I've come for and look within the pool to see how my husband fares this day!"

The beast appeared to understand her and it moved far to the other side of the large body of water and obediently fell still and silent. As she waved her hand above the water and began to attempt to summon Killian's image, she once more heard the loud flapping sound which disturbed her concentration.

Looking upward, she wasn't able to locate the source of the sound. And before she had time to further dwell upon it she heard another unusual noise. This was surely the sound of hissing…very loud and distinct hissing. There were no snakes to be found in Ireland so Alainn had never ever seen an actual snake. She had read about them, seen images of them, and also heard of their distinct hissing. After viewing the two creatures that remained within the cave, she was fairly certain she would not care to fall upon a snake that was anywhere near as large as these two beasts. The sea serpent and earth lizard both turned their large heads toward the direction of the sound and then looked back at Alainn as if she should decide what must be done.

"I do not wish to make acquaintance with an enormous snake no matter how seemingly pleasant the two of you may have turned out to be!"

The hellhounds growled and snarled, but slowly moved forward to stop short before a location not far from where the earth lizard had emerged. They, too, looked at her in anticipation of her next move and they actually began wagging their tails.

She shook her head and stood, once more distracted from her original purpose. She followed the canines and was startled to find an invisible barrier blocking their path. She placed her hands upon it and imagined what might be preventing them from moving forward. Almost immediately four walls could be seen, four translucent walls that formed an impenetrable chamber surely made of a peculiar type of crystal. Alainn continued to touch the beautiful stones and soon the image of what was secretly encased inside the chamber could be seen.

She gasped aloud once more, for it was, again, a creature that was surely only straight from her imagination or from ancient myths. It was huge, and reptilian in nature, but a bright red color and its eyes were large oval slits. It stared unblinkingly at Alainn and when it hissed and snorted she saw that smoke escaped its large nostrils. It attempted to move closer to her and to the hellhounds that surrounded the chamber, but when it unintentionally touched the side of the encasement, it shrieked and pulled back as though the very touch caused extreme pain for the creature.

"Who would entrap you within these walls and why?" she asked aloud as she viewed the creature.

The beast turned its large oval eyes toward her and it was clear he was observing her as carefully as she was him. She noted he was covered in large plates that were possibly huge scales. He had distinguishable ears as well, which set it apart from the other two beasts she had already encountered. She nearly fell backward when she heard the creature within the walls actually speak and in a language she was capable of understanding.

First there was a hiss and then a deep sigh of resignation and then actual words came from the beast's mouth.

"It was the Fomorians," he clearly stated.

Alainn's eyes widened as the creature spoke on.

"Many millennia ago when the two races of deities the Fomorians and the Tuatha De Dannann waged war with one another, the Fomorians won the final battle. They banished the Tuatha De to the underworld and entrapped any mystical creatures that had banded with the Tuatha De. I was placed within this Fomorian crystal prison along with the many other beasts you have seen within this magical realm," he explained. "But I must ask; how is it you have been allowed to enter the chamber for no gods or deities are allowed to pass through the veil that surrounds the passageways?"

Alainn cleared her throat and swallowed hard. "I am not a god!" she said in a small voice.

"Then what being are you?" The animal stared at her and repeatedly blinked its huge eyes.

"I am a woman, a human."

The creature narrowed its large eyes and dared to move closer to her yet steered clear of actually touching the walls.

"How could a human enter the realm of the gods?"

"I was brought here by Aine."

"Ah, so Aine still lives, she has survived the great war, though I suppose she was never in allegiance with either side." He spoke more to himself than to her. "But to what end, why has she allowed you to be present in the realm of the gods?"

"I am her descendant, and I am here for she believes I am in need of protection." She offered.

"So, you are not truly human?"

"Aye, sure I am human."

"But you must possess great magical abilities else you could not enter this cavern. The Fomorians charmed the entrance, no gods or any other creature from this realm can pass through the veil. Not one being has been allowed within or been capable of locating this place in eons. So because you are not a god, but a human who is capable of strong magic, you could pass through the veil of binding. You are a witch then?"

"Aye, it has been presumed to be so," she replied.

Alainn stood there still, staring at the mythical creature before her.

"And what is it you are to be protected from?"

Alainn sighed. "Because of my abilities, there are apparently dark forces that have taken an interest in me and what I may be capable of."

This quieted the beast as he seemed to need time to contemplate this information.

He finally responded. "Always, no matter the realm of the gods or human, or the time, ancient or present, there will be dark beings that choose to prey on the powers of others, to take them for their own to do their bidding. And never is it done for the betterment of any world; always it is to encompass evil. If Aine believes you are in imminent peril, then best you stay here and be surrounded by the protection of the gods."

"But my life and my only love are in the human world… and truly what life would it be to live here when my heart is elsewhere? I would be no less imprisoned than you are now, fire beast."

"There is truth in your words, but perhaps not wisdom, they are seldom intertwined. Tell me, magical woman, what name is it you have been given?"

"I am called Alainn."

He dwelled on that for a time before he responded and he looked deep into her strikingly blue eyes.

"I have heard of you."

"How is it possible that you would have heard of me when you have been imprisoned for all this time and I have lived but seven and ten human years?"

"I have heard of a human woman with magical abilities, that one day you would exist and that your name would be Alainn, you are the first in the line of three such supernatural beings."

Noticing the expression of displeasure and uncertainty on the woman's face at hearing this, the clever and insightful dragon changed the topic.

"Alainn, I see you have already met my brother and sister."

She looked back at the sea serpent and the earth lizard.

"I did not know they were your kin or that they were connected," Alainn admitted. "Why is it you speak when they seem incapable?"

"Why do you have arms and not wings?" He oddly reasoned.

"All people have arms and if I had siblings they would all speak."

"But humans possess defined qualities as well. Some possess brawn, some intellect, some swiftness, some intuition. We are not so very different."

She shrugged and looked back at the other two, smiling as they gazed at her with obvious fondness.

"Well 'tis little wonder you are at each other's throats, literally!" she stated. "If you have been locked up together for such a very long time."

"They do tend to battle each other from time to time. My sister can escape within the depths of the water and my brother can wander the boundaries of the earth and the extensive caverns, but still they have been forced to endure each other's company for too long. However, it is me trapped within these confining walls and my other sister who is tethered above, who have suffered the most through the many millennia!"

"Your other sister?" she questioned and then heard the loud flapping above once more.

"The veil ensures my earth brother and water sister are kept within, but because my air sister and I can fly, we have been further imprisoned."

"You can fly, how truly wonderful. I have always yearned to be capable of flight. How might I free the two of you?" Alainn asked without hesitation.

The creature eyed her suspiciously for the first time.

"Why would you feel compelled to free us?"

"No creature should be so imprisoned, 'tis sorely wrong! And I bare no loyalty to the gods, the Tuatha De Danann, or the Fomorians."

"And what if when I am freed I do you unspeakable harm?"

"I do not sense you would do so."

"And does your intuition never steer you wrong?"

"Seldom."

The creature looked at her intently and seemed to be assessing her abilities. "If you are so inclined to assist me, I might instruct you on how it might be done. You do not seem adversely affected by the magical crystal. It is apparently only harmful to dragons."

"Dragons?" Alainn repeated in disbelief. "You are a dragon; all of you are dragons?"

The beast before her looked at her with some annoyance and for the first time its voice held a hint of impatience. "You have premonitory abilities, yet you do not have the foresight to determine we are dragons?"

"Well, in my own defense, I have never laid eyes upon an actual dragon before and until this very moment I believed you were only creatures of myth. Though I am capable of magical abilities, I am human and in the human world, dragons do not exist."

"Is that truth?" The dragon seemed saddened by this, and he spoke in a somber tone. "Perhaps it is so, then, but at one time dragons existed in every realm, even that of humans. I am long since out of touch of the human realm and every other, but for this dismal cave and these formidable crystal walls. Where then in the human world do you lay claim to be your home.'

"I am from Ireland," she said her voice steeped in both pride and longing.

"Ah, the land of the endless enchanting green hills; I have a distinct fondness for that location. I often took much joy in flying above that magical land. Perhaps if you agree to free me, I might return there one day, after my brother and sisters and I first see to it each one of the Fomorians' bodies lie mangled, charred, and blackened beyond recognition."

Alainn noted the deep contempt and loathing the dragon held for its captors and though she understood the reasoning, she remained hesitant to free the beast.

"Tell me fire-dragon, if I free you what of the gods that still exist in this realm, will they be in peril as well?"

"Not if they do not interfere with our vengeful intentions, no harm shall befall them."

One of the hellhounds grazed her hand and she could clearly hear its worrisome thoughts.

"And what of the hellhounds, would they be free from your wrathful ways?"

"We would cause no ill will to the hounds that have shared this location with us for so many millennia. It is certain if the Celtic god Arawan still lives, he will be searching for his thirteen hellhounds. He is their handler. They aid him in tracking down lost souls and taking them to the Otherworld."

She wasn't certain that would be proper inducement to free the hounds either, but she spoke further to the dragon. "If no harm should befall me or the hellhounds then, aye, I shall assist you, dragon!" she agreed.

He was about to further instruct her on how she might accomplish just that, when she instinctively placed her hand to the crystal wall and began to speak in the language he well knew to be that of the ancient druids. She continued to strategically move her hands along the crystal and she traced the outline of a large portal. That done, the portal began glowing brightly and soon the entire doorway burst into flames. She jumped backward to avoid the scorching heat. As quickly as it had begun the fire was extinguished and the crystal crumbled to the ground in thousands of jagged pieces.

The dragon within screeched distinctively and immediately burst forth through the now open portal. Its eyes glowed bright red and it shrieked loudly, rejoicing in his freedom and at stretching his wings and flying after having been prevented from doing so for an eternity. It flew upward, backward, and upside down. It flapped and squawked and roared disturbingly. Alainn watched on in fascination, which swiftly turned to horror as it widely opened its mouth and breathed a long stream of fire that nearly filled the cavern. She backed up to avoid the flames and fell over one of the hellhounds who were also obviously fearful of the newly released creature. It glanced back down at Alainn, flapped its enormous wings, breathed fire from both its nose and its mouth and dove wildly at a rapid speed directly toward her where she remained lying on the floor of the cave.

Chapter Six

A LAINN HUDDLED CLOSE to the hellhounds, who now
encircled her, as they snarled at the dragon in attempt
to protect her.

When the flying beast drew perilously close to her,
Alainn glared at the creature and screamed. "This is the
appreciation you would show me for freeing you?"

"One should never trust a dragon entirely, young witch,
Alainn."

"One should never trust a witch entirely either!" she said
as she stood threateningly holding tight to a large shard of
crystal in her hands.

The dragon lurched back and then flew upward where
Alainn could hear the loud flapping of wings and then
muffled voices. She strained her eyes and she could just make
out the beautiful bluish gray shape of the dragon above. She
flapped frantically and Alainn watched as the fire-breathing
dragon attempted to use its fire to burn through the tether
that held his sister. But nothing the dragon did proved
effective in severing the magical rope.

Alainn had thought to leave the cave immediately and to

wish herself back to the castle before the unpredictable and dangerous red dragon returned, but he flew back down and landed beside her once more, this time more slowly and carefully.

"I must ask for your assistance once more, young witch!" he humbly said.

"After you nearly frightened me half to death and created perilous flames all around me, you would dare to ask me for further aid?"

"Not for me, but for our sister," he admitted.

The other two dragons looked on, silently requesting she help the air dragon as well.

She huffed aloud and rolled her eyes, yet she couldn't abide the poor dragon being incapable of moving for even one moment longer if she was able to prevent it, so she agreed.

"But how am I to assist your sister in any way when she is tethered so high within the cavern. I am not capable of flying and if you can't sever the tether with your fire, I won't be capable of slicing through it. 'Tis doubtful I will be of any use to you."

"But you were able to enter the cave, and the tether appears to be charmed magically, so no creature of this realm can break the tie that binds her. If you could find an object that would possibly sever the binding then you may be capable of cutting through it."

Alainn glanced down at the many shards of crystal upon

the floor of the cave and the earth dragon's broken tooth as well. She placed several of the sharpest pieces and the earth dragon's tooth within the pocket of her frock.

"And however do you suggest I reach your sister? I am of fairy lineage, but I bear no wings!"

"You must climb upon my back and I will take you up to where you can hopefully cut through the tether. But you must not allow the crystal to touch my skin or we may both fall to our deaths."

She placed her hands upon her hips and eyed the dragon with fury in her eyes.

"And you believe I should trust you when you yourself advised me not to do so? And it is not only me I must consider, you must assure me the child I carry within me remains safe as well."

He nodded his head in agreement and she intuitively sensed she would not be in danger. Alainn pulled the crystals from her pocket, tore a strip from her gown and wrapped them several times, then placed them back within. The dragon lowered itself so she could climb on its back and she attempted to avoid the many sharp and pointed scales.

Her excitement soared along with the dragon as she felt herself being carried upward inside the cave. She was exalted at the magnificence of flight. When they nearly reached the top, she saw the beautiful sleek feminine air dragon. She gazed at Alainn with apparent gratitude and lowered her head as if to bow to her. Alainn nodded back and smiled.

She saw the tether looped around her neck and the other end was tied to a spiraled formation on the side of the cave wall.

The fire dragon flew nearer to the tether and Alainn leaned over with the crystal in her hand and attempted to cut through the strands. As soon as she did so the air dragon shrieked painfully and the tether began to glow around her neck. Alainn stopped immediately and dropped the crystal back in her pocket. She pulled out the tooth and attempted the same with it. This time there was no shrieking or glowing, but after what seemed to be an insufferably long time, she still only managed to saw through a portion of the tether.

Calling upon her powers, she created a small fireball of her own that capably burned through the remainder of the magical thread. The air dragon shrieked once more, but this time in delight as she darted and soared freely about the cavern and she flew toward her brother, who remained hovering in midair. She nudged his nose in joyful reunion after such a lengthy time apart and then she whispered in a voice clearly much quieter and more feminine.

"I thank you, Alainn, young witch. My brothers and my sister and I all thank you, and we shall truly remain indebted to you for all time!"

"I was happy to assist you." Alainn whispered back and then the two dragons flew downward, settled on the floor of the cave, where Alainn climbed down. All four of the dragons frolicked together for a time, clearly pleased at finally being together once more. When the air dragon drew near to Alainn she found since the tether was no longer connected to the wall it held no magic and she was simply able to untie it and remove it from the dragon's neck.

As she stood looking at the sight before her, she beamed and realization finally dawned on her.

"You are the powerful magical dragons that once belonged to the ancient druids, the dragons of the four elements: fire, water, earth and air! I often used to dream of you when I was a child and sometimes I felt it was more of a memory than a dream."

"If you are of the line of Aine, and you possess knowledge of magic, perhaps then it is a memory passed down from her for Aine was once our designated keeper for a time, or perhaps indeed you have lived before!" The air dragon explained with a mysterious and unreadable expression in her long-lashed eyes.

Alainn turned when they were interrupted by a loud pounding outside the entrance of the cave and then she heard a high-pitched whistle. The hellhounds all eagerly bounded toward the entrance, but stopped short unable to pass through. She followed the canines and when she got to the portal she saw a large male outside the door. The hellhounds appeared as happy as young puppies as they stared at the being outside the entrance. They barked and howled, clearly wanting to get to him and by the longing expression on his face, he was just as eager to get to them.

Alainn walked past the hellhounds and easily stepped

through the portal. "You must be Arawan?"

He cast a wary glance in her direction, nodded politely, but did not speak.

She tried to call out the hounds and get them to follow her, but they came against an invisible barrier and when the god attempted to enter, it was clear he could not. Alainn wasn't certain how to reunite the hounds with their owner if neither could penetrate the veil.

She reached within her pocket once more and with the magical crystal she tossed it against the open air and the entire entrance glowed brightly. Within moments the hellhounds leapt out to their handler and it was clear they were well pleased to once more be together as they tumbled about joyfully reunited.

Alainn's heart caught in her throat though, when she saw the entire lot of them roll over the edge of the mountain. She screamed out in dismay, but then looked on with relief as the god and the beasts disbelievingly ambled happily across the clouds. The first hellhound she had encountered momentarily returned to her and affectionately licked her hand once more and wagged its tail before joining the others and disappearing amongst the clouds entirely.

When she went back within the cave all four dragons remained, but she knew they were excited to be free to do what they would. She mentally noted how happy she was that the dragons had been freed and most especially that she was not a Fomorain, for together the four of them would surely be an unstoppable force.

"I'll say farewell then." She smiled though admittedly she felt an undeniable and unexplainable sadness at knowing it was unlikely she would ever see them again.

"Magical creatures of all varieties share a bond that makes parting difficult!" The most emotional of the four, the air dragon said, for she had surely heard Alainn's thoughts.

"Aye!" she whispered as she gently touched each of the four creatures, the fire dragon last for she still harbored some displeasure at his earlier fiery display.

"You fear fire, young witch Alainn, but you can create it as well. Perhaps you lived during the times of the great druids when dragons were commonplace, for we each feel the same connection you now feel."

"Perhaps," she agreed. "Now be off with you then," she whispered, not wishing to prolong their parting. "But how will the earth dragon move down the side of the mountain and will the water dragon not remain confined to water at all time?"

"We are magical, Alainn, anything is possible with magic!" The fire dragon almost smiled and then winked at her as he spoke.

And, as if to confirm this, Alainn rubbed her eyes disbelievingly as the fire dragon dove beneath the water, the earth dragon presented wings and flew upward, the air dragon lowered her head and capably dug down into the earth, and the water dragon blew fire out of its nostrils, immediately sprouted wings and also flew away through the now open portal.

She shook her head at all the wondrous events that had transpired, sighed reflectively at all she had witnessed, and then finally once and for all knelt down and stared into the now quiet water.

Chapter Seven

ALAINN CLEARED HER mind of all the recent tumultuous happenings and finally forced her conscious mind to envision only Killian. She was quickly rewarded with a clear image, but her relief was soon changed to horror as she witnessed Killian and Danhoul rushing toward their horses. She gasped aloud as she saw the despicably malevolent beings chasing them and the churchyard behind them caving into the ground. Then the vision grew cloudy and was returned once more only to water. She reasoned she must discover a way to leave this realm at once. Regretfully, she mused, perhaps appeasing Lugh by revealing her powers would truly be the very measure needed to ensure she could return to Killian. She imagined the bedchamber within the castle walls in the realm of the gods and within little time the walls of the cave faded behind her and she was magically carried back to the castle.

After calming her usual dizziness over moving from one location to another, she attempted to form a strategy. She needed to know that Killian was well, that he had escaped the perilous time at the churchyard. Surely, if she was able to remain unharmed amongst hellhounds and capable of freeing mythical dragons, she could do other remarkable magical feats here in this realm as well. Since she'd had no success in transporting herself back to her own world through all of her numerous attempts, she resorted to an entirely different strategy, one she'd never dared to consider before. She concentrated on the memory of the last image she recalled of Killian and Danhoul racing toward their horses, and calling upon all the powers she could summon within her, all the abilities she had ever known to be hers and beyond, she willed Killian to come to her.

ALAINN FELT HER stomach grow queasy and her head spin; she gasped for air as she fell back upon the bed. She believed she might fall unconscious, for this time the dizziness refused to abate. As the room spun round and round unrelentingly, she heard the voice beside her.

"Alainn, what has happened to you?"

Though the voice was familiar to her, and certainly welcomed, she despaired at knowing it was not Killian whom she'd summoned. She felt the gentle touch upon her arm and she slowly opened her blue eyes to look into the face of the young druid, Danhoul Calhoun.

She forced a smile and slowly moved to a sitting position before she spoke.

"Is Killian well?" she finally managed as she tried to right the dizziness.

"Aye, he's well enough, but for his concern for you."

"The two of you escaped those hideous creatures at the churchyard?"

"Aye, just barely," Danhoul admitted, "They did not seem able to follow us far beyond the graveyard."

"I am much relieved," she said with a voice that trembled.

"But how did you manage to bring me to this realm, Alainn? And why do you look so unusually pale; are you unwell?"

Before she had a chance to reply he noticed the many dark bruises on her arms and the angry reddened welt of the burn.

"What has happened to you?"

Frustrated tears began to slide down her cheeks and the calamity of her day, combined with the relief of finally seeing a familiar human face got the better of her. She began to weep in earnest. The young man unsurely sat down beside her on the bed and put his arm around her shoulder till her sadness appeared to ebb.

"I was attempting to call Killian to me, but it seems I was incapable of accomplishing that feat." She informed him, but avoided his queries regarding her injuries.

"Aye, well, I've never known of any human who could summon another to their location! Your powers are immeasurable, Alainn, and apparently ever growing! One moment I was standing with Killian discussing our narrow escape, and then a ray of light encircled us. I did not experience fear or discomfort, but I felt myself being pulled through a strange tunnel filled with a thick mist. I believe I may have momentarily lost consciousness."

"Is it because you possess supernatural abilities of your own that I was able to summon you, but not my husband?"

"Perhaps it is so," Danhoul agreed.

"How much time has elapsed since I have been gone from our world, Danhoul?" she whispered in a forlorn tone. "How many days have I been held captive here?"

"You have not been gone days, Alainn." He reassured her. "Perhaps nearly a day. Dawn approaches now in our world, but it was only just this day Aine took you to this realm!"

"But Lugh informed me days ago that many days had already passed while I slept."

"Lugh is a powerful god and, I'll admit full well, he is capable of much, but he is often an arse and not above spinning falsehoods to suit his needs. However 'tis true time in this realm is not calculated as it is in our world."

"In the fairy glade 'tis true time is measured differently and it passes faster than in our world for I can spend what I think to be an entire day in the fairy realm and it in truth it is only hours in our world, but in the realm of the gods time evidently moves much more swiftly?"

"Aye! That seems to be an accurate observation."

He continued to glance down at the blisters upon her arm, which had been eased greatly by the dragon's slimy saliva, but Alainn saw Danhoul's most aggravated expression. He held his hand over the burns and closed his eyes. Light radiated from his fingertips and the blistered red welts disappeared entirely along with the painful burning sensation. The only evidence remaining from the deep burns were tiny pale white lines. Alainn's serious eyes quizzed him without words.

"Our powers are truly greatly exaggerated and magnified here in the land of the gods," Danhoul offered. "Have you not found this to be true?"

She glanced toward the doorway, expecting Lugh to appear.

"I've mostly tried to keep my abilities hidden from that arrogant dolt, for I have no time or desire to be assessed or instructed by him, but, aye, I can move from one location to another with relatively little resistance." She considered relating to him all that had happened with the dragons but, for now, she thought it better to keep that concealed. "I attempted to heal my arm myself, but you have managed it much more successfully."

"Aye! 'Tis much more difficult to heal one's self than others…even here in this magical realm."

"So you have been here before, Danhoul?"

"Aye, more times than I could count," he admitted.

"So, you've seen the many creatures found in this realm?"

she asked.

"Aye, I've seen some of them. There are many peculiar beings, giants and trolls, and such, and some with names issued by the gods that no human would truly understand or comprehend without having witnessed their like."

"Giants and trolls?" She smiled, considering the notion if not for the great desire to be back to Killian and their life together, not to mention the many daunting concerns regarding their unborn child; she would be intrigued to stay here in this realm to witness all the many creatures.

"And there are certainly many different locations that are home to the gods; for, of course there are the gods who were long ago banished to the Underworld. Others have the ability to come to our world and freely move from one realm to another. And each realm of the gods, like each fairy glade, is unique and filled with a diversity of creatures and beings."

"You have great knowledge of this topic, Danhoul. You have spent much time here?"

"Aye, here and in many other realms."

"What age are you then, Danhoul, for I thought you perhaps younger than my age.

"By what measure, Alainn? In human years, aye, I am six and ten, in truth, born upon the exact day as you, but one year later. I have spent much time in the lands of the gods, so I have lived many more years than what my age in our world would suggest."

"You hold many secrets within, Danhoul?" She mused.

He simply nodded.

"And where do your magical abilities stem from? I have learned I have fairy and druid lineage, which apparently deems I am a witch, but what of you? My grandfather believes you to be from a strong druid ancestry."

His smoky blue eyes took on a sad and regretful quality "I know little of my lineage, I possess some magical abilities common to druids, and the gods have assured me it is so, but 'tis also from the gods that I have recently learned of the date of my birth and the circumstances that followed. I was apparently left upon the steps of an abbey when I was scarcely hours old. I know nothing beyond that."

"Where were you raised then, and by whom?" she dared to ask one more question.

He turned his melancholy eyes from her and did not respond.

She chose to change the topic to one she hoped to be less disparaging. "So, would you be able to inform me as to whether dragons are found in all realms of the gods?"

"Aye, well there are said to be many dragons here as in many realms, but they aren't creatures that allow themselves to be seen often."

"Unless they're trapped within a magical cave and need to be freed by someone not of this realm!" Alainn smiled tellingly.

Danhoul's eyes grew as wide as shields. "You've located and freed the four druid dragons?" He slowly asked the nearly impossible consideration.

She nodded, but had no time to reply for, as she'd earlier suspected, Lugh appeared within the chamber.

Chapter Eight

"HOW DID YOU come to be here, young druid? You are not permitted to be present in our realm at this time!"

"You're aware my name is Danhoul, and you have no control over me. I'll certainly not be ordered about by you, Lugh! You should know that by now! And I have a bone to pick with you. Why did you allow Alainn to be harmed when she is under your watch? What punishment shall befall a god who risks peril to his charge when he is to be guarding and protecting her?"

"It was her and her stubborn unwillingness to cooperate that caused her mishap. If I am to train her and to mentor her she must reveal her powers. She refused and so I was compelled to force her hand."

Danhoul had obviously used his magical gift of second sight to learn what had caused Alainn's wounds.

"And so you chose to use fire, to direct your pitiful fire-balls at a woman who is of fairy lineage? Sure even you must be aware of what dire consequences befall fairies when fire is allowed to touch them? Do you suppose that was a wise choice, a choice Aine would desire or approve of?" Danhoul's voice grew quieter yet clearly more threatening as he spoke to the god.

"I'll be damned by all the Celt and druid gods who have gone before me if I'll be guided by what Aine desires or approves of! I did not request this impossibly thankless task of guarding or training this woman!"

"And are you not bound by the Council of the Gods decisions and what they desire?"

Danhoul was well aware he'd caused the god to feel great unease. The tension spread palpably throughout the chamber and Alainn glanced at Danhoul. Lugh's face wore a grim expression and his eyes filled with loathing. He took one step toward Danhoul and the young man defiantly pulled his sword from its scabbard.

Although Danhoul was a tall man, and stronger than his slight build would suggest, he was young. She felt her fear soar tenfold at seeing how Lugh obviously relished this physical challenge.

"You would dare to fight me?" He laughed in a nearly maniacal manner.

"I assure you, *I* will have no need to do battle with you," Danhoul confidently replied.

Although his eyes revealed his doubt, Lugh glanced around as if to see what army of humans might come to the young druid's aid. As he took another step toward the man, Danhoul glanced at Alainn. He caught the glint in her eye, saw the mystical light surrounding her and then watched her arms rise of their own accord. The massive bed that nearly filled the entire chamber lifted as though it were a feather and flew directly toward the god. He jumped to one side to escape the heavy object, and raised his arms to hurl it away, but the bed had begun to spin erratically at precisely the same time and trapped his arms in the iron headboard. Soon the metal spirals twisted further and whirled around his head as well. The bed spun several more times until it slammed against the wall, sufficiently pinning the god against the stones. His eyes grew wider and wider in astonished disbelief.

Alainn was shaking violently when she finally allowed her arms to rest at her sides. It was at that moment Aine appeared inside the chamber to view the melee. She glanced from the naked god who was evidently rendered harmless, to the two young humans. She arched her eyebrows and although she was quite obviously not one given to humor, she fought to control the urge to smirk at the absurdity of the situation.

"Lugh, have you perhaps *tangled* with the wrong female this time?" She cleared her throat to suppress her laughter. A low growl was his only response.

"Danhoul, I was not aware you had secured access or been summoned to our realm this day?" She directed her next query to the young druid.

"I had no intention of entering the realm, Aine. That, too, was apparently Alainn's doing. Though she may have been reluctant to reveal her abilities to Lugh, she inadvertently showed him what she can achieve and then some, I'd wager. I believe that is only a small degree of what she can accomplish."

"Perhaps you would have been wiser to listen to my warnings, Lugh. I asked you to remain concealed. You possibly believed it was so you would not be driven to fall into your lecherous habits with females but, in truth, because we had no indication what degree Alainn's powers would measure in our realm... I had thought to protect you."

"But...how could a mere human, a lowly woman, be capable of this?" He glanced down at his precariously unenviable predicament.

"My great-granddaughter may indeed possess human qualities for that encompasses part of what she is, but how quickly you forget or how very slowly you learn, Lugh. She is of my line—my father was the greatest of gods, my mother the queen of all fairies. Alainn's great-grandfather, the man I mated with to create, Ainna, her grandmother, was a most powerful wizard. And my daughter Ainna's mate, was an esteemed warlock. And that is simply Alainn's maternal line. Her paternal line is of an ancient druid lineage and an uncommonly strong and mystically gifted line at that."

Although the explanation was being offered to Lugh, it was Alainn that Aine cast her serious eyes upon as she continued to speak.

"Alainn was born of the full moon, at midnight, during

Samhain when the planets were in the perfect alignment, conceived of the new moon, when thirteen of the brightest stars aligned with another. Each and every one of these conditions can bring about unusual and unprecedented greatness, but to put them all together, the sum of each of them...it is unimaginably extraordinary! No other human has ever existed with all these elements! Only a combination of all of these conditions could create such powers and abilities. Even I am uncertain what she may be capable of. Alainn is undoubtedly the most unusual human ever created, the most powerful witch that has walked the earth. She is surely the one of legend!"

Alainn swallowed hard and attempted to blink back the tears in her eyes as she listened intently to all Aine was revealing.

"By now, Lugh, you will surely have observed Alainn would not be compelled by personal threat to reveal what supernatural and magical abilities she might possess. However, should you threaten those whom she loves or cares for, she will be driven to protect them with forces even you or I may be unable to harness or withstand. She possesses a keen ability to detect what weaknesses others may have. She knew you were immortal, that she is surely no match for your strength and so therefore she would be incapable of causing you physical harm. And yet she knew iron is your one weakness and that you could be confined by barriers of such a consistency."

Alainn attempted to comprehend all that Aine was speaking of. She felt her fears reaching unhealthy proportions and she slowly lowered herself to the floor in desperation, taking in all the snippets of information she had not known till this time, her ancestry, her legacy. If all Aine spoke of was truth then how was she ever to lead a life of normalcy? As if sensing her despair, Danhoul went to her. He nervously touched her head and softly patted her blonde locks to comfort her. Aine looked down upon her.

"Do you now understand why we must keep you from dark entities? Should they find a way to reach you or turn you to the darkness, lead you into the Unseelie Court, they would have a distinct advantage!"

"So you mean to keep me here indefinitely, to imprison me forever? For always there will be temptation, and till the end of time there will be those who unite themselves with darkness. And if it is to be so, if that is your intention that I must live out my life here in this realm away from all those who are dear to my heart, I implore you to assist me in finding a means to abate the curse that is upon the O'Brien line. And should we manage that great feat, I would further ask that when my child is born he be allowed to return to his father. Then I request you end my life for to live out my life here without my Killian, without our love, that is no life at all!"

Aine stared intently at her descendant and finally spoke. Even gods are not capable of endless feats, it is not within our power to simply undo or eradicate a magical curse that was not our doing, and we certainly have no desire to end your life. Though you may not care to hear it, your child may possess powerful abilities as well," Aine reasoned.

Tears slid down her cheeks as she spoke. "His father is human! Surely our babe will simply be a normal human child!"

"Aine, if you do not allow Alainn to return to our world, to her time, I sense there will be no hope of ending the curse and her unborn child will be doomed at any rate! You cannot keep her here against her will. You've seen what she is capable of when she is displeased," Danhoul begged the god's understanding.

"I did not think to keep her here till the end of her days; that was never my intention… nor that of the Council of the Gods. I have been gone this time, accompanied by many of the other gods permitted to leave our realm. We attempted to seal the many portals to the dark side. We have not managed to seal them all. Surely that great feat would be unattainable, but we have closed many with spells of magical enchantment. Perhaps now, together, you and Mara, your mother, may ensure the curse is ended."

Alainn's blue eyes filled with a newfound hope. She stood once more and walked cautiously toward Aine.

"You will allow me to return to my home, to my husband and our life together?"

The goddess looked upon the young woman with a

sternly maternal expression and bade her fair warning. "Aye, to keep you here would only create a discontent and darkness within your soul. I see that now, Alainn. I will attempt to watch over you when I can, but I regret I cannot protect you always nor am I able to keep you from harm's way indefinitely. It is as I have previously informed you; I am the protector of all women. My tasks are insurmountable and in truth impossible!" She sighed deeply and reflectively. "I will do what I can for you, to keep evil at bay, but you must do what you will and what you can to stay away from evil as well. As you have surely learned, your powers even in your world are unpredictable and ever-changing. Though magic is often a great asset, it is not without imperfections and not always to be trusted or relied upon. You must allow your husband, Killian O'Brien, and young Danhoul to be your guardians and protectors.

"And what of me?" Lugh grimaced with a downcast voice as he struggled against his iron encumbrance.

"Perhaps you might need a guardian yourself, Lugh!" Aine suggested as she slowly moved her hand through the air and the man was finally released from his twisted prison. He glared at Aine and then looked almost respectfully at Alainn.

Aine's authoritative voice resonated throughout the room. "If Alainn should need your protection or your guidance, though you as so many others are banished from entering the human world, you may be capable of offering some form of assistance when and if she desires it. You are most assuredly bound to this duty until her time on earth has ended!"

He only nodded in nonverbal agreement.

Alainn looked up uncertainly at Lugh who stood by the young man. Danhoul was a tall man, and yet Lugh stood at least a head and shoulders taller than him. The god remained completely unclothed, even now. Alainn waved her arms toward him and immediately he was donned in kingly attire.

He glanced down at his recently acquired garments and smiled at the young woman. "Ah, enchanting woman, well at least you chose for me garments fit for a god and not a pauper!"

Aine approached Alainn and spoke. "I must inform you that your new husband will retain no memories of having met me during my time upon your earth. They will fade entirely and soon he will have no recollection of having seen me or of me taking you to the realm of the gods. It is a condition governed by the Council of the Gods, no human can know of our visits to your realm." In an uncommon display of affection Aine took Alainn's hand in her own. "Go now, my kin and keep you safe!

She placed her fingers to Alainn's forehead, closed her eyes, and began to speak unusual antiquated words when the sound of much loud barking just outside the castle appeared to interrupt the god.

"Is that not the sound of hellhounds?" Lugh queried, his voice filled with disbelief.

Aine's eyes had grown wider and she cocked her head toward the doorway.

"It cannot be, for they've not been heard in this realm for...

"Millennia?" Alainn finished the sentence.

Aine cast a wary glance toward her kin and with her serious eyes asked an unspoken question.

"Aye, I released them from their prison and the four druid dragons as well," Alainn hesitantly admitted.

"You did... what?" Lugh stammered.

Alainn looked from Aine to Lugh and back again as the sound of the barking and howling drew nearer. Danhoul also wore an expression of uncertainty.

"Was it wrong of me to have freed the magical beings?" Alainn suddenly felt unsure.

"I do not take quarrel with the fact you released the dragons or the hellhounds. They have done me or mine no wrong, but sure if they are freed then the Underworld will now be opened as well and the Tuatha De Dannan will have escaped and will seek certain revenge on the Fomorians."

"The realms of the gods will again know a time of war!" Lugh revealed disparagingly.

"But the dragons informed me they will swiftly seek the end of the Fomorians so surely no there will be no need for war," Alainn nervously suggested.

"The dragons actually spoke to you?" Lugh appeared uncertain once more.

Alainn nodded.

Aine remained deep in thought and when she spoke it sent a chill through Alainn's body. "There are never actions without consequences," Aine whispered.

"Am I to be kept here then to face the consequences of my actions?" Alainn forlornly asked.

"No, you may leave now." Aine assured her. "I have removed the enchantment that has kept you bound to this realm. No harm will befall you because of your actions, for Lugh was to have been watching over you. The Council of the Gods will most assuredly desire to speak with him regarding this turn of events."

Alainn held no loyalty or admiration for the god, but neither did she wish for him to suffer harm because of her deeds. "I do not care for Lugh to be held accountable for my misdeeds, though I admit I do not regret freeing those magnificent creatures; surely a thousand millennia is long enough to be imprisoned!"

"Aye, perhaps it is time once again to allow true and ancient magic to have free reign here in our realm!" Aine suggested. "You go now, my kin; return to your world and the quandaries you face there, leave us to deal with all that will transpire here."

"How do I accomplish the return journey to my world?" she hesitantly questioned.

"Think of your husband; simply wish yourself back to him."

Alainn gazed once more out the open window to notice the astonishingly beautiful splendor of the sky being filled with the crimson glow of four suns setting simultaneously. Though she'd had no say in coming to this unusual place, and she could scarcely contain her relief and excitement at being allowed to return to Killian, she knew many of the sights and experiences in this realm would forever be etched within her memory.

"And what of Danhoul?" She glanced over at the young man beside her and questioned with some concern in her voice.

"He'll be sent back to your world in due time!"

Alainn curtsied gratefully to Aine, nodded to Lugh, and waved to Danhoul before she closed her eyes. Her thoughts went to Killian; she smiled to herself and was gone.

"WHY DID YOU simply allow her to leave?" Lugh asked.

Aine replied to Lugh, but her eyes met Danhoul's as she spoke. "It has already been determined in the future she will be direly needed! Should we keep her here against her will, we will never be capable of ensuring she will come round to our way of thinking. She would resist us and oppose us, perhaps even lean toward the darkness in rebellious retaliation. Allow her this time with her husband, perhaps she will one day recognize her fated purpose and she will come to us of her own accord!

"Nay, 'tis most unlikely, Aine. Alainn shall never willingly choose to do your bidding, not if it takes her away from Killian, for their love is uncommonly rare!" Danhoul openly disagreed.

"But her destiny was long since decided all those years ago, as was yours! And so therefore it shall be!"

"Perhaps!" Danhoul glanced at the two gods clearly not in agreement. "Now, since it appears for the time being I remain incapable of moving through the realms by way of magic, I'll need your assistance to return to my world."

The goddess nodded to the young man and watched him disappear.

Chapter Nine

ALAINN STEADIED HERSELF upon her feet, inhaled deeply and turned to see Killian there before her. Her heart leapt with joy! His back was to her and for a moment she allowed herself this time to feel relief in her return and to revel in looking upon his appealing form. He was leaning against her horse, the brown mare she'd chosen from the stables at Castle O'Donnel. It seemed like an age had passed since then.

He ran his hand through his thick, dark brown hair and sighed deeply which was always a sign he was severely concerned. She inhaled slowly and pinched herself to make certain this was not simply a dream. She smiled at the immediate pain for it indicated she was truly here, back in her world, in her time, and with her only love.

It had seemed an insufferably long time they'd been kept apart, but by Danhoul's assurance, she had been gone less than a day. The morning sun was now rising in the east. The sky was aglow in lovely pink tones, spreading out gloriously in promise of what wonderments the day might hold. She glanced down and observed that she was once more donned in the gown in which she'd worn when they were joined in marriage. She touched her hand to her hair and felt the flowered wreath as well. It had been one day since they'd been wed. And less than hours later they'd been forced to be separated. They'd not spent their first night together, not consummated their marriage.

She now realized she was standing before the entrance to the fairy glade; the very location where Aine had appeared and insisted Alainn must go with her until it was safe for her to return. Now that she was back she hoped Aine had been correct. Alainn prayed the goddess had truly been successful in closing and sealing many dark portals, extinguishing much of the threat. Aine had believed Alainn was in danger of being pursued with those who allied side, and the unsavory beings within the Unseelie Court, one of the many malevolent portals to hell.

Killian sighed once again and Alainn was shaken from her dismal thoughts to her much cherished reality.

She softly called his name. "Killian?"

He turned abruptly as though he'd been seared by her voice. "Alainn? Alainn, is it truly you? Am I only dreaming, seeing a vision brought forth by the urgent need of knowing you remain unharmed?"

He started toward her, clearly hesitant to touch her lest his vision be proven to be just that, one brought about by fanciful desire and need of sleep. She walked to him and he met her partway. He dubiously placed his hand upon her face and it was warm to the touch. Tears streamed down her cheeks and he softly wiped them away. His breath caught in his throat in discovering she was actually before him.

"No, 'tis me, Killian! I am no vision; I am truly here with you, my only love!"

"Ah, Lainna, how I have fretted about you, and how you might have fared after you were taken by Aine."

Aine had told her Killian would not recall seeing her, yet clearly he remembered everything. Alainn had once put an enchantment on Killian so he would never be adversely affected by her magical abilities. Perhaps it had ensured he was unaffected by Aine's magic as well.

Alainn would no longer dwell on Aine or Lugh or her time in the distant realm. She was here now, back with her man, and being protectively held in his strong arms. The tears of relief continued to slide down her face as she lifted her face toward him and he placed his lips upon hers. They shared a tender kiss, a kiss filled with relief and joy and jubilance at being together again. He lifted her into his arms and they walked, once more, toward the entrance to the fairy glade.

"Now, my sweet Lainna, we will finally have our time together, nothing shall keep us apart, mark my words! We'll have our honeymoon!"

"Aye, Killian, my darlin' husband, it shall be so!" She crooned as he placed his face in her sweet smelling hair and inhaled the loveliness of her scent. The horse followed as they stepped toward the portal of the glade.

"Oh, sure I'd forgotten, Killian, you'll be disallowed to carry weapons within the glade. The fairies adamantly disapprove of violence and of the killing of any living creature."

Killian's eyes filled with unspoken doubt. "And where would you have me place my sword then, Alainn. It's been accurately formed and weighted for me. I've trained with it for years now, I'd not care to have some unsavory type think he'd found grand fortune by discovering it and thinkin' he'd take it for his own."

"Aye," she agreed and she looked toward a nearby oak tree. She spoke in a language Killian had begun to recognize as used by the druids. Soon a small doorway appeared in the tree and Killian witnessed his sword being magically removed from its sheath and capably placed within the hollow of the tree. Then, as quickly as it had opened, it closed and vanished. He shook his head yet again in appreciation of her endless abilities and smiled down at his enchanting young wife.

"I'm trustin' you'll be capable of returning it to me when the time comes?"

"Aye, my love, but I assure you, husband, there'll be no time for swordplay in the next days," she whispered and cast him a most alluring look.

"I'd be most inclined to agree, Lainna."

He beamed down at her as they stepped through the

glowing portal that led to the fairy glade with his horse obediently following behind.

⌘

As Danhoul returned to the human world he caught sight of the happy reunited pair entering the portal to the magical glade. He walked toward the portal himself. As he, too, spoke in the antiquated language of the druids, he uttered a protection spell to ensure the portal remained closed for a time, so that no one or nothing untoward could follow them inside.

⌘

The magnificence that surrounded them as they walked into the fairy glade was even more startlingly evident than Killian remembered, and this journey through the perimeter was not accompanied with unsettling sounds, only profoundly beautiful, poignant music.

Alainn watched his face closely as he gently set her to her feet.

"Why is there no wretched humming; no horridly unpleasant din this time?" he questioned.

She ecstatically threw her arms around his neck with unhidden passion and force, as though he'd uttered the most pleasing words in all of history.

"Whatever did I do to deserve that?" He smiled as he spoke.

"Besides capture my heart and create the most beautifully romantic wedding ever known, you have just proven to me you truly have no qualms about marrying me. You are content, at peace, and truly happy even with all the many quandaries we face... for if you are able to pass through the portal with no disagreeably ill effects, it is assuredly so."

"You doubted that, Alainn, after all I have spoken to you?"

"How could I not, Killian? You are wed to a witch with unusual powers, who carries your child, whose very future is uncertain at best."

He held her close and kissed her soft and fragrant tresses, leaning forward so he rested his chin upon her head as he spoke. "I believe we will be happy, my sweet Lainna, that the future will be kind to us for surely the past has not always been so."

Alainn recalled the sad and sorely wounded boy whom he'd been when first they met a decade earlier. It was true he had experienced a great deal of grief and loss in his two and twenty years and she intended to do all within her power to ensure there would be no more for him. As he observed the glade he felt his heart gladden at the sights that beheld him. She sensed his awe and looked around as well.

"Aye, 'tis indescribably beautiful and magical; such enchantment is ever present during this time, from now till Samhain and beyond 'tis a glorious place."

Killian stared intently at the beauty that surrounded

them here in the glade. There were many vibrantly colored trees and flowers. Even the grass seemed to sparkle magically and, above them, the sky was aglow with magnificent colors that shone and danced unusually brightly across the sky.

Many different creatures filled the glade, so many more than when last they were here. There were the tiny colorful fairy orbs that had been present then, but in far greater numbers, and there were beautiful, unusual creatures of varying sizes and distinctly different appearances. They all seemed to come to greet them at the same time and Alainn smiled brightly at them.

They spoke to her in their peculiarly unfamiliar language and Alainn whispered. "You must speak in English or Gael for my husband should hear your kind wishes as well."

Some looked at her with doubtful expressions as though they were incapable, but she held her hand out to them and in little time Killian was able to understand them. He chuckled softly at their many tiny high-pitched voices.

They appeared most curious to learn more about Killian and many flew near to him and stared at him with interested wide eyes. They seemed in awe of his size, his height, and his broad muscular appearance. Many of them buzzed about him and whispered to each other.

They were all clearly moved by Alainn's beauty, for although she had been uncommonly beautiful ever since she was a young child and first began to visit the fairy glade, now she was even more captivating for her cheeks glowed with health and radiance and her eyes shone with love. Her unbound waist-length hair lustrously framed her noticeably elated face. Her wedding garment was enchantingly lovely. Some presented her with more flowers that she added to the wreath she took from her head. Killian was startled to learn that many of the fairies were much larger than he'd always imagined fairies to be.

"They're all fairies, Alainn?" he questioned.

"All liken to fairies, for there are many varieties of magical species. There are sprites, gnomes, elves, and nymphs as well."

Each species moved forward, spoke, or waved when their names were mentioned, so Killian might differentiate between them. Killian noted the shapes and appearances of each were vastly different. Some were remarkably lovely and others somewhat frighteningly unusual. The sizes varied much as well from the wee orbs he could surely hold in the palm of his hand to some that were nearly as tall as Alainn.

There was a rustle in the bushes behind them and when they turned toward the sound, they saw a small creature, who had clearly been eagerly watching them. He looked like a man, but perhaps a third of the size. He was a strange-looking little creature, oddly dressed in a green overcoat and a hat, but when he realized he had been spotted he shrieked and dove into the bushes.

"What was that?" Killian asked, and many of the other creatures laughed.

Alainn explained. "I believe we have just witnessed one of the wee solitary creatures. They are very curious, but completely elusive for 'tis well known they desire to keep their existence secret. They are mischievous little imps, but are said to bring good fortune. They've not actually been given a name yet as they are so seldom seen. The other fairies claim that this type of creature is only found in Ireland."

"And why by God's nails is Aine here again?" Killian whispered in his wife's ear.

Alainn glanced in the direction he had indicated and was startled to see the Celtic god. She wondered if she'd changed her mind and had come to ensure Alainn paid for the unrest she'd caused in the realm of the gods. Aine stood there tall and proud, a magnificent female of uncommon beauty.

"You told me I couldn't bring my weapons into the glade, Alainn?" he questioned further, though she had yet to answer his first query.

"She is permitted, for since Aine is the defender of women and all females, weapons may be a necessity wherever she roams. She is, after all, whom men and males of many species answer to for their misdeeds toward women. As you recall there are various myths and legends about her?"

"Aye, of course I know what the legends claim! And is it me she wishes to deal with this day?" Killian answered, his hand automatically going to the empty scabbard on his belt.

"No, I sense it is me she has come to see, though I am uncertain I care to know the reason."

The fairy approached and her eyes shone a deep blue to match that of Killian's wife. He couldn't help but see the distinct similarity.

She noticed his deep stare. "Aye, O'Brien, you have surmised your bride and I are kin!"

"I'm not daft nor on the verge of senility, Aine! I've not surmised it. You told me so yourself outside of the fairy glade when you took Alainn away with you. You claimed she was of fairy origin?" Killian quizzed.

Aine was clearly taken aback that Killian remembered any of what had transpired and she seemed deep in thought regarding that matter.

"Your man is uncommon, my kin, both in appearance and in ability. You must hold tight to him, for there will be many who would wish steal him from you, but equally many who would desire to take her for their own, Killian O'Brien! You are to be her guardian and protector, for never before has there been a being on earth as powerful as your new wife. During the time of her conception, all the necessary elements were in place, whether by chance or by design it still remains to be seen, but whatever the reason, she is remarkably uncommon and she may be a peril to her very own existence without you to keep her grounded.

Alainn and Killian held tight to each other as Aine issued her many words of wisdom and warning.

"Keep her close and guard her with your life if necessary. It is by no coincidence you were drawn to one another.

Creatures of her kind, with her unusual levels of ability will always throughout time attract and be attracted to tall, strong, and heroic men, men who can ably protect them and men who often possess a degree of magical ability of their own. But wield your power over her wisely and carefully, O'Brien, for though I am now aware she has created a protective magical charm for you and ensured you'll not be touched adversely by her magic, you can wound her as no one ever can or will. Treat her as a precious treasure, for if you hurt her you'll be made to deal with me. Though I cannot be near her always nor keep her from harm's way as I would desire, I will eventually deal harshly with all who might cause her pain or do her wrong!"

Killian looked at the serious, beautiful, yet frightening female before him as he continued to comprehend her warnings.

"He would never hurt me, Aine! His love for me is indisputably great."

"Aye, perhaps not intentionally, but the very love you share allows him power over you and permits him to sear you to the depths of your heart and soul."

Alainn appeared most distressed at Aine's ominous words and the fairy goddess responded. "Don't allow my harbingering warnings to cloud this cherished time you have together. This is to be your time of joy and private union. No harm will befall you within the boundaries of this realm. I and all of my legions will see to your safety. You may enter all portals of time, space, distance, and location, but use wisdom and caution for the return journey is not always possible."

"We'll not be crossing any of these portals. Our place is here, our time is now!" Killian firmly declared.

"You display great wisdom in that decision, O'Brien."

"Why is it you appear little older than Alainn, if you are apparently generations her elder?"

"Fairies never age. I have lived for numerous centuries, in truth, millennia, gods and fairies are oft immortal beings!"

Killian glanced down at Alainn, a new concern evident on his face.

"You needn't worry; although your new bride is of fairy blood, she is predominantly human. She'll grow old with you should fate allow it."

Killian breathed a deep sigh of relief, and Alainn smiled, thinking it ironic at how pleased they were that she would one day grow old.

A large group of tiny, lovely fairies approached and they flitted about the armored woman and she smiled for the first time since she'd been in the presence of the young couple.

"Your marriage bed is now prepared for you. The creatures here have made it most appealing, I'm certain, for fairies are great lovers of romance and long for lovers to be happy and content always. I wish you well, my youngest kin. I see in your eyes and hear in your thoughts you have great uncertainty and many questions. One day they will be answered, I'm confident in that truth, but now is not the time for queries, now is the time for love and pleasure!" she added as she appraisingly glanced one more time with a long and lascivious gaze at Killian. Alainn caught the look and sent a nasty glare at the goddess.

"Mind your jealousy and keep it in check, Alainn, for you have powers even you are not yet aware of and for your quick temper and your unhidden jealousy you may pay for dearly, but not this day."

With that, she smiled fondly at Alainn and touched her shoulder, the spark that arose was loud and Aine quickly pulled back her hand. This time Killian noted there was an unmistakable fear that surely seldom presented itself in the eyes of the female warrior. She glanced at Killian this time as if longing to say more, but instead she nodded to them and slowly vanished in an ethereally hazy glow.

Killian looked down at Alainn and his eyes held a distinct seriousness she wanted to see entirely gone. The many tiny creatures waved to the happy couple and appeared to be sending them off with well wishes, but the fairies pulled at Alainn and she started off with them. Killian followed and he was entirely bedazzled by where they led them, and the enchanting sight before them. It was the location by the magical spring where they'd once made love, but it was far lovelier than before. It was lush and verdant, and the flowers were all abloom. The colors were beautiful and many. And an elaborate bower had been formed into a soft canopy. It was draped with a silky material also consisting of many lovely pastel colors.

Alainn pulled back the filmy fabric and she beamed appreciatively. Inside the chamber was an immense bed covered with softly perfumed flower petals. The abundant pillows were large and the quilts appeared invitingly soft and comfortable. Within the canopied chamber were surely hundreds of candles not yet lit, but arranged in a beautiful manner. They all looked toward Alainn and urged her to do her magic.

Killian wondered aloud. "Why are they so eager for you to light the candles?"

"Fairies are inexplicably drawn to fire; they adore it, are even mesmerized by it, but unable to create fire themselves and are also unable to tolerate it. If it so much as touches their skin or most especially their wings, they are sure to perish!"

"By Christ, Alainn! Because you possess fairy blood within you that is why you said you don't want to be set afire at the end of your life, and why you reacted so adversely to the flames that caught your skirts in your bedchamber those weeks ago."

"Aye, and 'tis why I have not healed entirely from the burns when I typically heal at an unusual rate from other maladies." She pulled back her skirts to show light scars where the fire had grazed her ankles. She also glanced down at the pale lines upon her arm where she'd been burned by Lugh's fireball while in the realm of the gods. Each and every fairy gasped or screeched in horror at the frightful sight.

"I am a contradictory creature, I think," Alainn continued, "for the witch and druid in me can create fire, the fairy in me is drawn to it yet cannot tolerate it, and the woman is in a constant state of torrid fire within me whenever I think of my strikingly virile husband." She looked at him seductively and indicated to the others she desired to be left alone with her new husband. They apparently had other intentions. They tugged on her sleeve and pulled her toward the other side of the bed.

Killian was uncertain. "I thought you said they wouldn't try to steal you away."

Alainn giggled, "They aren't trying to steal me away; they are preparing to ready me for our lovemaking."

"Ready you, is it? Well, you can tell them straightaway the only readying you'll be needin' will be done sufficiently by your husband, for 'tis clear to me not all the fairies are female," he said, as he only then seemed to notice there were definite gender distinctions.

Alainn spoke in the fairy language and Killian noticed the male fairies stayed behind with him as the females led her to a concealed area beyond the canopy. He could hear much excited giggling and merriment, and when they finally presented her to him, he felt himself grow hard at the very look of her.

She wore a garment, that surely might as well have been invisible so sheer was the fabric, it barely covered her lovely bottom and it left half of her breasts bared, and her nipples were almost entirely visible and obviously peaked beneath the transparent cloth. He thought it fortunate her hair was so lengthy for it covered her far more adequately than the sheer garment. She still wore the flowered wreath in her hair as she walked toward him, which made her appear most angelic and beguiling. He heard the strange sounds coming from the other fairies that were closest to him and saw their eyes were bulging at the sight of her. He did not care for the fact that any males even of the fairy variety were seeing her like this. He quickly pulled a quilt from the bed and covered her with it.

"Alainn you are donned or rather partially donned in a manner only fitting for your husband's eyes. Tell the wee impish creatures they're to leave us alone now. Be off with you, then, the lot of you!" he tried to shoo the fairies away as they whimsically flew and darted around him dizzyingly.

Alainn remembered they remained waiting for her to light the candles. She raised her hands and slowly moved them in methodical, circular movements before her and soon the many tiny flames flickered in a romantic fashion. She looked toward the sky and the brightness of midday immediately turned to twilight. The candles softly illuminated the bedchamber and the enchantingly lovely woman who stood there. Once more Killian moved his hand toward the fairies and gestured to them to be off. The males of the species did as instructed and flew off out of sight, but the females remained.

"What are they waitin' for?" Killian asked.

"Perhaps they wish to steal a glance at what impressive manly attributes my new husband is blessed with?" She jested.

"And would you glare at them in jealously if they dared to look at me with lust in their eyes?" He returned the mischievous banter.

"Coupling with these females would be clearly impossible....with Aine it would not!"

"Aye, well, I've no desire to couple with your great grandmother! Although, sure, she looks like no grandmother I've ever seen, 'tis nearly unbelievable even here in the fairy realm. But, Lainna, I've no plans to couple with anyone other than my new bride for the next century or so, and it feels as though it's takin' a century to get to it!"

Chapter Ten

ALAINN LAUGHED AT his growing impatience, and made a gesture of her own for the fairies to leave them to their privacy. Before they left, they pulled a frayed ribbon from the canopy cover and wrapped it several times around Alainn's wrist. They tugged on it until she moved close enough to Killian that they could wrap it around his wrist as well. With that, the fairies hummed happily and finally flitted off, leaving them alone.

"A fairy version of handfasting, I'd suggest!" Alainn explained.

Killian stared down at her and whispered, "You are truly a vision, Alainn, surely the loveliest woman ever born in the human world or any other." He reached out to touch her cheek with his hand and let it slowly, sensually slide down her throat and to her breasts. He noticed the two small distinct openings in the back of the garment and questioned her with his eyes.

"To allow for fairy wings, I believe!"

She glanced up at the grove of trees surrounding them and the magical spring. She moved her hands before her as she turned around several times in a circle and chanted a mystical charm.

"What is it you're doin', Alainn?" he questioned for he could see no reason for or results from her actions.

"I am creating a barrier to surround this area so no prying eyes will be capable of looking within. I am making certain we will, indeed, have privacy, for I tell you plain, fairies are most curious and I'd be inclined to believe they might long to watch us."

"But we have the curtained canopy to form a chamber around the bed." He reminded her.

"Aye, but do you suppose when we're in the throes of passion during our lovemaking that we would notice if a dozen wee fairies decided to pull back the curtains and look within?"

Killian looked at her with doubtfulness at the oddly perverse consideration, but he was certain Alainn knew much of fairies and their ways.

"In truth, I doubt I'd notice if a herd of giant Irish elk stomped through the entire chamber when I'm in the act of lovin' you, Lainna!" He beamed at her and she knowing returned the smile.

"I also desire for us to walk about freely and swim in the spring without benefit of garments during our time in the glade." She spun around three more time and then she smiled proudly. " 'Tis done!"

She gazed at him with a sultry expression and then stood

on her tiptoes and kissed his lips, a kiss of promise, then she moved from him as far as the ribbon would allow.

"Hold on awhile will you, now? Where do you think you are off to?"

"I thought I might take a rejuvenating swim in the spring, it looks most inviting?"

"By God, Lainna, have you truly no notion how badly I want you, then?"

"Oh, but did you not once tell me the anticipation is half the pleasure of it?"

She glanced toward the ribbon and it slowly unfurled without her touching it, then as she'd suggested she swiftly moved toward the spring and dove in the inviting warm water. She left him standing there his mouth agape.

"You wee tease, get yourself back here and service your husband."

"Get yourself in here and service your wife!"

He could barely make his fingers move as he hastened to unfasten his tunic and his trews. She stood watching him and reveled in every taut muscular part of him and when he removed the trews entirely she witnessed the great need he had been speaking of.

"You are a most impressive man, Killian O'Brien!"

He glanced down at himself and then at her in the water.

"If the water's cold at all, you know it'll ruin this perfectly good condition necessary for lovin' you."

"Then I'll warm it most assuredly," she said in a voice

laced with her own arousal. She closed her eyes, willed the water to grow warmer still and when he tested it, he pulled his foot back out."

"Well, now you're liable to scald me, Alainn!"

"You're a wee bit demanding, milord; you haven't changed much since you were a boy." She said as she magically caused beautifully formed snowflakes to land upon the water where they created a light mist on the water.

He made his way deeper into the warm, inviting water. She swam near him, grazed his chest and then playfully moved out of the water, her garment pasted firmly to her skin and now entirely transparent. He followed her, entranced by her beauty and seductive behavior. She shook her hair so that the droplets landed on him and she stood close enough to him so her nipples brushed his chest. He crushed her to him, no longer capable of even pretending to stem his insurmountable need. She returned the passion as they shared a dizzyingly fervent kiss. He slowly removed the wet garment and it fell to the ground and then he caressed her skin as they kissed once more. He lifted her into his arms and carried her to the bed, making certain to close the many finely curtained layers around them. When he lay beside her, she was quick to fondle him and to set his body afire further still. His hands roved up and down her body as well, caressing every part of her and making her heart race and her skin tingle.

"Perhaps you've changed a wee bit at that!" she said as

she caressed his manhood.

"And when would you have seen me such as this when I was a boy?" he questioned, his voice raspy as his arousal heightened further.

"Once when you were swimming with Rory and Riley, I watched from behind the concealment of a grove."

"You were a wanton young women even then, were you now? And you saw your cousins without clothing, as well?"

"Well I didn't know at the time they were my cousins, and I would say I was more curious than wanton, though even then I was intrigued by the look of you unclothed and I did not find them to be appealing!"

By this time he found it difficult to hear what she was saying for she had not stopped caressing his manhood and he had to move her hand away. He gently turned her so she lay on her back as he looked deeply into her mesmerizingly blue eyes.

"My god, I love you, Alainn. More than I can ever tell you or show you, and I've a need for you that often disturbs me; it is ever constant and all-consuming!"

She felt him hastily and fully enter her as he spoke and she gasped aloud.

"Have I hurt you?" He worried and began to move from her.

"Hurt me? Killian, are you mad? You're on the verge of pleasuring me greatly, but I swear if you even think of discontinuing this when we have waited so long to finally consummate our marriage, there'll be hell to pay!"

He heard a distant thunder begin to rumble lowly above them, but not as loudly as his heart beat at this moment, he wagered. Feeling reassured, he began to move above her and she cooed and moaned in appreciative response to his movements. Her hips arched to meet his thrusts and she cried out as her body quivered and tingled with pleasure. His breath became more ragged and his thrusts quickened and when they'd simultaneously reached their glorious crests, he began to move from her, but she held tight to him.

"Need you be leaving so soon, my love? I adore bein' here like this, still joined, still as one."

He allowed himself to relax, but shifted his position so he would not rest his considerable weight upon her small frame. She caressed his hair and he nuzzled her neck softly and brushed his lips along her throat.

"Refrain from that, Killian, or you'll be made to love me again, sooner than later!"

She felt his body growing steadily firmer within her and she smiled as she looked deeply into his familiar green eyes.

"What power you have over me, Lainna? Do you purposely bewitch me or does it just come so easily and naturally to you?"

"I have never used my powers to attract you, Killian, only my womanly wiles, not my abilities as a witch."

"Aye, well whatever powers you hold over me, you wield them well," He spoke in an aroused tone and soon they were impassioned once more.

⌘

WHEN THEY HAD slept for a time, Alainn glanced up at Killian and found him curiously wide awake. She heard his stomach grumble its protest and realized they had not broken fast, and that Killian surely would have had little opportunity to eat the day previous. He typically possessed a hearty appetite even when he'd not expended as much energy as he had this day.

"Sure you must be nearly famished, Killian?"

"Aye, I could eat a horse, I'd wager!" They heard a loud insulted snort from outside the enclosure and when Alainn pulled back the coverings she saw Storm nosing his way toward them. She softly nudged his snout and he affectionately rubbed her hand in response.

"We are disallowed to eat meat of any variety within the glade, for fairies are great lovers of all of nature's creatures. They believe in eating nothing that once breathed or had a heartbeat."

"Shite, I'll starve for certain!" Killian complained.

"Well, I'll see what I can manage but, for now, I see they've set out a tray of nuts, berries and fruit, ah, and some enticing breads and cheeses. They must know you have worked up a fierce appetite, Killian."

"And that you are needin' food to nourish our son!"

"Aye!" Alainn beamed at the proud tone Killian used

when referring to the child they had conceived.

She stepped out of their enclosure and retrieved the tray without stopping to locate her garments. Killian watched her every move and thought he must be in heaven to be wed to a woman so lovely and graceful and with an appetite for lovemaking that matched his own. Her golden, tousled hair fell softly to her prettily formed round bottom and he felt his body responding to the sight of her appealing nakedness. He reasoned he was going to be exhausted if they kept up this pace and frequency.

When she came back to the bed with the large tray, she placed it beside him and they happily began sampling the tasty food.

"And how is that the wee fairies are able to send us sustenance through the barrier you created if they cannot come within this location?" Killian wondered aloud.

"By way of magic they are able; they simply cannot enter within the barrier themselves."

"And is it not a bit uncharitable of us to disallow them from entering this area when it 'tis their own glade?"

"In truth, the glade is enormous, Killian, almost incomprehensibly so. They will not feel slighted that I have secured this small private haven for the limited days we have together here. I am most certain regarding the matter."

He grinned at her in agreement and continued to eat heartily.

" 'Tis such a welcome relief to be mostly done with the

putrid stomach for it was not a pleasant consideration to either retch continuously or to experience the unsettled stomach constantly. Now I often feel ravenously hungry!" she admitted.

Killian watched her eat and found that only proved to further enhance his arousal. He continued eating himself and then responded to her previous comment.

"I would have much preferred it if you'd informed me about the child earlier, Alainn. I understand your reasons for keeping it from me, but I feel I have missed a lot already."

She attempted to make light of the situation. "You have missed seeing me spew and retch a good deal of the time. The journey to Galway took ever so long, stopping so frequently that I might retch fitfully. I think Pierce and Cookson were never so glad to get anywhere as when we finally made it there." Alainn noticed his sudden serious expression, and she questioned him. "What has you so deep in thought, Killian?"

"Do you believe in a predestined fate, Alainn? With all your magical, mystical powers, do you believe we are surely destined to live a life already long since predetermined?"

Something in his words caused her great unease and she shivered, attempting to push the disturbing thoughts far back within her mind as she responded. "Aye, to some degree, I think we are fated to live our lives a certain way. I most certainly believe you and I were destined to be together, to fall in love, but I try not to dwell on that too intently for I become consumed with the enormity and the complexity of it all.! It leaves me feeling most unsettled"

"Why is that, my Lainna?"

"Well, if we were fated to be together, is that what led to the grievously tragic chain of events that ensured you were made to come to live with your aunt and uncle; was that the reason your mother died, or your father's castle was attacked and he taken away never to be located? I pray that is not so."

His green eyes narrowed and he shook his head, not allowing it to be something he would dare to consider. "No, I can't believe that would be so. Our love is far too perfect, too rare, and precious to be the reason for death or devastation. But, I do believe if I had not seen you on the beach in Galway that we would surely not be together now. I think you would have done all things possible to elude me, and to have me wed Mary." His brow furrowed and his eyes filled with pensiveness as he spoke further. "I don't know if it was fate, but it was an unexplainable feeling, an incredibly strong indication I experienced that I absolutely must go to Galway. The others were in favor of it for the day grew late and all welcomed a break in the journey, but it was I who suggested we travel out of our way to go to Galway. And when I saw you standin' on the beach, lookin' radiant and lovely, surrounded by all those wee children, I knew why I had been urged by some unknown force to journey there. I do believe it was destined to be so!"

"I believed Mary was a better match, would make a better wife. I thought I would cause you undue tribulations and endanger you by connecting my life with yours!" Alainn quietly confessed.

"But you already carried our child, Alainn. How could you consider leaving me or not telling me of the babe?"

"I feared for you and was uncertain about the babe because of the curse."

"And now?" He dared to question.

"For now, I suspect all is well with the child, but my most immediate fear is for you, Killian. I maintain anger and trepidation that you felt you must issue the challenge."

"No talk of that now, Alainn. No talk of anything unpleasant. Now, would you be in favor of a swim in the spring?"

"Aye, I would gladly welcome a swim with you, Killian!" she agreed and they eagerly headed out to the water.

⌘

THE DAYS PASSED rapidly and soon they'd been in the fairy glade over half the time they would be allowed. Their days were spent making love, happily walking unclothed hand in hand by the spring, swimming and playing within the water, and lying on the water's edge, talking endlessly of the past and, more importantly, of their future. They had seen or heard no sign of the fairies or any other beings other than Killian's horse. Often soft, sweet enchanting Celtic music would drift over to them, and always there would be trays of food left for them morning and evening.

One morning as Killian stared down at the food upon the tray that had come to be their staple diet, he looked up at Alainn and his desire for something more substantial and more to his accustomed taste, was clear on his tanned face. Alainn searched for the garment she'd worn to the glade but it was clearly nowhere to be found. She noted Killian's clothes were also missing. Improvising, she selected a section of the drapery around their bed and wound it around herself so that her intimate areas were covered in a fashion. Killian was curious as to what she intended, but she assured him she would be back directly. When she returned she wore a broad smile on her face.

"What has you lookin' so entirely smug, Lainna?"

"I have been granted permission to serve you meat. The fairies have agreed as long as the animal's life is not taken here within the glade, they will allow it."

"But how do you intend to get it here?"

"I have my ways!" she merely stated as she closed her eyes and thought of Cook, she envisioned his kitchen and the many platters that would be within. She was soon rewarded with a large platter filled with ham and eggs, scones and cheese. She opened her eyes and could see Killian staring at her, his mouth fairly watering as she handed it to him. He ate it as though he'd been completely famished, and then he lay down beside her and felt himself growing sleepy in his contented state.

"So, how did you convince the fairies to allow meat here in the glade?" he asked as he absentmindedly played with the tresses of her hair.

"I told them you'd not be able to keep up your...husbandly duties if you didn't eat more heartily," she added playfully. "I told them human males need to keep their stomachs full in order to have enough strength and endurance to frequently pleasure their women."

He chuckled lowly and opened one eye to gaze upon her. She had moved closer to him and was presently caressing him again in a very pleasing manner. When his body responded without question, she positioned herself above him, capably guided him within her, and began to slowly ride him. Killian grasped her hips and arched his body to meet hers. He closed his eyes and felt himself attempting to contain his ever-mounting passion. He was entirely stunned and dismayed when she unexpectedly moved from him entirely and simply lay down beside him.

"What exactly are you doin' to me woman, you cannot simply stop in the middle of it. It leaves a man in a rather unenviable position. So tell me can tell me plain what it is you're up to, for you never do anything without a specific reason."

"I intend to keep you in such a lustful, needy state of arousal that you will love me as you once did!"

"As I once did? Am I to take this as an indication you are criticizing my way of loving you after only days of being wed to you?" She sensed he jested in part, but her words had wounded his male pride. "I've never had any complaints before!"

She sneered at this, realizing he was assuring her his other lovers had never voiced anything but praise for his lovemaking mastery, but she went on to explain.

"I do not criticize, Killian, and these days have been unquestionably wonderful. You are a gifted lover and you have well pleased me, you've been tender and loving and gentle and made certain I know well how very much you love me. You have treated me like a treasure and I do most assuredly require that, but sometimes I need more than that."

He maintained a wounded look as she furthered her explanation.

"If I'd never been with you previous to these last days, I would know no different, but sure you forget, I have. I know you willfully withhold your passion. You purposely bridle your deepest needs and keep your desires in reserve. I believe the next few months will seem insufferably and unnecessarily long if that is the way you intend to love me till after our babe is born. If it is in concern for the child, I assure you his safety will not be jeopardized by loving me more passionately."

He looked at her seriously, an obvious skepticism in his green eyes. He knew well enough she was a learned healer and would surely know much regarding such topics, and she'd not willingly do anything to purposely put their unborn child at risk. He mulled it over within his mind as his mind and body waged battle. He made no attempt to touch her further, so she moved from the bed and pouted prettily as he watched her walk away.

"Suit yourself then, Killian. I admit full well, I shall sorely miss the intimacy we share most assuredly."

"I'd say you're cuttin' off your nose to spite your face then, Alainn," he said in a stubborn tone.

"It has absolutely nothing to do with my nose or my face!" she said as she neared the water and her bright blue eyes looked back at him seductively and she bent forward ever so slightly, her long shapely legs and round bottom in clear view to him. She sensually drizzled the warm water down her bare breasts. He could not tear his eyes away from her when she lay down upon the soft grass, and then looked back at him as if to question what he intended to do about the impasse they had reached.

"Surely you can't mean you'll truly not allow me to bed you simply because I won't love you as roughly or take you as passionately as you would have it done."

"Aye, I can and I mean to!" she said as she began to tilt her hips erotically. When she moved to stretch and then rest on her hands and knees, he knew he was done for. He left the bed and approached her with a hungry look upon his face that had nothing to do with food. He knelt beside her and touched his hands to her firm breasts. She did not prevent him from doing so. She gasped as he came up behind her and pushed inside her with a suddenness she reveled in.

But soon she noted he was once more purposely restraining his passion. She turned around and met his passionate gaze. "I know you have a strong faith, Killian!"

He did not respond, but slowly moved steadily within her. She began to pull away, but he held tight to her hips.

She spoke to him in a breathless manner. "Do you truly believe we are expected to produce children…to not be unfaithful…yet that we are not to be allowed to adequately display our love and our passion in all the many months a woman carries a child?" She managed through moans of extreme pleasure.

"By God's bones, Alainn, would ye quit tryin' to reason with me while I'm tryin' to love you?"

"Then love me properly and well, without hesitation, for you're creating a madness within me that I cannot control." She moaned loudly as she skillfully moved to meet his thrusts.

She smiled as they began to increase in intensity and duration. She cried out as she felt herself taken to the edge and beyond and when she succumbed to the greatest of physical pleasures, he persisted with an urgency she recognized and welcomed. When he finally achieved his release, he lay beside her exhausted, and she touched her hand to his scar as she always did after their coupling.

"Was that more to your likin' then, wife?" he breathlessly

asked as he kissed her hand.

"Aye, that was entirely what I needed!" She sighed contentedly as she felt herself drifting off to sleep in his arms.

"Aye, and me as well!" he whispered as they fell into slumber.

Chapter Eleven

T HE NEXT DAYS, Alainn and Killian spent growing ever closer, entirely comfortable with each other, and more intimately connected than either of them imagined possible. They talked of subjects they'd never broached before. She informed him of the many happenings in the realm of the gods and discussion of her magical abilities was both common and sometimes a cause of dissention between them. And when they argued, he realized she remained unsure of his intent of being with her for all their lives, even though he'd vowed to do so on the day they'd been wed. One morning their words had gotten heated and he determined he needed a time away from her to clear his mind.

" 'Tis time we spent a few moments apart, Alainn, for clearly we'll never come to an agreement on the subject."

"But why was I given these unusual powers if not to assist you and those I love, in both simple and complicated matters?"

"The why of it may surely never be known, Alainn, but how you choose to use your powers is no longer entirely up to you."

"Aye, well it has surely never been left entirely up to me. It was always Morag who insisted I not use them, but because of that they have not been developed or understood as well as they might have been. She instructed me to keep them hidden and guarded, at times forbade me to summon them at all, but if I have been given these magical abilities, there must be a purposeful reason and surely they are to be enlisted. You once assured me you'd not prevent me from using them."

"Aye, 'tis true enough, but you will absolutely not employ your powers to assist me in the challenge against my uncle; it would be an unfair advantage and completely undermines what it is I need to prove and what he needs to learn!"

"But it is he who has made the challenge so clearly unfair. 'Tis true you are younger and unquestionably more capable than him, but he remains an able swordsman and he is still a strong man. Given his recent use of an unsafe combination of remedies and his near madness, he is not to be underestimated. Even Mac said his strength was most unusual."

Her cheeks had grown pink with her fury in attempting to make him see things her way. She pushed her long hair from her eyes impatiently and raised her chin in defiance as she continued mincing words with him.

"And you will have the weight and weariness of two other challenges behind you. I've no doubt you can best the other two opponents if you fight with skill and wisdom as always, but the pith-axe and the morning star are heavy weapons and one missed step, one wrong move, and you will not only be sorely wounded, you could be killed. And in the battle with your uncle, I think he will not show quarter!"

"I don't believe he'll actually kill me, Alainn, even in his unpredictable state. 'Tis only to first blood. That is the condition of the bout!"

"But first blood with a broadsword leaves no room for error and most certainly can bring about death; we've both seen it before. You know it with no uncertainty, and your uncle may love you well, but he possesses a violent temper he oft cannot control, especially if he continues to consume the potions he has been taking. And 'tis plain he intends to teach you a hard lesson. If you simply allow me charm your sword or hex his, perhaps then it will truly be a fair match."

"Alainn, you're missing the entire point of it, and sure you're bein' as unreasonably stubborn as he is. When he hurt you and he attempted to violate you, it was to get to me. He wanted to punish me for opposing and defying him. He needed to show me he is not to be disobeyed or, that his word is not to be questioned, but he should not have tried to force himself on you!"

"Women are often taken against their will, 'tis not an uncommon happening!" She retaliated and downplayed her ordeal.

"Not my woman! And not by my uncle! You can't truly

believe it was by sheer coincidence that he picked that time to try to have you. You've possessed a beauty and sensual appeal for years now, and he never made a solitary move toward you until I told him of my intentions to marry a commoner."

"But *you* did not tell him it was me!"

She stood beside him with a determined look on her face, but by now his jaw had tensed and his eyes were filled with newly felt fury.

"You cannot imply he didn't know it well enough. And you would dare defend him in any manner after what he did to you? And to me?"

"It wasn't you there alone with him in the great hall, or your skin that crawled with the sensation of his unwanted hands upon it!"

His eyes revealed a stricken quality at her purposely cruel and telling words. "Maybe not, but it was done to me no less, for when you hurt, so do I. And he needed to strike at me with his power. He wanted to put me in my place, to emasculate me in his own way, and whether you know it or not, that is what you do, Alainn, when you won't allow me to protect you!"

He had gently grasped her by the shoulders and stared down into her eyes, needing to allow her to see the magnitude of the subject they were discussing and how compelled he was to make her see his reasoning.

"You appear to suggest your powers can right all wrongs.

They cannot! And if you think they're the solution to all injustice then you're dead wrong about that as well! Now where are my damnable clothes? I need a time apart from you before I say something I will surely regret!"

A tunic and trews instantly appeared in her hands and she threw them at him in a fury.

"Fine, Killian O'Brien, be off with you then, leave me whenever there is the slightest hint of unpleasantness or a trifle of disagreement between us!"

"I'm not cursedly well leavin' you forever! I'm only takin' a few moments to allow myself to calm my ire. Do you fault me even for that?" he said as he angrily pulled on his garments.

He clicked his tongue and Storm came to him. He mounted the horse without benefit of saddle, and looked back at her. He saw the displeased look on her face and the tears that brimmed in her eyes and threatened to fall.

"I won't be long away, Alainn."

"Oh take your time, milord; sure I'll welcome the blessed solitude!"

"I am now your husband and not your lord, and I've asked you not to refer to me by that title, for it riles me fiercely!"

"Then it serves my purpose well!" She sniped and snapped her fingers. He saw she was now clothed in a garment he'd never seen before.

"And where are you off to, then?" he questioned as his

horse reared obviously in need of a run.

"To converse with magical beings who do not condemn my powers and abilities!"

" 'Tis clear there is no use speakin' with you at the moment. I'll meet you back here straightaway."

"Don't make haste on my account, I am, after all, only your wife and this is only our honeymoon and soon to be our last day here together!" she sarcastically stated in a wounded tone as she began to hastily walk away in the opposite direction.

"Ah, so I'm not to be allowed to take a piss without ye with me then since we're now wed; is that how you see it?" He blared.

"Go you to hell, Killian O'Brien!" She hollered angrily as she glared at him.

"Sure, you're already seein' I'm livin' there, Alainn Mc—" He caught himself using her former name. She smiled at that, closed her startlingly blue eyes and disappeared before his.

⌘

ALAINN BRUSHED AGAINST the flowery bush and inhaled the sweet scent of the blossoms. She saw the clouds above her clear, and the soft rain stop. A bright and beautiful rainbow formed across the sky. She smiled at the magical sight, uncertain how much her powers determined the weather within the fairy glade.

Many tiny creatures had accompanied her on her walk. Some spoke, others simply flew near her or gently touched her to dispel her uncertainties. She shouldn't have allowed her quick temper to present itself, not here where the harmonious balance needed to be maintained, not now when their time together was so short. She glanced about and saw the dozens, no surely hundreds of magical beings that were gathering here, and Samhain was still months away. Perhaps her increased powers simply allowed her to see what had always been.

She longed for a place and a time when she could truly test her powers and see what limits or pinnacles she could reach or achieve with them. She doubted that would ever become a reality. She'd clearly had just such an opportunity in the realm of the gods, but at that time Lugh was demandingly obstinate and attempting to control her, and all she could dwell upon then was the need to be back with Killian.

Now she knew she must protect those around her, though that, too, oftentimes required the use of her powers no matter what Killian said or how he felt on the subject. Did he truly believe she could simply allow him to possibly be mortally wounded; or taken from her when their lives together had just begun? Yet, if she interfered, he surely would see it as a slight to his masculinity, a disservice a wife should never do to her husband. Perhaps he would not know, but that in itself would be entirely too deceptive. And he *would* know, for he knew her well, even before they'd been joined by her magical protection charm and by matrimony. Therefore, she would be forced to stand by and let fate deal whatever hand it had in store for them, to keep her husband's love and to ensure she knew what deep respect she held for him.

She tried to envision the results of the challenge between Killian and his uncle. It would not come to her for all her attempts and her continued efforts only made her head ache fiercely as though she was not meant to know the outcome. That disturbed her as well. The child moved inside her and she shook her head.

"You, wee imp, are you so like your father; you are already determining I should not use these powers?"

She jumped when she saw Lugh suddenly materialize before her.

"Why are you here?" she questioned in a rude tone, which was replaced with trepidation when she considered what the reason might actually be. "Are you here to take me back to your realm? Has the Council of the Gods deemed I should be punished for my actions during my time there?"

The male god dismissed her concerns. "No, they do not seem interested in your part of the happenings and though they have discussed the matter with me at length, they have yet to issue sentence to me, as well. I am here for I simply needed to look upon you once more. I am admittedly most attracted to you, enchanting woman! It's been millennia since I've felt such an attraction and never before to a human woman!"

"You well know I am a married woman!" she insultingly retorted.

"And at odds with your husband after less than a week of being wed; perhaps he is not truly suited to you after all or simply incapable of satisfying you!"

"I most certainly will not discuss this with you! Killian and I have often been at odds for half our lives, because we sometimes disagree only indicates we are strong-willed and of opposing opinions at times; it does not change how we feel about one another. It certainly does not give cause to question if our love is any less because of it, and I am well satisfied, I'll have you know!"

"Ah, but you've never been pleasured by a god!"

"Nor will it ever be so!"

She pushed past Lugh and, when she looked up, she saw Aine standing before them.

She was scowling disapprovingly at the male god. "Once more, Lugh, you refuse to listen to reason or commands, even after the events when last time you acted so negligently. You were not to make contact again, only to look down upon Alainn. Once more you are overstepping your rights and ignoring your responsibilities."

"Aine, you are far too serious, perhaps it is you who needs an erotic time with me to ensure you are duly satisfied?"

She glanced at him briefly, but soon shook her head.

"Not by destiny or desire!" She rebuked him, but smiled at her descendant.

Alainn questioned the other woman. "You told me Killian and Danhoul are to be my guardians. This most distasteful being is no longer required, 'tis doubtful he ever was!"

Aine smiled at the Alainn's open and shared dislike of the male god.

"On earth, when all is well with you, your husband and Danhoul, the young druid, will be your protectors and guardian of your powers, but destiny may determine a time when you are and your husband are parted. And your kind often requires many guardians. There are also worlds and times where your husband cannot venture, and not all gods, creatures, or even angels can enter into the realm of humans. And though you may not believe it now, this arrogant, distasteful male will be needed.

"Destiny be damned, I'll not ever be long-parted from my husband, and I assure you I'll never need the likes of him!"

When Alainn heard the sound of a horse's hooves in the distance, she knew Killian was near and she felt her heart gladden.

Lugh noticed. "You truly are in love with the man?" He mused in complete astonishment.

"Entirely in love, evidently beyond what you are capable of understanding," she whispered and she saw the god vanish before her. Soon Aine was gone as well.

⌘

KILLIAN ESPIED HER standing by a laurel bush and he smiled a broad smile at the enchanting sight of her. Her hair shone even more lustrously than usual, here in the glade, and her eyes were a sparkling, magically luminous blue as she lovingly turned to meet his gaze. He leaned over and effortlessly pulled her upon the horse with him.

"Your rancor has cooled, then, Killian?"

"Aye, and has your own vexation lessened as well, Lainna?"

"It has!" she whispered as she turned and her lips grazed his throat.

"Then I've a notion we'd best take advantage of this time and this place and continue with the more favorable aspects of bein' wed, for I've missed ye even in this short time we've been apart!"

"Aye, milord! I've missed you as well!" She cooed teasingly as she leaned back against him and his hands moved upward from her waist to her breasts.

"If I'm your lord, then surely you're my servant! Do you intend to service me?"

"Aye, but to be serviced as well!" She chortled seductively.

He nudged his horse in order to hasten them to their private haven.

⌘

THEY SPENT THE remainder of the day and the evening in their marriage bed. They'd made love once in a slow, gentle, tender fashion and the next time in a torrid, reckless, uninhibited manner. The third had begun in the water. Alainn had taken a scented soap to bathe in the warmth of the water, where Killian joined her on the intention of merely soaping down her back. Of course, it had led to something much more primal and pleasing. When the gloriously sensual joining was completed, they'd slept…in each other's arms, entangled in intimate embraces, but always, always touching. Alainn sensed neither of them really wanted to dwell on the time they would be made to leave this place.

As she began to drift off to sleep, she heard him whisper to her though she'd been almost certain he was asleep.

"Promise me you won't interfere with the challenge, Alainn!"

"Mmmmm…" she simply whispered back pretending she was mostly asleep.

"An unintelligible mumble will surely not serve as a binding promise, Lainna!" He caressed the back of her neck as he spoke. "I need to hear you pledge the words to me on this!"

She turned to face him and looked into his serious eyes.

"Swear to me!" He pressed.

She sighed resignedly and glanced up at him with doubt upon her lovely face. "I don't pretend to like it and I am greatly fearful of the upcoming challenge, but I will do as you wish. I swear I will not interfere with your challenge in any manner, including by way of magic!"

He smiled a serious sort of smile, and kissed her hand as he held tight to it.

"I require further time in the spring," she interrupted the solemn moment. "Come join me, Killian! Let us gaze upon the stars and forget our woes while we bathe in the warmth of the enchanting water?"

"Aye, that sounds like a fine notion, Lainna!"

Chapter Twelve

WHEN THEY'D SPENT a considerable time basking in the warmth of the pleasing spring waters, Alainn made a further suggestion. "Might we walk in the glade and see what can be seen through the portals."

"I promised your kin and the fairies we'd not venture through the portals or into any other realm, and I intend to remain true to my word."

"I agree, Killian. I do not wish to go through the portals, for we must remain here to ensure the curse is truly lifted, and our child remains well, but would it not be of interest to you to simply gaze into other realms, or other times?"

"Aye, indeed it would! I'd be most intrigued by that. I know well enough with your many abilities you are able to see these magical places, but will I actually be capable of seein' through the portals?"

"If you take my hand and I envision a sight, I believe I can show you. I have not attempted it often but I believe I am capable. In truth, I believe you could envision something and I will be able to manifest the image so we can see it before our eyes, as though we were there in the location, actually present where the memory was created."

"How could that be?"

"Come here, sit beside me and we'll give a go!"

"Would it not be best done in daylight?" he questioned.

Soon the stars above them shone brighter and the entire area surrounding them was lighted with surely a thousand lightening bugs, then magical lanterns appeared that cast an ethereal glow. She smiled at being able to use her powers openly and gestured for him to join her on the edge of the water.

He did as she'd instructed and sat beside her on the soft, green grass, their feet still trailing in the water. They'd become so entirely relaxed and contented with each other that being unclothed had become completely natural to them. She took his large hands in her own and told him to close his eyes and think of an image of something she'd never seen.

She sat still for a time, but finally spoke. "I haven't actually seen it, but I've been near it?" she questioned.

"Aye, you're correct!" He grinned, enthralled by this entertaining pastime.

She summoned all her powers and her mind filled with the vision of the sight he'd seen within his mind's eye. When she finally told him to open his eyes, he gasped and almost let go of her hands, but she told him to remain as they were. When she opened her eyes, it appeared they were in an immense bedchamber. The walls were stone and the bed that stood before them was adorned with rich brocade fabrics. The furniture was grand and elegant and of a dark, colored wood.

"Where is this place, Killian?"

" 'Tis my parent's bedchamber. I'd always imagined we would spend our honeymoon here. God willing, this is where we shall sleep and love for all our married life after we make the journey to our castle," he promised, barely able to believe she had formed this image simply from his memory. "How is it you can't read my mind, but you can see my thoughts of this place?"

"I don't begin to attempt to understand my powers any longer. Perhaps because we are touching or because you were willing to have me see this, it is possible."

"But I would be willing to have you know my thoughts. Well, most of the time" he added as an afterthought.

"Not this afternoon during our quarrel?"

"No, I think I told you well enough what was on my mind! You didn't need to hear my thoughts"

"Aye, sure you didn't seem inclined to keep your anger within!"

"I can't, Alainn. God help me, I do try, but with you I can't conceal the good or the bad of what I'm feelin', and you make me feel the both of those extremes, and on a regular basis."

She nodded with understanding and trying to dispel his seriousness, she spoke. "Would you like to see somethin' I envision within my mind, the very day when first I laid eyes upon you?"

"The day in my bedchamber, when you healed me?" He wondered.

"Nay, 'twas before that, Killian. Would you like me to show you?"

"Aye, I would!" He held her hand and softly caressed it as they sat there together.

She closed her eyes once more and visualized a time several years previous. She brought the image to her mind and when she opened her eyes, he was staring even more disbelievingly than he had before.

" 'Tis me, when I was only a young boy. I would have been perhaps eight years of age yet it is at Castle O'Brien. My God, Alainn, my parents are there, and my siblings, Cian and Nola as well. She's so young then. How is it you remember this?"

Alainn pointed to the small child in the corner hiding by the castle gate.

" 'Tis you?" Killian exclaimed, looking at the wee girl with the long golden hair and the large, frightened blue eyes, holding tight to Morag, the old healer's hand.

"Aye, I remember it well for it was the day the farrier took me to live with Morag. I was fearful and felt great despair and uncertainty. I saw your family arrive for a stay with the chieftain and his family. I remember wishing to have a family like yours, wondering what it would be like to feel so entirely loved. And you gazed at me, your warm green eyes looked at me so intently, and it was as though you knew what I was thinking. You smiled at me, and I think then, Killian, that very day when I was but three years of age that was truly when I fell in love with you."

"Why don't I have a memory of that?" Killian wondered aloud.

"It was of no consequence to you at the time and why would you remember a young servant child?"

"If you looked as sad as you do in this vision, then surely I should have remembered you!"

"You were only young yourself and on your way to spend time with your cousins whom you hadn't seen in a goodly while. You were overjoyed and excited, you couldn't wait to be with them, and I was excited for you. After you smiled at me and I felt the warmth of your eyes, I was no longer afraid. And even then I knew we would one day be close, perhaps even then I knew one day we would fall in love."

"And that is why you believe you somehow caused the events that led to me coming to live at Castle O'Brien?"

"Aye, at times it plagues me still, Killian. What if the desires of a powerful, wee girl capable of magic were the cause of your family's tragedy and despair?"

"I don't believe it, Alainn, not for a second, and you shouldn't either. You must dismiss that grim and disturbing line of thinking entirely. You can make me another promise this night; that you'll not dwell on this, not ever again. Will you promise me that?"

"I can hardly control what I think or what I fret about."

"Well you're not doin' yourself or me any favors by worryin' regarding this, Alainn. So tell me when these dark and unsettling thoughts enter your mind you'll think of an enormous blue dragon who belongs only to you…a dragon whose only purpose is to be there to do your bidding and protect you from fears and perils."

"Have you gone completely daft, Killian O'Brien?" she asked as he rattled on adding more and more to the fanciful statement. "Were you too long in the water or too long distanced from humans?"

He chuckled loudly at that. "No, 'twas something my mother used to say to my brother and me, but most especially me because of my often troublesome imagination. I would lie awake at night afraid of what might be hiding under my bed or what despicable monster might visit me in my dreams, so my mother tried to reason with me. She'd tell me every time a fearful thought entered my mind to envision a large dragon, usually green for I had an affinity for that color, but I thought since you have mentioned your preference to blue, I'd change the details a wee bit for you. And now that I know you've actually seen dragons you should have no difficulty imagining such beings."

Alainn smiled warmly and looked into her husband's eyes so filled with fondness in his memory of his mother and her nurturing.

"At any rate, she had me dwelling on what the dragon would look like, how big it was, how powerful, and of course he was mine so he would be willing to fight off any monster or horrid creature to protect me. I'd go to sleep with that image in my mind and it proved effective every time. And it helped throughout my life whenever I worried unduly about something of which I had no control. It still does, except now when my thoughts go to a dark place or a dark time, my dragon has beautiful long golden hair and large expressive blue eyes and a lovely enthralling shapely body that would make any man want to die just to have a glimpse of the heaven of it. And of course she is mine so she's willin' to do anythin' for me."

He leaned over and kissed her and saw tears in her eyes again.

"Aye, I'd do anything for you, Killian. Sure I promise you that!"

"Then come now, Alainn, let's go look through the portals and see what we might see, for by my estimation we've only tomorrow and one more night after this one before we must leave this lovely place and …"

"What if I caused it to rain for two fortnights, Killian? The challenges would need to be postponed much longer. Could we perhaps spend another moon here in the glade?"

His eyes became filled with anticipation that soon gave way to doubt.

"How does the different measurement in time affect our

child, Alainn? Does he continue to grow at a similar rate within you when time nearly stands still here?"

"I am uncertain of that truth, Killian. As you know, because of my unusual abilities, I felt movement unusually early and he continues to move strong and often, but sure I have no clear answer to your question then."

"Then best we make the most of the time we have here and then leave when we intended."

She sighed deeply and nodded. "Aye, for I would do anything for him as well," she whispered as she lovingly placed her hand to her belly.

Killian bent over and placed a soft kiss upon the spot she'd touched. It tickled and she giggled and the baby moved yet again.

"He knows you love him as well, Killian!"

"Aye, I do, Alainn, for he is a part of you, of course I will always love him and to know we created him together from our love, it causes me to experience a deep unfamiliar emotion I did not know I was capable of."

"I think I could spend an eternity with you, Killian, and never tire of hearing you speak to me. Even today when I was so angry with you and you with me, the love I felt for you was growing with each moment. Is it right to love another so completely, so intensely? For I love you more than life, Killian. I could not bear it if something untoward should happen to you. How could I live on if..."

"I think you'd best call upon your dragon, Alainn, for

you do have a tendency to fret about things you cannot control, and if you cannot then surely no one, bar God himself, can. So wipe the maudlin look off yer lovely sweet face and get some form of garment on you, for we've other realms to see, my beautiful Lainna."

He stood and extended his arm. She rose as well and she snapped her fingers again and she was dressed in a lovely green gown.

"You said you favored green!" She commented when he looked at her still finding it unusual seeing her using her powers so often and so effortlessly.

"And have you some other garments for me as well then, though you've assured me the fairies can't enter through the barrier you've created, the wee creatures seem to keep stealin' mine.

She soon held out her arms and was holding a rich gold set of tunic and trews for him. She started to pass them to him then thought better of it, she closed her eyes, waved her hands and he was clothed in the outfit.

"That does seem to save considerable time!" he simply said as he took her hand.

Chapter Thirteen

KILLIAN FOUND HIMSELF completely in awe of all that he was witnessing. He was being allowed to see a realm that few humans could ever lay claim to. He was surrounded by hundreds of fairies and unusual creatures of varying sizes and shapes. Some were startlingly beautiful, some undeniably quite homely, perhaps even frightening, but all mystical and enchanting.

Alainn smiled at his reaction to the various creatures and when his eyes bulged at the sight of a radiantly and captivatingly beautiful young fairy nearly the size of Alainn, and with considerably less clothing, she held her hands over his eyes and scolded him.

"Never you mind gazin' at her with that look. You're a married man now, Killian O'Brien, and should act accordingly." She taunted.

"Well, 'tis a wee bit difficult not to look at her, Alainn. She's flyin' right before us."

"Then close your eyes!" she stated simply, but laughed when he seemed unable to pull his gaze from her. "So it would appear I might be glancin' into other realms and times alone, for you seem content to remain in this spot. 'Tis fine. I'll see to it Lugh accompanies me. He would not turn me down, I'd wager!"

"What?" Killian managed as the young fairy sensually batted her eyelashes and smiled suggestively at the handsome man on Alainn's arm.

Alainn glowered at the fairy and chastised her. "Don't flirt so openly with my husband, Tara! Be off with you, go find another to entrance!" She glared at the fairy as she spoke, and Killian caught the displeased look.

The fairy openly challenged Alainn and drew closer to Killian with seduction heavy on her mind.

"Would you like me to place a spell upon you, Tara, to ensure you appear hideously unappealing to males of all species?"

She glared at Alainn, but did not move from her position where she continued to eagerly eye and openly appraise Killian from head to toe.

"So be it!" Alainn raised her hands and began to chant in a combination of druid and Gaelic. A swirling wind formed around the fairy and she shrieked and flew away before the whirlwind drew nearer to her. Alainn dismissed the spell and the wind diminished.

"Don't be jealous, Alainn!" Killian shook his head and seemed to be capable of clear thought once more. 'Tis you I am married to, I'll not risk losin' you, no matter what a woman or a fairy might look like. I was just admirin' her wings."

"Aye, well, fairy wings are indeed quite the sight to behold, but if her wings were on her chest, I might actually believe you, and Tara is a love nymph so her sole purpose is to entice, enchant, and to mate, repeatedly, so I suppose you would be drawn to her, you are a man, and I can't fault you for looking, but sure if you were ever to do anything more than look, Killian…"

The thunder rumbled threateningly to the north and Killian saw the sky darken, as did her blue eyes.

"You can't truly be questioning my faithfulness so early on in our marriage, Alainn. 'Tis a ludicrous consideration, so get those damnable thoughts out of your mind straightaway!"

"And later on in our marriage I might be warranted in having suspicions?" She quipped, only partly in jest, despising her jealousy yet, driven by it as well.

"Do I need to repeat my vows daily then, to reassure you I intend to remain faithful to you all the days of our lives, Alainn?"

"Not daily, but I would welcome a reassurance occasionally that it will always be me your heart yearns for and your body responds to for 'tis a certainty there have been others before me whom you have shared a passionate time with."

"Aye, we have discussed this previously, Alainn, and you're well aware I've bedded other women. I've not ever attempted to conceal that from you. But that was in the past."

"Aye, I know it, Killian, but it does sadden me to know you've shared with others what we now share." She morosely lamented.

He threw his arms up in exasperation and placed his palms out toward her in attempt to prove his point. "Nay, Alainn, that is untrue by every measure known to man. I assure you what we share is unusual and exceedingly rare. I tell you plain, what I share with you I have never shared with anyone else. Bedding someone for simple gratification to still a physical urge is by no means anywhere close to what you and I share!"

She wore a pained expression and a look of uncertainty in her blue eyes as he continued to speak.

"When I love you, of course I gladly love you with my body, but I love you with all that I am, with my heart and my soul. You cannot continue to let my past indiscretions interfere with the great love we share now. Perhaps, I should then be jealous of the young druid, Danhoul?"

"Danhoul? Why ever would you be jealous of Danhoul?" She appeared almost amused, "Sure I barely know him, and I've certainly never entertained the notion of sharing his bed, much less actually done so."

"Aye, but you share much with the boy. You can hear his thoughts, you can speak to him telepathically, you are both capable of many magical feats and you are both druids. The two of you are able to travel to other realms. I can never be part of any of that, Alainn."

She glanced up at him with new understanding, "But 'tis not entirely the same, Killian. And how can you know for certain you will never tire of what we share, that you won't require the variety of women you once knew? What if one day you should find our time together with all the many uncertainties that come with my magical abilities, too difficult to bear any longer?"

Killian's face took on a much more serious expression as he clasped her hands in his and he looked deeply into her unsure eyes. "You must trust in me and our mutual love, as I do. How do I know for certain you will be content in our marriage, that one day you won't long to journey to the realm of the gods once more to ride upon a dragon?"

She shook her head. "Killian, you are being ridiculously absurd! When I was in the realm of the gods all I could think of was getting back to you."

"So no part of your experience there was intriguing or exciting?"

"Not enough to warrant being parted from you, Killian!"

"Then sure you must not doubt me, Lainna! He spoke on with words of understanding and reassurance. "I well know the man you believed to be your father abandoned you when you were only a wee girl, and the woman who is truly your mother handed you over to strangers when you were only days old, but don't judge me by their actions, Alainn! I love you with every breath I take, with every time my heart beats! I'll never, ever disavow you, and I don't know how to calm your jealousy or quell your uncertainty."

His green eyes filled with seriousness and his handsome face pleaded with her as much as his words. "Even though we both know our union isn't likely to be without its trying challenges or uncommon obstacles, I'd never willingly choose to do anything to put our marriage in jeopardy. I'll be with you till one of us no longer lives. I'll not ever do you wrong. You've heard me speak the vows before God, but I'll do whatever pagan ritual you require if it will make you more confident and secure in my love and my word. So draw my blood if you must, but never again question my love or fidelity, Alainn. I promise you, there'll never be another woman in my heart or my bed!"

He remained standing there his hand still extended to her, but she smiled instead.

"I have no dagger with me just now!" She dismissed his offer and stood on her tiptoes, placed a gentle kiss on his lips and then took his strong hand in her own. "I'll not question nor mention your fidelity again, Killian!" She pledged.

His eyes registered relief at appearing to have finally managed to settle her many doubts.

⌘

THEY WALKED ON together hand in hand, Alainn offering further explanation of what type each fairy and creature was, where each had apparently originated, and what powers or magical abilities each possessed. He was entirely intrigued with every detail. When they came upon a dark shadow on the ground, Alainn carefully took a wide berth and guided Killian around it.

"Never step into the round shadows for they are portals to other realms, usually to darker worlds!"

Killian seemed filled with disbelief. "I thought it was only in the edges of the glade that the evil creatures were found.

"Many congregate in the Unseelie Court, but there are openings to other worlds within the fairy realm and even within the human world."

"And are there people who simply stumble upon them mistakenly and are carried off to other worlds?"

"Not often, but aye, I have heard it has happened so."

"And are they able to get back again?"

"Sometimes the portal reopens and they are allowed to make their way back, other times those with supernatural abilities, appointed searchers or guardians must pursue them and right the wrong. They must see to it that they are brought back to their own realm or to their own time so the future will not be adversely affected."

They came upon a vast, rounded hill that looked like any other, but Alainn gestured to Killian to peek through a tiny opening and to look within.

"What is this place?" he asked his voice laced with curiosity.

" 'Tis this precise location, but another time…a time

very, very long ago."

Killian curiously peered in once more and noticed how remarkably beautiful it was. The grass appeared even greener than usual, there were many more trees, and there seemed to be an all-encompassing serenity and peacefulness to the place. He could see no buildings, not a castle or cottage, not even a stone wall or a roadway. Alainn leaned closer to him and they looked in together.

He grew extremely excited at what he next saw. "Jesus, Mary and Joseph, Alainn, is that a…"

"A giant Irish elk?" she excitedly answered. "Aye, when you made mention of that animal the other day, I thought you might like to view one since they've been gone from this earth since long before man inhabited it. Aren't they stunningly majestic creatures and even more immense than simply looking upon a set of their broad antlers pulled from a peat bog would indicate?"

"You've seen them before then; lookin' through this magical portal you've seen these enormous beasts on other occasions?"

"Aye, I've always been drawn to gaze upon them, and they can see us, too?"

Killian remained doubtful even after all he'd seen, so he moved his hand before the portal as if motioning to the creature. The giant animal slowly turned its massive head and knowingly looked straight into Killian's eyes.

"Shite, you're right, he can see us. Could he come

through the portal?

"It is doubtful. He knows where he belongs, what time and what place. I think it is only humans who make the mistake of heading to another time. Of course, sometimes it is not a mistake. There are those who deem it adventurous to head off to other times."

"And you've never gone, Alainn? I find that difficult to believe; you were always so desperate for adventure when you were younger."

"I have looked into the past many times, but never ventured back for I was always fearful of being unable to return to you. And the future is less appealing to me. I have taken quick glances, but it does not hold my interest."

"And what frightens you about the future, Alainn?"

"I did not say I was frightened."

"You didn't have to speak the words, Alainn. I can see well enough you are fearful to look ahead in time."

"Well, sure I'd not care to look upon myself on my own deathbed or, worse yet, on you at the end of your life."

"And can you not look far, far ahead into the future, perhaps many centuries ahead then? We will only be dust by then so your fears would be unwarranted."

"I suppose," she whispered, but it was obvious it was not a consideration she desired.

They walked on again, Alainn pointing out several other portals. Some were actual arched doorways, others oval-shaped windows, and some appeared only as a shadow or a circle of light upon the ground.

"And so we are to avoid the dark shadows, but what of the circles of light upon the ground?"

"They usually indicate a place where the veil is thin between our worlds, they lead to magical lands, but even they are not without danger, for not all magical beings can simply be classified as good or evil, just as humans I suppose. Some are capable of both!"

"And how are you able to distinguish between the portals that lead to other worlds and those that lead to other times?"

"The past is often found in a hill, for the many secrets lie deep within, memories and events layered one upon the other... the culmination is often a rounded hill. The future is sometimes in a gulley for the events have not yet produced distinct memories, but not always. Doorways to the past are also simpler to open for they have been opened before. The portals that lead to the future are more deceptive, for to dare to go into the future you risk changing events in the past and that can have irreversibly tragic results, I am told!"

"And where does this doorway lead then, Alainn?" Killian pointed to a small circle liken to a ray of light from the sun.

"That is the past, but the recent past, and it is lighted with such an appealing glow because it holds a pleasing memory for you and me."

Alainn closed her eyes and moved her hand gently over the spot and soon Killian saw the two of them standing before the priest, exchanging their vows. He listened to every word and he noticed how Alainn's eyes were glistening with tears when they watched their first kiss as husband and wife. She moved her hand again and the image was gone.

"Why is it women tend to weep so at weddings, Alainn?"

" 'Tis a time of great emotion, to give oneself to another forever. Sure it can be the happiest, most meaningful time in one's life or perhaps the saddest, most disparaging day for many women…and men, I suppose!"

She showed him many other portals, some held memories of his childhood, others were their shared memories, and they laughed and talked together of happy times in days gone by. She passed an especially dark circle on the ground before them and hurriedly moved from it without directly looking down at it. This only proved to pique his curiosity.

" 'Tis a most dark memory!" she simply stated as she continued to hurriedly walk away.

Chapter Fourteen

"A DARK MEMORY for me?" he questioned, undoubtedly curious.

"Aye, for you Killian. 'Tis the day your father's castle was pillaged, your brother, Cian, was killed, along with so many others, and your father taken away. The day you were wounded so severely by the invading clansman's sword and you were nearly killed yourself…the day your uncle found you hidden amongst the dead bodies."

"I must see it!" he demanded.

"No." She shook her head in adamant disagreement. "It would not be a wise consideration, Killian. I have viewed it before. 'Tis bloody and brutal and left me grievous and heartsick. It is nothing short of miraculous that you survived the harrowing ordeal at all!"

"And why did you feel compelled to watch it, then, Alainn?" His tone was soft, but his voice had a distinct coolness to it.

"I needed to understand all that had happened, all you'd experienced before I could attempt to heal you."

"You watched it when you were a small child; even before you healed me?"

"Aye!"

"Well then, as a grown man, I suspect I'll be able to bear it if you were able to withstand it when you were only a wee girl!"

Her eyes were sad and solemn, she remained doubtful of the wisdom of allowing him to witness it, but she knew he would not be dissuaded. She held tight to his hand while he viewed the gory spectacle, but she kept her back to the gruesome scene. When he'd obviously seen enough, he turned his head away and slowly lowered himself to the ground. His face had gone nearly void of color and his entire body shook with emotion at the painful memories that had been stirred by the vision.

She sat down upon his lap and gently wrapped her arms around his neck trying to ease his great pain. She tenderly ran her hand up and down his lengthy scar and finally took his handsome tanned face in her hands.

"You were unusually strong and valiant even then, Killian…at two and ten, forced to fight like a man when you were scarcely more than a boy."

"Could I go back to that time, Alainn? Would you be capable of allowing me to journey back through time to that dismal day?"

"It is unlikely, sure I'd not be capable of taking you back to that fateful time," she said in a voice barely more than a whisper.

"But if I might save my brother, or see what was actually done to my father."

"If your brother lived through that day, he would surely not live long, for it must have been fated to be."

"How can you of all people say that, Alainn? You saved Rory from the fall to certain death at the round tower several years ago, and he still lives today."

"But sure I must have been meant to save him. I was allowed to view the portent vision of his impending misfortune because he was not actually meant to die. It was not what fate had in store for him."

"So you think every step of our lives is already mapped out ahead of time, that we are simply pawns or puppets acting out a great drama…that no matter what we do in our lives, no matter what our choices, that the consequences are predesigned, everything is already aptly charted and accurately predetermined?"

"I don't know what I truly believe, not entirely, Killian, for it oft seems contradictory and ever-changing. I do believe God has a specific plan for all of us!"

"What God, Alainn? My God, Lord God Almighty, our Christian God, or one of the Celtic gods that you now know exist?"

His tone was angry and challenging, and she knew he was becoming uncommonly argumentative. She reasoned that seeing the past had left him sorely tormented and she regretted allowing him to witness it and to relive it.

"I do believe in our God, Killian. 'Tis how I was raised; same as you."

"But what of the other gods you speak of?"

"Perhaps they are not truly gods, just entities, or lesser deities. I am uncertain, Killian." Her voice grew weary as she spoke. "Because I possess magical abilities clearly does not ensure I have definite answers to any of these great quandaries!"

"And when you interfere with the grand scheme of God or these other entities are you not riskin' catastrophic consequences?"

"I do not know for certain, Killian. I don't always use my mind when I employ my powers, but often my heart. If we went back to attempt to save your brother, perhaps a far worse fate would befall him!"

"Worse than a painfully brutal death at the age of three and ten?" His tone was sarcastic.

"Aye, he might have been horribly maimed. He may have been left alive, but never able to recover, unable to live as freely as he once did. He may have lost his legs or his eyes, had a mortal wound inflicted upon him that became purulent. He might have suffered in grievous pain for days, weeks, perhaps even months only to die at any rate. And what would that have done to your own heart, Killian, to watch on without possessing the ability to assist him or heal him?" she whispered, sadly knowing well enough what torture Killian would have endured if that had been Cian's fate.

"And why then could we not simply watch what happened to my father; to learn what fate befell him, for not knowing, the damnable uncertainty has been slowly eating away at me for so many years."

"Sure, I know it well, Killian!" She held him tight around his neck and though she was pleased he was opening up to her regarding this subject often too painful to be broached, she had few answers. "I have tried, Killian, so many, many times through the years, I have attempted to see him, to conjure an image of him, but it eludes me. Not so long ago, I spoke to Morag about it and she does not see your father or mine in the spirit world."

"You've gone back there, Alainn, back to the spirit world, after what happened last time when you very nearly were unable to leave the spirit world?" His voice was raw with emotion.

"I wanted to be able to tell you I had news of your father one way or the other, and I sensed that your father and mine were together somehow. I thought the only place they could be together was in the spirit world."

"But Mara says you might not be capable of returning from there and yet you still go when I have forbidden it."

"It was for you I went. And Mara does not understand everything about my magic. 'Tis true she is a witch and possesses powers, but they are not of the same strain or magnitude of mine for I am of fairy and druid lineage."

"Don't go back there, Alainn. Not for me, not for anyone. I swear if you attempt it one more time, I'll..." His voice was shaking now, so distinctly displeased was he, and Alainn sensed his entire body growing tense in his fury.

"This was a grave mistake, coming here, looking back or forward. 'Tis surely not meant for a human to witness." She pondered more to herself than to her husband.

She moved from him and as she stood above the dark shadow on the ground before she held her arms out and then chanted lowly in words he could not discern.

"What is it you are doing now, Alainn?"

"I am creating a spell to permanently close this portal. No one shall ever be capable of entering or looking into it again for no good can come of looking upon the tragic events of that day. I should have done it long ago. If I'd known how to manage it as a child, I might have done it when I saw it back then."

"Why not simply close them all, then?" Killian remarked in a less than pleased tone as he angrily gestured to the area surrounding them.

"A lot you know!" She griped in an equally displeased manner. "If I had a hundred years and there were a dozen of me, I might be capable of accomplishing sealing some of the portals."

"There are that many?" he asked, this time more interested than displeased.

"More than even I could imagine. And some I cannot see

or am not allowed to witness. If they pertain to me or involve me directly and I might attempt to alter the outcome, past or future, I am usually not given access to viewing them."

"Forgive me, Lainna!" he whispered as he gently caressed her cheek. "I was wrong to grow so angry and to direct my rage at you."

" 'Tis what a wife is for, no? To share all, both good and bad?" She smiled, but sadness remained within her eyes.

"No, a wife is to cherish and treasure, to love and to honor."

"That would clearly not be a wife, but an angel or a goddess, not realistic, not included. I would rather bear the brunt of some of your displeasure and be included than to be shut out of what hurts or angers you. For surely together, united always, we can get through whatever life and fate has in store for us."

"Surely!" He smiled and held her tightly to him.

"Shall we go back to our bed, then, Killian? I think we have seen enough of other times."

"Aye!" He nodded in relieved agreement.

As they began walking back arm in arm, a large indentation in the ground seemed to appear before their eyes. Within the center, an oval opening appeared liken to a looking glass.

"Does that opening indicate you are to look within it?"

"So it would seem!" Alainn did not seem entirely overjoyed with the consideration.

As they approached it and peered inside, the noise and confusion nearly overpowered everything else about the vision. There were buildings that reached far into the sky and coaches that were swift and noisy, and some that disbelievingly flew through the skies. The air was filled with a pungent scent and the sky was enshrouded in a vaporous dark cloud.

The wide streets were filled with crowds of people all donned in unusual garments and all seemingly in a hurry. The unfamiliar sounds roared in their ears and Alainn glanced at a window in one of the enormous buildings. She noted a face in the window looking back at her and she felt a violent repulsion at the sight. She pulled away from the vision and fell back to the ground.

"What the hell was that place, Alainn, and what did you see that frightened you so?"

"I am almost certain the place was England, but I believe the time was centuries from now. I think I shall never again look into the future. I do not care to see what violations have been done to our world by then. I have seen quite enough!"

"Aye, well 'tis true it wasn't pleasant. The din was enough to make a person's ears protest, and the smell of it was acrid, but why did it frighten you so? Did you see something I was not aware of?"

"I don't care to discuss it, Killian. If that is what the future holds nearly five centuries from now, then I am most pleased I live now, here in an era I adore, for even though it is not a time without peril and uncertainty, it is much preferred to that atrocity, and besides I *am* here with you in this time and that is all I shall ever desire."

He noticed how her hands trembled and her voice quavered as she spoke. She'd obviously seen something more that disturbed her, but she wasn't willing to discuss it and he would not push the issue.

They would go back to their bed, share another night of love together just the two of them, for soon they would need to leave this strange and beautiful place. They would need to face their world and their troubles, which included his uncle and their upcoming challenge, not to mention all that he'd seen at the graveyard with Danhoul and the spirit woman, Ainna. He had yet to speak of that to Alainn. He wasn't certain he would ever be truly ready to relive that. Dwelling on those dismal thoughts left him as shaken as whatever it was that Alainn had seen in the far off future.

Chapter Fifteen

ALAINN AWOKE TO find Killian gone from their bed. She pulled back the silken fabrics that surrounded the bed and ensured they kept the bright morning sunlight from shining within. She spotted him on the other side of the water. He was wearing only his trews and his brawny chest glistened. He held a large tree branch in his hands and he was pulling it through the air as if it were a sword. She watched as his arms, taut and well-formed, strained with the weight of the branch and the speed with which he thrashed it through the air. He was practicing for his battle with his uncle, she was certain. He would be facing one opponent later this morning and another this afternoon. It may well be Riley that he faced this afternoon, for it was often the two O'Briens that battled it out for championship of the tournament.

As the standings stood the day before their wedding, Killian held first place and Riley second, they would battle the third and fourth opponents and the winners battle each other to be declared the champion. Killian had won the last three years, but this year because of the grand celebration the opponents consisted of even greater numbers.

Although she seldom watched when Killian took part in a challenge for she despised the knowledge he might be in imminent danger, Alainn delighted in viewing him when he was in mock battle. She thrilled in watching his chest and arms and back as he moved with a rare agility for the size of man he was. And his thighs and buttocks were most commendable as well. She smiled as she thought of what lie between those muscular thighs. It was still a wonder to her that not so very long ago she'd been virtuous, then only dreamed of being with Killian in that manner, but never actually believed it would be so. And now they were married, she carried his child, and they shared a physical relationship that brought a fire within her when even she thought of them being together.

She felt her cheeks grow warm as did every part of her at the thought of what it was like when they were joined in physical intimacy. She pulled herself from her lustful thoughts and continued to watch her husband in mock battle. She heard him cuss out loud when the branch splintered as he struck the ground with it. Alainn closed her eyes and aptly summoned his sword. When she opened them he held it in his hands.

"Ah, so you're awake then?" He said when he saw his wife looking out from the canopied bed.

"Aye, I've only just wakened and seen you so busily training."

"And what of the ruling of no weapons within the glade?" he called to her from across the spring.

"We will need to leave soon enough and I doubt you'd ever actually desire to cause harm to the creatures here in the glade. 'Tis important you hone your skills to the utmost."

"Now you're not makin' me feel entirely confident with that bit of concern evident in your voice."

"No, I am most confident in your abilities, but you have not held a sword in many days, and I know how regularly you prefer to train. And you could use a partner to spar with."

"And did you have some wee fairy in mind?" He jested.

"There are others who might be enlisted who are capable of giving you a fair bout."

Alainn remembered seeing the muscular form of Lugh, who was supposedly her guardian. He boasted often of being skilled in all forms of weaponry. Perhaps he would be willing to spar with her husband if she wished it to be so. As her guardian she hoped he would be willing to assist her. She'd barely allowed that thought to enter her head when he appeared before her. She remembered she wore no clothing so she quickly pulled the sheer curtains closed around the bed.

"Did you summon me, woman? Have you already tired of your human? Do you long to spend time with a male who could surely satisfy you more adequately?"

Alainn searched for her garments. They had been in rather a hurry to disrobe last night and she couldn't recall where her gown or chemise had been removed. And Killian was correct, the fairies seemed to delight in magically stealing their garments and keeping them in a perpetual state of nakedness. Killian had taken to hiding his trews under his pillow so he would be ensured clothing in the morning. Alainn had not done so and she tried to summon some other garments, but she saw the curtains being pulled back and she hurriedly grabbed the quilts to cover herself.

"You needn't hide your alluring loveliness from me, enchanting woman!"

"Aye, I certainly must!" She quickly assured him as she envisioned garments and they appeared on the bed beside her.

"What did you call me here for if you don't want me to mate with you?"

"I didn't call you here, I only thought about you."

" 'Tis surely commonplace for females to lie within their beds and think of me, I would imagine," he stated with a distinct conceit Alainn snorted at. The loud voice behind them caused both their heads to turn.

"What is the damn meaning of this? Why, by God's bones, is there a mostly naked man gawkin' openly at my entirely naked wife?" Killian blared.

"I am well covered, Killian. I assure you. He has viewed no part of me."

"But I have imagined every part of you, enchanting

woman and most often!" The being declared without thought of hiding such lewd confessions.

"You've a lot of nerve, man, admitting such adulterous thoughts and leerin' at my wife so openly. Whoever or whatever you are, I suggest you draw your sword for I intend to teach you some manners in dealin' with another man's wife."

The gigantic male seemed entirely unfazed by this open invitation to do battle, but he did turn to assess the man. "You are a fairly adequate specimen for a man, I must admit, but I have not entered this realm to do battle. It was your wife who called me here, so I would suggest taming her some if I were you."

"You called him here, Alainn? What the hell is he talkin' about, and how do you know this man?"

"I am not a man!" The male seemed completely insulted by the suggestion.

"Well, whatever you are, I assume you are male, that you possess the objects that make you a male?"

"I do, indeed, and I'll reveal them to you should you require proof!"

He proceeded to begin to unfasten the cloth that covered his loins, but Killian and Alainn both discouraged it openly and Alainn looked away and felt her cheeks grow pink.

"I only just met him recently and I did not summon him, I merely thought of him."

"And why were you lying in our bed unclothed and

thinking of another man."

"I am not a man!" He vehemently repeated.

"Whatever the hell you claim to be, you can leave this instant. My wife and I have a few matters we must discuss."

"Do you truly wish me to leave?" He looked at Alainn and indiscreetly raised his eyebrow suggestively.

"My God, I have never seen anyone so entirely full of themselves. I thought of you because I thought you might serve my husband, not me."

"What?" both males yelled with matching looks of uncertainty and disdain on their faces.

"Not in that manner! Though I am well aware and by no means opposed to the fact many people are attracted and indeed hold deep love and longing for their own gender, that is not what I was referring to."

Both men had not lost their chagrined expressions which only proved to further amuse her. Alainn giggled in earnest and then found herself unable to stop laughing at the very thought of what they'd believed she was implying.

"He has a weapon!" She managed through her uproarious laughter.

"Is that the terminology humans have given to such bestowments?" The man glanced down at the barely adequate triangular garment covering his masculine attributes.

"No, you oaf, you possess a sword. My husband needs someone to spar with for he must do battle this day and he has been without training these past days."

"I would suggest he may well have been doing some endurance training for the amount of time you've spent within this space." He waved at the area of the spring. "This veil ensures no beings can see within, and your time behind it has been quite lengthy."

Killian finally seemed to grasp the meaning of what she'd been trying to tell him. A smile crossed his face.

"You would do battle with me, man?" the other being asked.

"And why wouldn't I; do you think I fear you?"

"He is immortal, Killian!" Alainn announced. "Pass me your sword, husband!"

"You don't need to shelter or protect me, Alainn. I'm not afraid to participate in sword play with him."

"But if you allow me to charm your sword then it can wound him!"

The god's eyes widened and he glanced at the woman who remained wrapped in the bedclothes, looking most alluring.

"Alainn, get yourself dressed before I have to cut out his eyes for the way he's starin' at you."

"Pass me your sword and then I will get dressed."

"And how do you mean to hold tight to the bedclothes and take hold of this heavy sword?" he queried.

She snapped her fingers and the bedclothes were instantly replaced by a gown. Killian passed her his sword, she worked her magic on it and then gave it back to him. Then a sword magically appeared in Lugh's hands as well.

"Now you must fight with skill, Lugh. But if you hurt my husband I swear you'll deal with me."

"And if he hurts me?" he asked in a voice filled with obvious mockery.

"You will bleed!"

The male was not entirely convinced but Killian deducted it was the first time he actually believed the other male began to take the bout seriously.

"I won't stay to watch, Killian, but I am secure in your abilities."

"But where are you headed, Alainn?"

"There is something I must attend to, but we'll break fast together when I return. For then we must leave this realm."

"Aye!" he agreed and the look of resignation on her face matched how he felt regarding the subject as well.

⌘

ALAINN COULD HEAR the steady clanking of the metal swords as she started out. She dreaded what she must do next, but she reasoned she needed to do it just the same. She found the location where she and Killian had been the previous night; the place where she had looked far into the future. She dared to look once more. Again her distaste for that time grew evident. It assaulted her senses. She searched through the many buildings she had seen the night before. She found the one she was looking for and her eyes skirted the many windows to the exact window she'd seen the previous night.

And, once again, she was terrified by what she saw. The eyes that stared back at her were most certainly her own.

Chapter Sixteen

ER HEART ACHED at the sadness of the eyes within the reflection for they appeared fearful, lonely, and confused. She tore herself away from the portal, and struggled to understand what she'd just seen. Obviously, she would be made to travel ahead in time. Apparently, one day that was what was fate had in store for her. Well, she was adamant she would not go willingly. She would fight it with whatever powers she could summon, for she would not leave the life she had, the time she lived in now, and, most importantly, she would not leave Killian.

When she turned to make her way back to Killian, Alainn saw Aine staring at her.

"You have seen what is to be then?"

"I have seen what might be. I will simply not allow it to come to fruition."

The goddess looked at her with obvious consideration. "Some things are not within our power to change, Alainn. And perhaps it is the very powers you possess that will deem you must journey to places or times you would not choose to if you were truly given the choice!"

"There is always a choice!" Alainn rebelled.

"And if the choice is death?"

"Then I would die in this world, and my time, with my husband." Alainn glanced at Aine with a new seriousness and another inquiry. "As a powerful being do you hold within you the power to remove the magical abilities I possess?"

The female goddess stared at her with a stern expression on her face and deep thoughtfulness in her eyes. "Nay, your powers are of an ancient origin and, as I mentioned before, there were any number of elements present to create your unique magical abilities. I possess no knowledge of any god or mystically enchanted being capable of simply dissolving your abilities or rendering them completely ineffectual. It is as I have previously explained; the conditions and events of your conception and birth created the many magical abilities you retain and lay claim to. They cannot simply be undone. There is surely a destined purpose for your powers and a charted destiny."

Alainn's eyes filled with profound sadness and uncertainty.

"And my kin, you have healed not a few and in truth saved many humans and often times those dearest to your heart because of your gifts and powers!" Aine stated, well aware of the truth.

Alainn nodded in agreement, but added, "Aye, but perhaps I have endangered as many with drawing and attracting dark beings because of my abilities as well."

"There is never a gift without consequence, or an asset without responsibility, not for humans or for gods. In truth, your powers may possibly endanger you and those around you, but more often they will clearly ensure your safety and benefit you and yours as well. Do not question them, revel in them, learn from them and one day, you will surely relish the fact you have been bestowed with such powerful, enchanting magic!"

They had no further time for discussion although Alainn longed to ask many more questions of the goddess, her ancestor who appeared to possess infinite knowledge as well as supernatural capabilities. Their conversation was cut short when Killian and his opponent were seen walking toward them. Alainn was relieved to see Killian had no wounds and all vital parts seemed to remain intact.

The male beside him appeared to be viewing Killian with new appreciation and respect. "He is an able swordsman and a capable warrior! For a man!" He added for Killian's benefit.

"And was Lugh able to challenge you adequately, Killian?" Alainn taunted the god.

"He'll have to do until I can spar with an actual man, I suppose!" Killian returned the jesting on the other male's account.

"Humans have absolutely no notion of what is humorous!" Lugh declared before he aptly vanished.

ALAINN FELT A deep sadness settling in her heart and her soul as they prepared to leave the glade.

Killian recognized it and, as they walked hand in hand across the fairy glade, he tried to reassure her. "At week's end, as soon as we have attended Riley and Rory's marriages, we shall leave straightaway for our castle. Then, after I have seen to some necessary matters at Castle O'Donnel, we will take an entire moon if we choose and never leave our bed-chamber. It will be as perfect and wonderful as it was here. Well, nearly at any rate, perhaps not so magical, but we can make our own kind of magic when we are alone together, aye?"

"Aye!" she whispered, but tears glistened in her eyes as she spoke.

"Don't be maudlin, Alainn! I know you fret overly much regarding the challenge, but you needn't worry so. I am confident I will defeat my uncle!"

They had reached the opening to the human world and Alainn felt her magical protective triquetra amulet grow warm and begin to glow. She knew it would not be a pleasant crossing for her this time for she had many concerns that plagued her mind.

When they reached the other side, she felt weak and her stomach reeled. She attempted to conceal this from Killian for he had more than his share of concerns to deal with. He led Storm as they slowly walked together through the stone close.

"I think it best you remain at Cook and Margaret's cottage this night. I will miss you most assuredly, but tomorrow night, after the challenges are concluded, we will never spend another night apart. I will tell my uncle of our marriage then. We will spend tomorrow night in my bedchamber in the castle."

"Aye!" she agreed but spoke no further, keeping her concerns and fretfulness within.

Killian continued speaking and informing her of what he believed would assist her. "This day, Alainn, you must go about your daily tasks as you would any other day. Go tend to your herbs and I ask again that you refrain from using your powers. Above all, you must attempt to avoid my uncle and his priest. Sure if we get through the next two days then we'll be through with all of this unpleasantness. We will locate the missing crest that belonged to your father. It will prove you are Teige O' Rorke's daughter, and sure soon we can then begin our journey to our castle where you will be living next to your grandfather. You'll be able to get to know each other as you should."

She wanted to tell him she didn't believe locating the crest would be a simple task, and they would surely never be able to leave Castle O'Brien with the curse still upon them. She wanted to reveal that she must also attempt to locate the record of her parent's wedding, and somehow make Hugh O'Brien, his brothers and all of the O'Briens recognize and accept her as nobility in order to ensure their child would live. Of course she spoke of none of these dismal topics for he had bouts and challenges that he must concentrate on.

She simply put her arms around his neck and was content to have him hold her for a moment longer before they would need to be parted. Finally they reluctantly pulled from their loving embrace. He escorted her to Cook and Margaret's cottage, where they held tight to each other once more, neither one wanting to let go. He finally began to walk away from her at Cook's gate, but then returned straightaway and he eyed her suspiciously.

"My sword, Alainn. Whatever you did to it by way of your magic, it must be undone."

She nodded and while he held it she touched the blade. It glowed, turned a bright golden color and then returned to its normal silver shade.

"I love you more than you could ever truly know, Killian O'Brien!" she whispered.

"And I you, Alainn O'Brien!" He smiled lovingly as he left her there and she inhaled several times in hope of calming her fears and stilling the tears that threatened to fall.

Chapter Seventeen

ALAINN STOPPED TO spend some appreciated time with Molly and Margaret. She was most happy to see them again and as she and Molly lovingly embraced, the younger girl's eyes filled with easily recognized happiness for her friend. Upon seeing her Margaret, she beamed widely and she, too, gathered Alainn close to her bosom for an affectionate moment of motherly doting.

Alainn was pleased at how quickly the morning passed. The three women sat comfortably together, enjoying a hot herbal drink while the many noisy Kilkenny children each came to claim their time with Alainn.

Cook and Margaret had thirteen children in all. Alainn's friend, Cookson was the eldest and he and four of his brothers, who were of an adequate age to work, were off in the castle's kitchen where they were employed with their father, who was head cook.

The Kilkenny's cottage was not large by any measure, and it always seemed bursting at the seams with playful, energetic children. Alainn smiled at their enthusiasm and their sweet, affectionate mannerisms.

She held the youngest babe upon her lap and noted, as always, Margaret maintained a happy home and a loving disposition toward her family. Although she could be stern when necessary and had clear expectations of her children, she did not agree with the common belief that children should be seen and not heard. She was never unduly sharp or impatient, and she often allowed her children to be raucous and willful. Because of this, their home was oftentimes chaotic and undoubtedly noisy, and there surely was never a dull moment.

As the women attempted to speak, the playful din around them made it seemingly impossible. Margaret finally stood, cast a strict maternal look, and gestured to her many children. Without so much as a commanding word spoken, they all obediently congregated to the other side of the cottage and soon partook in a quieter game.

"Now, we may actually be able to get a word in edge-wise!" Margaret smiled.

"You wedding was so very lovely, Alainn. I was greatly pleased and honored to be able to attend. And you truly spent your honeymoon within a fairy glade, Alainn!" Molly gushed. "It must have been a magical time."

"Aye, well, we weren't allowed an actual moon within the glade, but it was truly enchanting. If not for missing my friends, including the two of you, I think we might have stayed there indefinitely."

Margaret smiled at Alainn, clearly pleased at how radiantly happy she appeared.

"What news have you of the chieftain?" Alainn finally dared to ask.

"He has returned." Margaret assured her. "The captain and much of his army searched for him for no less than three days with no success in locating him. Then he returned of his own accord with no explanation of where he'd been. The physician apparently assessed his condition and found he had no obvious ill effects, although Seamus tells me the chieftain himself has no clear memory of his time away. Lady O'Brien and their sons were understandably wrought with concern at his absence. Myself, I was thinkin' maybe it would be better by far if he'd just stayed away for good, I was, the feckin' arse that he's been as of late!" Margaret admitted, and Alainn smiled at the woman's off-color language. "And sure then there'd be no cursed challenge between the earl and your Killian!"

Alainn nodded as she glanced at the seriousness in Margaret's eyes and, but for the fact Hugh O'Brien was quite possibly needed to do his part in ending the curse by accepting her, she would have much been in agreement with the other woman. The thought of the upcoming challenge left Alainn fearful once more.

"The chieftain did not appear to be overly enraged regarding Killian's absence then?" Alainn inquired.

"Da says from what he's noticed the earl seemed somewhat more agreeable since his return. I pray that continues, perhaps he'll simply cancel the damnable challenge."

Margaret glanced disapproving at her usually shy daughter and her uncommon use of unacceptable language.

"Not so becoming of a young lady!" She declared.

"Well 'tis a dreadful challenge and sure all present here at this table would be much grateful if it was cancelled."

"To be sure!" Her mother concurred.

Alainn thought that was highly unlikely and it was doubtful Killian would ever agree to it even if his uncle suggested it. She longed to have the worrisome topic out of her mind and she hurriedly changed the subject.

"Molly, have you and Pierce had occasion to spend further time together?"

Molly's cheeks turned crimson and she nervously twirled her finger in one of her many lovely, red ringlets.

"Aye, we've spent some time together." She blushed as though she longed to speak more freely with Alainn, but didn't elaborate since she was in her mother's company as well.

"Aye, they've requested time together on more than three occasions, never alone, mind you, for you'll know Seamus and I would not allow that consideration. The young man was here to dinner just last evening." Margaret related. "Sure, he's a brave sort for the lad withstood a meal and an entire evening at the Kilkenny table without complaint, which as you know is no easy feat!" She winked at the young women at the table beside her. "And her brothers were a might irksome toward their sister and her new beau!"

"Ardan and Carrig were ever so disagreeable, Alainn! Sure, they were horribly embarrassin' and they taunted Pierce unmercifully for they found a lovely poem he'd written for me. Even Cookson joined in the great delight of pokin' fun at the situation. When Pierce took leave, I gave them all a good tongue lashin', I did!" She smiled as her cheeks colored once more and the affection for her brothers was obvious no matter how often they chided her.

"And sure the lad must not have objected too severely for he's asked if he and his father might stop by this evening. So, I've invited the captain and his son for dinner this night. Come to it, best I'd better quit dawdlin' and get busy preparin' the meal."

Molly's hazel eyes brightened at the prospect of seeing Pierce again and Alainn sensed her friend's infatuation with the captain's son was changing to a more mature affection and possibly even love.

Alainn bid the women fond farewell and set off. The next stop she made was to the kitchen. She saw Cook and went to him upon seeing him.

"You look happy, Alainn!" He commented as he affectionately gathered to him the young woman whom he thought of as a daughter.

"I am happy, Cook…sure I am elated!"

"I am glad for you, Alainn! Truly, I am."

The kitchen was as always an undoubtedly bustling location and with so many guests remaining in the castle and present for the games and celebrations, Alainn noted there was little time to keep Cook detained. He glanced over at the herb-chamber that bordered the kitchen.

"I think the physician will be most pleased to see you. He's been made to deal with a lot of drunken clansmen who've been at each other with both fists and swords. The rainy weather and the lengthy time together has left the men all a bit edgy, I think. Now that the bouts have begun again, everyone will now find somethin' to do with their time."

"Aye, I hope the ground is not too wet for the challenges," she said to Cook, but in her mind she was already summoning a warm wind to dry the ground and ensure fewer injuries. She'd promised Killian she'd not use her powers, but surely this was not a magical feat anyone could possibly link to her.

When she went to check in on Thomas O'Donaugh, she found he was indeed in an uncommonly displeased mood.

"Finally, you've decided to come to my aid. I might have used your assistance in the past days. Where have you kept yourself hidden? I hope you were up to something important or interesting at the very least?"

She smiled at him and at his deep uncharacteristic frown. "Sure it was most important to me, and I'd thank you to keep it from traveling to the chieftain's ears just yet. I'll tell you straight where I've been. I spent my time away with my husband!"

"You were wed?" he questioned disbelievingly. "I thought you didn't end up marrying the farmer? Was I misinformed?"

"No, I did not marry the farmer." She smiled, suddenly giddy at being able to finally relate that she was a married woman.

"Then who?" he asked as he casually wiped the blood from one of his tools.

"I cannot say." She smiled again, enjoying the suspense she was causing.

"Well, sure you must tell me now! Shall I guess? It was the chieftain's nephew, wasn't it? I haven't seen him around these past days either."

"Aye, it is Killian I am wed to!" She confirmed the man's suspicions and held up her right hand to reveal the ring. "But, again, you must not allow the earl to learn of this until tomorrow evening. Please tell me you will not speak of this to anyone."

"Aye, sure I've no reason to tell him."

She assisted the man in readying the supplies that might be necessary in dealing with wounds from the bouts, all the while silently praying Killian would not be a recipient or require any medical healing. For the time being, there was little for her to do in the herb chamber and unable to keep her mind from Killian's challenges she was antsy and unsettled.

The physician noticed as she nervously rearranged the

vials and repositioned the bandages over and over again.

"Oh, be gone with you, then, Alainn, for sure you can't keep still for but a moment at any rate. In this state you're likely to be a detriment to anyone needing healing. I'm certain I could send someone to find you should I need your assistance." He good-naturedly smiled as he sent her off.

⌘

ALAINN NEXT WENT to see the state of her herb garden and was surprised to find it well tended. She was uncertain who might have been in the garden especially since it had been raining for the past few days, but she got her answer soon enough for when she knelt down to begin gardening she saw her mother walking her way, her skirts caked with the mud from kneeling upon the ground.

"You are back then from your romantic time in the glade?" She smiled at her daughter.

"Aye, only just this morning. I thank you for tending to the herb garden in my stead."

Her mother nodded to her. "It was much appreciated to be back within this garden, it has been some time!"

She glanced around at the garden she tended with Morag from the time she was a child. "Where is it you have been staying these days?"

"Lady Siobhan has been kind enough to allow me to stay in Morag's chambers, the same chamber where you have always stayed, where I spent my youth and many memories have come to me from days long since passed."

"And is there no longer a price upon your head, have the guards been instructed to show mercy after all these years?"

"Lady Siobhan has spoken to the captain, his guards, and the chieftain's army. They have been informed I am being employed to create a means to end the curse, so I am no longer in danger of being killed upon sight. The chieftain is still unaware I have been within the castle, for I have kept well-distanced from him, but Siobhan has assured me, she will not see me harmed."

"She is a good woman, an empathetic person!" Alainn commented.

"Aye, as was her brother," Mara added.

"I am now going to speak with the village priest to see if he might allow me to look through the records. I pray there is evidence that will confirm your legal and binding marriage to my father, for then the O'Briens will surely believe I am the daughter of a noble. If I am accepted as such then it will do much to undo the curse."

The older woman's eyes held a serious and doubtful gaze. "I would not count on it, Alainn. I am certain any documentation would have been long since destroyed. But if you wish to search, then so be it. And I have yet to inform you of the location of your father's druid amulet for that, too, may prove the deep connection between Tiege and me. For from the time we learned I carried you, he was insistent you, as a druid child, must bear an amulet of their father's clan."

"Aye, tell me then where within the dungeon I might find the amulet," Alainn asked with dubiousness in her voice.

" 'Tis in the southernmost corner; 'tis hidden behind the thirteenth stone, the number chosen often by those who possess magical abilities. It is often used in spells and enchantments."

"Aye, I know that to be truth and I certainly am well aware of the relevance of the number thirteen, but surely there must be a dozen different ways to determine what could be considered the thirteenth stone. You must explain it in greater detail than that, for I have never ventured down deep within the dungeon. I only made it partway down the steps last time I attempted it."

"Aye, well it's not a place you'd desire to be, I assure you. But, from the stairwell, it is in the sixth chamber to the right, 'tis the thirteenth stone to the left of the doorway and the thirteenth stone from the ground. And you will know it when you touch it for it was charmed with a protection spell, it will surely glow when you are present, and grow warm upon your touch. Once your hands touch the stone, it can be easily taken from the wall, and only you can remove the amulet behind the stone."

"Aye, I will try to find a way to get into the dungeon. Perhaps after the games are concluded and after Killian speaks to his uncle, I will be simply allowed to search the dungeon."

"You do not sound entirely certain of that, Alainn?"

"I do not trust his uncle, and I fear he will not accept our marriage any more than his father accepted yours."

"Pray to whatever god you choose, that is not proven to be so, daughter!"

Chapter Eighteen

L EAFING THROUGH THE many dusty volumes in the church cellar, Alainn finally came upon the documents that would have been signed around the time of her parent's marriage. The kind village priest had been most helpful as he had also looked through many bound booklets until he was called back upstairs by one of his assistants.

The cellar was dark and damp. She inhaled the scent of the dank air as she held a candle as close as she dared to try to make out the many faded scrawls. When she located the exact page where the entry should be, she was disheartened yet not surprised to learn a page had been torn from the weathered volume. It was as she'd surmised; the priest and the previous chieftain had left no evidence that could confirm her parents had ever been wed.

Well, she had certainly expected as much and the legitimacy of the marriage or of her being born a legitimate O'Rorke was surely not as important as now being declared an O'Rorke. If she found the other portion of the amulet which had belonged to her father, she felt Hugh O'Brien would believe she was a daughter to Teige O'Rorke. She prayed it would be enough, for if he believed her to be of noble lineage and she was accepted as nobility, surely it would be a means to end the curse.

The priest glanced over at her when she came up from the cellar and entered the abbey.

He spoke in his always kind and pleasant manner. "Were you able to find anything of relevance, Alainn, anything at all that might assist you in your quest of proving your parents were wed?"

"No, it was not to be so, Father, and in truth I was not overly hopeful the document would exist at any rate, but I needed to know for certain and I do thank you for your assistance"

"Sorry I am, you didn't find what you were searching for. I will pray some other form of proof will present itself. I must tell you I was most pleased to perform the ceremony when you and Killian were wed, Alainn." He smiled as he looked at her. "I believe your union shall be happy and blessed!"

She returned the warm exchange, but soon her expression turned to one of seriousness. "Father, do you believe when people possess unusual, unexplained abilities that they are born of evil?"

His gentle eyes filled with a solemn quality as he thoughtfully responded. "Do you speak of your own abilities to do magical healing?" he queried.

"I suppose they are the abilities most in question." She

did not attempt to conceal her powers for clearly the man already knew some of what she was capable of.

"I have known you your entire life. I have never sensed anything untoward or evil about you, child!" He gently rested his hand upon her head and then shook his own. "Sure, I do not believe you are evil, Alainn, and, in truth, perhaps your abilities stem from the Lord God Almighty. You have a most angelic disposition about you in dealing with young children, the elderly, the destitute, and the ailing. I sense the warmth and goodness within your heart, the natural empathy, unfailing compassion and unquestionable caring. And sure, you have saved as many souls as I with your various healing abilities. How am I to question but that those powers are heaven sent?"

"You hold a much contrary opinion to the chieftain's priest or of many men of God, I fear, Father Michael!"

"Aye, well I do not believe the chieftain's priest is to be trusted entirely. I sense an uncommon coldness, perhaps even an unholy darkness, about the man and I always have. We have been at odds since I came to the abbey. Unfortunately, many within the church are overly quick to point a finger at anyone who dares to reveal diversity. I cannot claim to know why men of the church or otherwise choose to declare any differences from the accepted, any unusual qualities and differing abilities as a harbinger of evil when so very many signs are perhaps given of and to angels and deities.

Man is surely too quick to condemn and seems more willing to hang on to long-believed superstitious nonsense. Why must it be assumed diversity is wrong, or that magic is of a dark origin or that those who possess the knowledge or means to affect others in a benevolent manner are somehow associated with evil and must be ridiculed and punished? We have clearly not learned so very much from our past wrong-doings and misdeeds in all these centuries."

Alainn shook her head unable to answer the man's man queries, observations, and obvious uncertainties. She was oddly both comforted and disheartened by their conversation.

⌘

AS SHE MADE her way back to toward the castle she was pleased to see Danhoul by the castle gate. She had not spoken to him since their time in the realm of the gods. She had many questions to ask of him and much to discuss, but there seemed to be a huge amount of people about the courtyard and the castle grounds. The crowd was boisterous and bustling, so she knew their conversation would most certainly need to be curt. She smiled as he approached.

"I am much relieved to see you were safely returned to our world!" she began, trying to be heard above the din of the courtyard, but not wishing to be overheard while speaking of such unusual topics.

"Aye, and you and your husband have taken leave from

the fairy glade so that he might partake in the clansmen's games?" Danhoul, too, had difficulty making himself heard.

"Aye." She sighed wistfully, as though wishing she were back within the magical glade.

There were surely few locations where they might hold a private discussion, and Danhoul appeared to have information he longed to relay to her. Although they were capable of speaking through telepathy, that, too, may well attract attention if they stood together staring at each other but not speaking. She finally led him to a small alleyway outside the healing chamber so their conversation would be kept secretive.

"Ramla has come to me once more, Alainn, as he did in the graveyard. He has spoken yet again of a dark entity or perhaps several dark beings, who insist on preventing you from speaking to the old healer, Morag. Although Aine has closed many portals, I sense there remains an unusually dark presence in our midst. Keep your wits about you and rely upon your powers of instinct to keep you safe!"

Alainn shivered, now unnerved by his revelations, and she glanced around suspiciously at the many shadows cast by the lanterns near the stone wall. She placed her hand to the charmed amulet that hung from her neck.

"Stay within lighted locations when you are able, Alainn. I intend to search the area surrounding the castle and nearest the graveyards to see what might be done to learn more of the dark demon, how to locate it, and how to alleviate its threat to you."

"I am most grateful to you for that, but you must promise me you'll be wise and cautious also, Danhoul. I would not care to have the guilt of your death upon my head as well."

"You needn't bear unwarranted guilt regarding Ramla. He was providing assistance willingly to a friend with akin abilities; he bears you no ill will because of his death. He has spoken to me of such and wishes to convey that message to you. And I am to be your guardian, so I will do what I can to protect you and see you safe. You must not question that."

"But you've admitted to me your young age? How can you be assigned such a perilous task?" She quizzed.

"Aye, and you are but one year my elder and have saved the lives of countless many and possess abilities never before witnessed. As I've aforementioned, age is not but a number to those who must do what they will to protect others... I learned that as a soldier in the kern, the Irish army, but 'tis true of being a guardian or a magical healer, as well, I would suggest!" He smiled at her with sincere assurance.

His smile and his words eased her in an odd manner, and his light blue eyes held such an unusually familiar quality. She stared deeply into those eyes and attempted to hear his thoughts. He knew immediately what she was doing and became uneasy.

"Have we met before, Danhoul Calhoun, for I've never felt such an indescribably unusual connection to someone I scarcely know?"

He looked away from her as though wanting to conceal something, but his words were put forth in a manner of jest. "Not in this life, Alainn O'Brien… sure it must have been in another!"

"Be wise and cautious, Danhoul!" She repeated but she stared after him long after they parted ways.

⌘

BACK IN THE herb chamber, Alainn brushed the dust from her garments, wiped her hands on her frock, and considered what she might do next. She had promised Killian she would not use her powers and she must remain true to her word. Yet she was much at odds within herself, for she distinctly longed to conjure the spirit of Morag, but knew it was impossible to attempt it in light of all Danhoul had warned of. Surely it would be unwise at any rate with dark forces ensuring they could not make contact. She momentarily attempted to summon the image of the missing portion of Tiege O'Rorke's amulet. Her head throbbed most fiercely whenever she dwelled upon any of those quandaries.

She held tight to the sprig of thyme in her hand and longed to have Morag back beside her in the herb chamber as in times gone by. How she missed the old healer who had been a mother to her all those years. She sensed well enough something dark kept Morag's spirit from coming to her. Killian had both spoken to her of the unusual and unsettling occurrence in the graveyard with the spirits of Ainna and Ramla.

Both Killian and Danhoul said Ramla had assured them Morag would continue in her attempts to reach Alainn, but that, too, caused a deep fearfulness within her at what malevolence the old woman's spirit may be facing in attempt to aid her. The woman deserved a time of peace after her passing. She had lived a very long life and earned this time of eternal rest.

Alainn was hoping to find a way to distract herself from her many various woes and pass time quickly while Killian was occupied in his bouts. She'd heard, through the castle's servants, both Killian and Riley had won their morning challenges, and that Hugh O'Brien was well pleased about the O'Brien's top position in the tournament. Now it only remained to be seen who would be named sole champion.

She heard the drums rumble and the pipes playing, which surely indicated the challenges between Riley and Killian was about to begin. First there would be jousting, then spear and darts, and lastly the broadsword. They were evenly matched in nearly all events, but Killian was usually dominant with the sword. Both jousting and sword involved a certain amount of danger and little room for error. She trusted Riley would not mortally wound Killian, but it was often not intentional when dealing with such dangerous weaponry. And on the morrow, there were still three challenges Killian must face. Alainn shook her head and, using the strategy Killian had done by his mother's wise advisement, she envisioned a large blue dragon, but smiled to herself as she clearly recalled the image of not one, but four dragons from her memory.

⌘

ALAINN EVENTUALLY SETTLED on returning to Cook's cottage. Perhaps it would dispel her discontent and agitation. Spending time with Molly and Margaret, who were as close to family as she could claim, always left her feeling at ease. The busy household with so many young and active children would if nothing else, be a most welcome distraction. She was so untypically nervous and edgy she couldn't seem to keep her mind on any one task at any rate.

Perhaps she and Molly would have time alone so Molly might elaborate further on the happenings with Pierce and herself. Sure Alainn might offer to assist the other women in occupying the children or in preparing the evening meal.

She wondered briefly if Pierce had a purposeful intent on insisting his father come to speak with Cook and Margaret. Had his intentions toward Molly become so serious he was possibly planning a proposal of marriage? She didn't attempt to use her powers of perception to discover the answer. If it were to be so she would much rather hear the joyful news from Molly, herself. She smiled at the pleasing prospect.

Deep in thought, while walking on the pathway near the stone wall that surrounded the village, Alainn heard the sound of children crying. When she listened more intently she noticed they were not simply crying, but wailing and not only in dismay, but in fear and in obvious pain. She hurried to peer through the bushes from where the sounds came. She was startled to see the chieftain's old priest earnestly beating two small boys. She recognized the two young lads as the blacksmith's sons. They were perhaps four and five years of age and she couldn't begin to imagine what they might have done to cause the priest to be assaulting them so viciously.

"So much for avoiding the priest!" She resignedly thought to herself.

She called out to the man, but so enraged and intent on his task was he; he did not appear to hear her over the wails of the children. He was brandishing his walking stick as his manner of discipline and Alainn finally loudly screamed to get his attention.

"Stay away from me, Maiden McCreary! This is none of your concern!"

She was further stunned to see him continue hitting at the boys unrelentingly.

"Stop that, this instant!" She hollered and without hesitation stepped between him and the two young boys.

She didn't stop to think that he might actually strike her, but that was exactly what he did, and with an unusual strength she would not have thought possible. He struck her across the upper arm and she winced at the immediate consuming pain. She put her other arm up to defend herself from the next blow, but this one came even harder and she thought she heard the sickening sound of the bone in her wrist snapping. She fought to control her powers and her temper.

"What could these small children possibly have done to deserve this harsh punishment?" She winced at her unrelenting pain and tried to reason with the deplorable man.

"They have spoken indecent profanities, taken the Lord God's name in vain; they have willfully broken one of his commandments!"

Alainn backed away from the man, but tried to keep herself between him and the children who were still wailing noisily and painfully. She partially turned to take a look at what damage had been done to them and saw that their backs were covered with huge welts and fresh bruises.

"They are only small children, Father. And have you ever heard their father speak? He cusses and curses continually. Do you not suppose they have heard that talk all their lives, and how are they to know it is wrong if the use of such language is commonplace?"

"Stay out of this; I will deal with these young sinners. You keep away from me with your interference and your evil ways?"

He started toward the children again and Alainn hastily turned to tell them to be off, to run to their father as fast as they could, when she felt the heavy stick forcefully strike her head this time. She felt herself growing dizzy and she knew she was about to lose consciousness. Her last clear thought was of her dagger within her pocket and then she slipped to the ground and into darkness.

Chapter Nineteen

WHEN ALAINN AWOKE, she was uncertain how much time had elapsed, but the priest had been knocked down, his walking stick was a pile of ash on the ground and she lay atop him with her dagger to his throat. He wore a terrified expression and that was what the chieftain's guard witnessed when he happened upon them. Alainn soon found herself being carried off by two guards with the priest close behind, accusing her of any number of crimes against him and against God. She closed her eyes and prayed the searing pain in her head and her arm would soon subside, and then she disparagingly fell into a dark sleep again.

She awoke in the dungeon. Well, pitifully attempting to remain optimistic, she had wanted to get to the dungeon, but not this day, and certainly not in this condition. She could barely move her wrist and her opposite arm and shoulder ached fiercely. Her head was throbbing and the smell around her was putrid. The chamber was nearly void of light. It was cold, damp, and musty. The distinctly pungent smell of human excrement was unmistakable. She was unable to see or determine how many others shared the stone and earthen cell with her. She looked up toward the tiny sconce upon the wall and tried to will it to burn brighter, even that seemed to take all her concentration and it simply made her head hurt more fiercely.

Alainn's thoughts went to the dark entity, the one she had once sensed within the dungeon. She used her powers of perception to determine if the creature was near. Although her head throbbed and her stomach reeled at the consideration of meeting that level of evil, especially in her wretchedly unenviable state, she wasn't entirely certain she could count on her powers of premonition in her present damaged condition. For now, she was reasonably sure she could not detect such a vile being of darkness in her location.

She longed to weep and call out for Killian, but he would not hear her and she doubted the guards would fetch him for her. Perhaps she could convince them she needed to speak with their captain or even to Pierce; they would see to it that Killian be found. Surely his challenges would be over with by now, and he would wonder where she was. But would he? He believed she would spend the night at Cook's cottage. They had not made arrangements to meet this day. When would she actually be missed and by whom? Only the priest and a small number of the guards knew she was here, and the other prisoners of course, but even they seemed unaware it was a woman that now shared their cell. Of that she was most grateful.

She thought of using her telepathy to call to Mara or to

Danhoul to assist her, but when she did so, she felt herself growing fainter and threatening to slip into unconsciousness yet again. She reconsidered and terminated her attempts.

When she tried to move her shoulder she realized her back hurt terribly as well, the despicable old priest had surely struck her even after she had fallen unconscious and that must have been when her powers had taken over. She felt the child move inside her and the tears rolled down her cheek. He remained well. How had she allowed this to happen to her, to them? And how could an aged man in failing health possess the strength to wound her so aptly and so quickly? She had misjudged and underestimated him. Perhaps the dark cloud she'd seen around him since she was a child was a sign he possessed and retained an evil quality.

Alainn felt something scurry past her hand and she unwittingly squealed. Now, regretfully, whoever was in the near vicinity, would surely know a woman was in their presence. She was thankful to see light at the top of the winding stairwell and hear footsteps approaching. A guard had come to retrieve her. She was to be taken to the chieftain for judgment. She learned the chieftain had not been summoned earlier as he was viewing the games and had been instructed not to be disturbed until the challenges had concluded.

She was led to the weapons storage room, for at this time the Great Hall would be filled with tables for the feast that was certain to begin soon. Alainn recalled this was occasionally the area where lashings were rendered. She was pushed roughly into the partially darkened room and she cried out when the guard squeezed her damaged wrist.

"Have you not secured her?" She heard the chieftain question.

"She is wounded, milord. Her arm is most likely broken and her other shoulder also damaged.

"You issued her a severe beating, Father!"

"Aye, she well deserved it for her interference in my duties, and the sorceress tried to slice my very own throat with her dagger!"

Hugh O'Brien approached Alainn. She did not lower her eyes from him as he expected.

"Maiden McCreary, you seem unable to keep yourself free from trouble. When last we spoke, we struck up a bargain that I am quite certain you have not fulfilled, and now you have attacked and tried to murder my priest? Are you so eager to swing from a rope? I think even the alleged granddaughter of an important chieftain could not escape entirely unscathed from this heinous crime. And that would only be if I actually believed you to be the granddaughter of a chieftain. That has yet to be proven!"

Alainn remained silent and that startled the man.

"What have you to say for yourself, girl? Why do you keep that bitter tongue still?"

"I think you will not listen to reason, and will believe nothing I say. And your priest could be found guilty of crucifying Christ himself and get off without so much as a sideways glance from you!"

The priest shuddered and gasped aloud at her startling blasphemous words and the chieftain laughed heartily.

"Now that's more like it, Maiden McCreary! That's surely liken to the feisty young woman I've come to know!" He put his hand to her cheek and she quickly turned her face from him.

"Now I wouldn't care for anyone to think me an entirely unjust man, so tell me your version of what transpired to cause you to attack my priest!"

The priest revealed his disagreement of the woman being allowed to speak to the accusations at all, but the chieftain silenced him and urged the young woman to go on.

"I did not simply attack your priest in an unprovoked manner as he has suggested. I defended myself against him and attempted to prevent him from beating two small, defenseless children. He chose to viciously attack them for speaking profanity, yet turns a blind eye to every other abhorrent sin committed here in this castle. I doubt he'd think to act so wrathful toward the children's large, imposing father though he consistently uses every profanity known to man and sure some he's invented himself."

"The priest has the right to issue punishment when he deems it necessary. That is surely not to be questioned even by you?"

"So, in truth, he wields more power than you here in your own castle?" Alainn dared to suggest.

"Not entirely!"

"Well then, look upon the bodies of the two small children he beat so willfully and tell me you wholly agree that his punishment was not harsh beyond what was necessary."

"You'll not tell me what I am to do, woman!" The man's commanding voice echoed loudly off the stone walls.

She turned away from him and glanced toward the door and then up to the barred window.

"Who do you think might come to rescue you, Maiden McCreary? The man you have bewitched into believing you are his granddaughter… or my own infatuated nephew, perhaps?"

Alainn did not answer him, but she tried to swallow the sob she felt rising in her throat.

"So, Father, what punishment do you suggest would be adequate for the woman?"

"She should be hanged, milord! Of course she should be hanged for attempting to take my life!"

The chieftain considered it for a moment. "There's never been a woman hanged at Castle O'Brien!"

"Clearly, there's never been a woman to attempt to murder your priest before!" The priest declared emphatically.

"Aye, 'tis true." The chieftain gestured for the guard to bring her closer and he glanced down at her deeply bruised and swollen wrist. He also pulled back the neckline of her dress and saw the severe extent of bruising on her neck and shoulders.

"My wife's father will not be pleased on this count, Father!"

"She is evil, milord; she deserves much worse. In truth, perhaps it would be best to have her burned at the stake for her association with the dark arts! Your own wife's father is surely truly bewitched by the girl. When she is dead, only then will he be capable of seeing how wrongly enticed he was!"

"She possesses strange, supernatural abilities, you and I both are both aware of this for we have witnessed them with our very own eyes, but if she was entirely evil I believe you'd be dead by now, Father, and come to it, so would I!"

He paced back and forth anxiously and looked from the priest to the young woman and back again several times.

"She will be lashed, five lashes as is the usual amount issued to a woman when she has committed a crime!"

" 'Tis not punishment enough, milord; surely not nearly enough for what she attempted."

"Do you presume to tell me how to conduct my judgments, Father? In truth, she has far more actual physical evidence of being attacked than you do. Perhaps I might have you lashed for beating children and the suspected daughter of an esteemed chieftain!"

The priest hastily snapped his mouth shut and openly glowered at the woman. The chieftain nodded to the guard beside him to get the whip. Alainn saw him retrieve it from the peg on which it was hung. She swallowed hard and vividly remembered how Killian had once described what it was like to see and hear someone being lashed.

"I wish to speak with the Chieftain O'Rorke!" she whispered in desperation.

"You believe he can save you from this punishment I have ordered?"

She trembled and avoided looking at the man. The guard nearest her pushed her down to her knees and it was Hugh O'Brien himself who raggedly tore open the entire back of both her gown and chemise and bared her back from nape to waist. With her injured arm she unsuccessfully tried to cover her mostly exposed breasts with the torn garment. She heard the guard unfurling the whip and, in anticipation of the pain, she could almost feel its sting upon her skin. She lowered her head and tried to brace herself for what agony would surely follow, when she heard determined footsteps outside the room, and the door being thrown open.

Chapter Twenty

"WHAT BY ALL that is holy is transpiring here, Uncle?" Killian asked in an enraged tone. "The black-smith's young sons told me Alainn came to their aid. Why then, is she to be punished?"

He went to Alainn's side, knelt beside her, and, in covering her, he noticed the dark bruises and her bent wrist. "Someone had better explain to me what has happened to Alainn or I swear to all of you here, there shall be hell to pay." He removed his overcoat and placed it around her shoulders as he glared at his uncle, waiting for him to reply.

"Stay out of this, Killian. This clearly does not concern you. Maiden McCreary has been judged and will serve the punishment. Five lashes for attacking my priest!"

"And how did Alainn receive these abrasions; did they appear out of nowhere?"

"Killian, you have no right to question any of this; she is not your concern! Because she shared your bed does not give you cause to defend or protect her."

"And does Niall O'Rourke know you intend to have his granddaughter lashed?"

"Killian, leave us to our business. The decision has been made, the judgment called. She will be lashed!"

"No, uncle, she will not be lashed! You can be absolutely certain, she *will not* be lashed, this day or any other!"

"You have no authority to question what has already been determined and judged!"

"Then I will bear the lashes for her! That is oft allowed!"

"You cannot. You are not blood kin to her, or of any recognized or accepted connection. You will therefore not be allowed to serve her punishment as that is my law!"

The two men glared at each other with austere expressions when Killian gently helped her to her feet and then openly took Alainn in his arms and tenderly consoled her.

"Aye, well, I have an indisputably strong and binding connection to her, uncle, for we are wed. Alainn is now an O'Brien for she is my wife!"

The man's face registered stunned disbelief as did that of the priest.

"You would speak falsehoods to defend this evil seductress?" The priest accused.

"You would stoop so low as to lie to protect her, nephew?"

"'I speak no lie, uncle! 'I swear on the grave of my mother, 'tis truth!" He held up Alainn's right hand and then his own to reveal the sacred rings upon them.

"By Christ Almighty, Killian, what the hell have you done?"

"I've done what I've longed to do for the past two years, what I should have done months ago. And now you can get on with your damnable lashings for it will be me who suffers them!"

"No, Killian, you must not! What of the challenges tomorrow? You cannot be injured and weakened by a lashing. You simply cannot do this!" Alainn gently pleaded with him.

"Aye, I can and I will, Alainn, and you'll question me no further on this!"

She held tight to him and began to quietly tremble as he held her.

"Get it over with then!" Hugh O'Brien ordered. "But it will be ten lashes then for that is the typical punishment given to a man!"

"No!" Alainn screamed. "Nay, you cannot do this, 'tis unfair. Is that how you choose to win tomorrow's challenge, to wound Killian so severely he has no chance against you, for surely everyone in the entire county knows that is the only possible way you could best Castle O'Brien's champion?"

"Shut your mouth, woman, before I order his punishment doubled or disallow him to take the lashes in your stead!"

At that moment Rory, Riley, and Niall O'Rorke entered the dimly lit room, demanding to know what was happening, and Killian soon alerted them as to what had taken place.

" 'Tis wrong, father, and sure you know it well enough!" Rory angrily declared to his father.

"If Killian feels he needs to suffer Alainn's punishment, that is understandable and acceptable, but don't add more strokes of the whip to spite him!" Riley spoke his opinion as well.

"Don't question me, lads! It will be as I have proclaimed!"

"Then I'll take the extra lashes myself!" Rory hollered.

"You are unable!" His father snarled.

"Killian is my cousin, and I believe full well Alainn to be my cousin also, so by blood law I can serve the punishment for either!"

"As can I!" Riley angrily announced.

"And I, too, will take the lashes for my granddaughter, Hugh, if you insist on being so unjust! Allow your sons to bear the five extra lashes you've added and I will take a portion of those originally ordered to be issued to Alainn!"

Hugh O'Brien stared at his two sons and his wife's elderly father in exasperation and in fury at their defiance and opposition of his word.

He finally proclaimed his decision on the matter. "My nephew shall receive only the woman's five lashes, but she is to be taken to the dungeon while the lashes are being issued, for I doubt she'll be able to still her unnatural powers while her *husband's* skin is torn from his back."

The chieftain ordered his guards to take her away and

they had to pull her from Killian. He removed his leine and leaned against the whipping post where the other guard secured his wrists.

Only partway down the corridor when the first lash was issued, Alainn heard the sound Killian had once spoken of and she screamed out in horror and in deep despair. She wanted to prevent the other lashes. She tried to move her arm and when the pain seared through it, she called upon her powers, but the throbbing in her head seemed to render her helpless and when she saw more guards heading toward her she felt herself growing faint and she collapsed against the startled guards who had been taking her off to the dungeon.

THIS TIME ALAINN awoke to a large group of curious men staring down at her. Remembering her torn garment and feeling the coldness of the damp air on her exposed skin, she tied Killian's overcoat around her waist to ensure she remained covered. The small window high above them allowed only enough moonlight within so she could make out the shapes of the other prisoners. As her eyes adjusted to the darkness, she was more accurately able to assess their condition. Many were obviously weak and sickly in appearance and surely had not eaten recently. She heard a voice from behind the bars in the next chamber.

"Ah, 'tis the evil sorceress herself, finally made to pay for her malevolent deeds?"

It was the voice of Richard McGilvary and Alainn silently thanked Mac for seeing to it she was not thrown into a cell with that vile and untrustworthy man. And she thought it ironic that he whom she had always felt was undeniably evil was referring to her as the same. She surveyed the crowd of men around her again. She judged that only two of them possessed strength or sturdy health enough to pose much of a threat to her. The two men were from a neighboring clan and at the moment they were leering at her in a most disturbing manner.

"Sure, we may as well take pleasure while we can and make the best of our present predicament!" The eldest and largest of the two poked his companion and she noticed the toothless smile the other revealed as he agreed.

"You hold her, brother, and I'll have a go at her, then you might have your turn with her!"

"And why should you be allowed to have her first?" the brother argued and shoved the other.

Alainn sat up straighter and pushed herself back against the cold hard stones of the dungeon wall. Her head was fuzzy and her pain so great she glanced down at her amulet and realized though it was meant to protect her, it surely prevented her from using the full extent of her powers.

Killian had asked that she not use her powers, but she was certain he would understand the necessity of doing so in preventing herself from being raped, and in protecting their unborn child. She forcefully yanked the chain from around her neck and stuffed the amulet within her pocket, all the while trying to decipher whether this was the cell her mother had claimed Teige O'Rorke's family crest was hidden within. Because she'd been unconscious both times she'd be brought to the dungeon, she was not able to discern her exact location within the chambers. She envisioned the many stones, thinking hard on the thirteenth stone, but none appeared to be glowing and she could sense no stone that had been charmed for her.

The brothers must have decided to forget about their quarrel and just get to something more pleasant. One of the unsavory two had reached for her just as one rodent ran between them, and another scurried behind her back and into a small hole in the wall. Alainn cried out at both the pain in her shoulder as he'd tried to roughly pull her to him, and the sight of the filthy, disgusting creatures. She wished within her mind that the many felines within the dairy shed could be here to rid her of at least some of the unpleasantness around her. The man released her when perhaps nearly a dozen cats appeared out of nowhere.

"The witch has called her familiars to her aid!" Richard McGilvary loudly warned the other prisoners from his location in the opposite cell.

"You're a witch?" The nearly toothless man stepped back and tripped over his brother as he posed the question. They both fell to the ground and upon trying to stand again stumbled over one other in attempt to put as great a distance as possible between themselves and the woman.

"Aye, I am a powerful witch, and I swear by all the many powers I possess, I shall turn the entire lot of you into toads if any one of you dares to lay another hand on me!" She raged in an ominous voice.

She chanted eerily and then spoke in first druid, then fairy, and opened her eyes wide as she moved her hands about dramatically for affect. She thought of the small pond not far from the castle wall and she envisioned the many large toads within. Soon she was rewarded when a goodly amount of the creatures appeared, all confused and croaking loudly, each hopping about wildly in their unfamiliar surroundings.

The entire group of men, even the ones which had previously seemed barely able to move, backed away and clustered tightly against the far wall. She was pleased by their reaction, and was nearly thankful to the horrid man in the other cell for alerting the others to her abilities. She concentrated some of her powers in attempting to heal her maladies. She sensed warmth radiating to her wrist and her shoulder. She thought the pain had eased at least somewhat.

Glancing at her companions within the cell, she noticed how filthy and perilously thin they appeared. As she'd done in the fairy glade, she imagined the many platters that now filled the tables of the Great Hall and she summoned some to her. They now rested on the ground before the men so obviously in need of sustenance, yet they failed to draw any nearer to the food she had provided.

"Eat! 'Tis safe, and assuredly retrieved from the O'Brien's very own table. Tonight you shall all dine like nobility." She smiled at them though they appeared to be frightened still.

Finally, one wretched old man dared to reach out and pull a scone from the tray and he ravenously stuffed it in his mouth. Soon after, the others followed his lead. Before long, the entire tray lay emptied of its larder. Alainn glanced at it again and they were further awed to see it filled once more. She also procured several jugs of water and goblets of a royal quality. She'd considered wine, but knew that would do little to keep the peace if they became filled with drink. While they ate and drank she scoured the entire area and tried to decide again what stone would be the thirteenth. Every way she calculated it, and with every stone she looked upon, she could envision no crest beneath it. Using her powers, she willed the stones possibly deemed to be the correct ones plucked effortlessly from the wall by way of her magic, but to no avail. None of the stones glowed as Mara claimed the charmed stone would do, and no crest was found behind any.

She rested her head against the stone wall of the adjoining cell, and tried to decide her precise position in the dungeon. She could sense no metal objects anywhere within the dungeon bar the chains that hung from the walls or were fastened to ankles of some of the prisoners apparently perceived as being the most dangerous.

Alainn closed her eyes, called upon her magic and was pleased to find herself in the next cell. There were only a handful of men in this one and they all backed up against the far wall when she appeared to walk through the stone wall as if she were an apparition. When she provided them with a tray of food as well, they all eagerly grabbed the food and stayed clear of her. She did this seven more times in seven more dungeon cells, and no thorough searching of the area provided her with any hint of where the missing crest could be.

Only one cell remained and it was presently solely occupied by Richard McGilvary. She did not attempt to go in there. She feared him even though he was surely still wounded from his fall from the tower wall. She sensed how utterly evil a man he was and she did not wish to make contact with him. And if the evil being who often dwelled within the depths of the dungeon was here, it was certain he would choose to be in the company of Richard McGilvary.

She tried once more to direct her thoughts to Mara, to ask for her telepathic assistance in locating the crest, but could sense no response to her query. Alainn felt completely disoriented down here and her muddled thoughts kept going to Killian. Where was he and how had he fared the lashing? She wondered if Hugh O'Brien had allowed him to be seen by the physician; if he might have applied water from the spring or healing ointment to his wounds.

She heard the sound of the upper door opening and saw the guards carrying a man down the winding steps and handling him in an unusually careful manner. When she glanced through the bars on the door she realized why. She saw the broad, muscular back and noticed the deep slashes upon it. She was in disbelief that they had brought Killian to the dungeon. Alainn gasped at the extent of his wounds. He appeared to be unconscious as his head lagged forward and his knees appeared limp. The two men struggled under his considerable weight and then she noticed the captain lend a hand to his men. They headed toward the cell that housed Richard McGilvary, but Mac discouraged that.

"No, you'll not put him in with that fiend. He'd surely want revenge for Killian's killin' his brother, and the lad is in no condition to defend himself at the moment."

"Mac!" Alainn pleaded as she placed her hands on the bars of the cell. "You must put him in here with me; you know I can heal him if I am allowed!"

"The chieftain has instructed you not be allowed to be together this night, lass!"

"Please, Mac, I beg of you! Name whatever favor I can offer you and I assure you it will be done. Killian must be healed for he'll stand no chance in tomorrow's challenge when he has been wounded so severely!"

Chapter Twenty-One

B EFORE THE CAPTAIN had time to consider Alainn's words, Richard McGilvary spouted his unwanted opinion. "Accept her offer, Captain; why not ask her for favors only a woman such as herself can provide. And allow us all to watch while you accomplish that surely most desirous feat!" The vile man lecherously advised the Captain of the Guard.

Mac furiously responded to the crass suggestion by smashing his fist against the face of the man leaning directly against the bars of his cell. The man staggered backward and held his nose which now spewed blood. The captain pulled a large metal key from his tunic pocket and unlocked the cell that held the steward's son. He roughly grabbed the frightened man who now cowered away from the large Scot apparently expecting a severe beating. But he was simply thrown into another cell and Mac gestured toward the now empty cell for the guards to place Killian inside. Then he opened the other cell and allowed Alainn to go inside with her new husband. She attempted to sense if the dark creature may be lurking in the shadows of the chamber. She was grateful that was not proven to be true. The guards had carefully lowered Killian to the ground and she noticed his eyes had begun to open and he moaned as he attempted to move.

"Feckin' hell!" Killian moaned once again and Alainn watched him as he tried to roll on his side so that his wounds would be less affected.

She had never before heard him use that type of language and she thought he may not even be aware of her presence. Mac had closed the door behind them and was turning the key when Alainn called out to him.

"Mac, I thank you greatly for this, but I must ask more of you, I fear. If you could arrange it, would you be capable of having the physician bring my ointments and elixirs? The remedies for deep skin wounds," she added as she knelt beside Killian and assessed the damage that had been done to him on her account.

The captain heard the tears in her voice and he looked in to see her tenderly touching her healing hands to her husband's open wounds. He winced and the chamber was filled with the sounds of her weeping. He turned away surely not wanting to intrude on this intimate moment as he saw Killian take her hand in his.

"No tears, Alainn! 'Tis not nearly as bad as it appears, I'm certain!" He attempted to ease her guilt.

" 'Tis worse than I imagined it would be, Killian."

Even in the moonlight as she looked down upon the five

lengthy gashes on his back, she noticed the blood had dried around three of the wounds. The other two remained bleeding profusely and had left bright trails of red down his trews and on the ground beside him. "You should not have insisted on having done this; I could have born the pain of it! It would have been better to have allowed me to endure it!" She whimpered as the tears flowed down her cheeks and dripped off her chin.

He moved in attempt to look at her and he grimaced and cussed once more.

"And have this lovely body scarred? It would be unthinkable!" He managed as he placed his hand on her shoulder.

"It would have been better, for I face no challenge tomorrow and I could have endured it, I swear it!"

"Aye, but I would not see you in pain, Lainna, and how could I risk a torment that might have caused you to lose our child? You've already suffered enough. Those welts and bruises are unforgivable, and sure the bone in your arm is broken!"

"Aye, but it has begun to mend, you know how quickly I heal when I employ my powers."

He opened one eye as he had closed them both again to conceal the intense pain he was feeling. Even to breathe sent searing pain down his back and when she gently lie her hands upon him it appeared he may fall unconscious again.

"Forgive me, Killian, but I must touch you if I am to attempt to heal you."

"Aye, do what you must, Alainn."

She tried to be as determinedly gentle as she could, but even the slightest amount of pressure sent his body into uncontrollable shivering. These were the deepest lashes she had ever viewed before and she had certainly viewed many through the years as her time as a healer. She fought to control herself and not cause the guard who issued them to die a painful death. She reasoned that he had only been following orders demanded by Hugh O'Brien and perhaps it was the chieftain who should be dealt with through way of her powers. If he died this day, there would be no challenge tomorrow. But by killing the chieftain would that bring about the death of their unborn son, for Hugh had not yet done his part in accepting her and ending the curse?

She felt her anger beginning to grow and she felt helpless to do anything about it. She would need to allow her own blood to mingle with her husband's blood. The guards had taken her anelace and Killian's weapons, too, of course. The blood from her head wound had long since dried and there seemed no item available to inflict a sharp slice on her hand. The stones in the wall were mostly rounded and worn with age so they would not cause a deep slice on her hand. She actually thought about biting her own arm and when she put her wrist to her mouth and Killian noticed, she noticed the horrified look that crossed his face.

"What exactly are you doin', Alainn?"

"My blood is necessary to heal you!" She explained, and

then she thought of her amulet within her pocket. She pulled it out and Killian noticed that as well.

"You dared to remove it?" he asked with a tone of disapproval.

"I needed to use my powers and it bridles them too severely!"

She took the rounded metal disc and rubbed it vigorously against a rough stone, hoping to create a sharp edge; when it began to glow brightly, Alainn hastily dropped it to the ground.

"Shite!" she declared as it burned her skin, "It has been charmed so that it cannot be defaced. Cursed druids!" she yelled so loudly the entire dungeon could hear her.

"Put the damnable thing back around your neck, Alainn, and just do whatever healing you're able with only your hands!" Killian ordered.

"It will not be sufficient and not quick enough to aid you in tomorrow's challenge. I know I have promised you I won't ask you to revoke the challenge but, Killian, in light of all that has transpired and your injuries…"

"The challenge will take place, Alainn!" He loudly exclaimed and then moaned even louder as he attempted to find a more comfortable position.

"Are you so damnably eager to make me a widow?" She objected.

"Sit yourself down here, Alainn, and let me lay my head upon your wee lap, for I'm feelin' as though I might need to rest awhile! Let me fall asleep to the closeness of your soft body around me and the sensation of our child against me."

"Killian, I need to heal you, and Mac will return with the healing balms and ointments, and an able elixir that will dull your pain and make you sleep."

"I'll take no elixirs, Alainn, for though they may be capable of dulling the pain, they will too severely impair my senses as well, and slow my reactions, and that would be detrimental to the bouts tomorrow."

"Killian, you will be in no condition to fight tomorrow. Allow me to see you even so much as attempt to lift your arm or shoulder, much less hold a sword!"

"By the morrow it will be much improved!" He winced and groaned even as he barely moved his elbow.

"That's horse shite and you well know it. Cursedly stubborn man, damnably headstrong Irish!" She declared as she stood and began knocking on and then pounding each stone along the doorway.

"So are you attemptin' to pull the castle walls down on us, then, Alainn? Is that how you plan to end my sufferin' and prevent the challenge from takin' place?"

"Never you mind what I'm doin'; I'm not speakin' to you at the moment!"

"Ah, so what's the lovely wee sound comin' out of yer sweet mouth then?" He attempted to lighten her mood.

She did not respond for she had been overtaken with a clear vision. She was a small child, so very young that she had not remembered this deeply suppressed memory. It was surely long before she had come to live with Morag for at that time she'd been three years of age. In this vision she was possibly not yet able to walk for Morag carried her upon her hip. She watched as Morag pulled back the glowing stone while she held her in her arms.

Then Alainn watched intently as her younger self removed the silver metal crest from within the hole in the wall. Morag had surely known the metal was charmed by Mara and that only Alainn would be able to remove it. How would she ever be capable of remembering where the portion of the amulet had been taken or placed when she had perhaps not lived yet one year on this earth at that time it was removed?

"By all that is holy, curses Morag, what the hell have you done?" she screamed aloud, causing half the men in the dungeon to quake in fear and Killian to open his eyes and stare uncertainly at her.

"You're cursing the dead now, are ye? Not content to simply direct your anger at the druids, me, or Irishmen in general? Alainn, look at the bright side of all of this."

"There's a bright side to this, Killian. I simply cannot wait to hear what could be construed as a bright part of this night!"

"Aye, well we thought we'd be spending this night apart and sure we're together after all!"

Alainn knelt down beside him once more and she felt the tears sting her eyes again as she looked at Killian and the love and warmth that remained within his pain-filled, green eyes. She tenderly caressed his hair and softly brushed her lips against his. He seemed relieved and she saw his lids close.

She had a sudden notion, but wasn't certain if it was actually a viable possibility. She carefully removed her amulet once more and placed it in her pocket. His eyes remained closed and he did not seem aware of her recent actions. She took both his hands in her own and quietly asked him to envision the spring in the glade. Although he seemed uncertain what she was attempting, he halfheartedly did as instructed. Alainn concentrated on it as deeply as she could, but when she opened her eyes nothing had changed. They remained in the dungeon. She wasn't certain what to do next.

She knew she could be transported from one place to another, but she'd felt certain she could ensure that Killian could be transported along with her. Once, in the realm of the gods, she had unsuccessfully attempted to bring Killian to her, but this was entirely different. She would be taking him with her. She dared to remove the amulet that hung around his neck. He called out in pain at even this slight movement, and it was clear he wanted to ask her what she was doing, but he was surely too weak and helpless to speak.

Once more, when she attempted to take them to the glade, nothing happened. She was nearly at her wit's end, when she remembered something she'd once told Killian. She could seldom hear his thoughts unless they were joined.

When they were one, her magic was the strongest and they had the strongest physical and supernatural connection.

She despised having his amulet off for such a lengthy time, especially when she was uncertain when or if the dark demon, who often could be found lurking in the dungeon, would appear at any time, but there was naught to do about it.

Chapter Twenty-Two

KILLIAN LAY ON his side and she wasn't certain what she hoped to attempt was a possibility at any rate. She placed his amulet in the pocket of her frock beside her own. There was no easy way to achieve what must be done and, in the dismal shape he was in, she doubted he would be capable of the actions that must be achieved. She edged closer to him and ever so gently placed another kiss on his lips, a slow tender kiss. She felt him respond, but only to calm her fears and reassure her he was not unconscious again. When she persisted with the kiss and began kissing him in a way that involved the use of her tongue in a distinctly sensual manner that was often done only when they were passionately making love, he opened his eyes again.

"Lainna, if you're thinkin' what I believe you're thinkin', yer about to be gravely disappointed, for there's no way we'll be spending' tonight together in that fashion. I can't image you'd think I would be capable of doin' what you're suggesting, nor can I believe that is what you really want, not here, like this, even though you've admirably arranged for us to have the chamber all to ourselves."

"Hush, Killian!" she whispered as she fervently kissed him, a long and lasting kiss again, and this time her hands went to the fastenings of his trews.

"Pain is surely not the greatest inducement for arousal, Alainn!" He groaned as he felt a slash on his back being opened further.

"You underestimate the great power of arousal to momentarily assist you in forgetting your pain, Killian!" she whispered as her kisses tasted the musky saltiness of his neck. Her hands continued with their intended actions and he was disbelieving to find himself becoming hard, despite his belief it would not be a possibility.

"And now what do you intend to do about this, Lainna. Sure, I can't move without bein' in a good deal of discomfort, and I believe you'd be hard-pressed to think of a position that won't hamper my maladies!"

She lay down beside him with her back to him. Careful not to disturb his position, she untied the overcoat and pulled her skirts up over her hips, resting her softness against him. She guided him within her as gently as she could manage, and he cried out once, but she soon felt his arms tighten around her and his hand found her breast. He slid it beneath her torn chemise and she felt her nipple harden at his touch.

The pain in her own shoulder screamed out wildly, but she moved slowly and then she spoke to Killian who had apparently become most intent in what they were doing.

"Now you must picture the glade, the water where we made love only this morning! Do you see it; can you feel the warmth against our bodies?"

"Oh, I feel a lovely warmth, Lainna, but it has nothin' to do with the water in the spring!"

"Killian." She gasped as she arched her hips in response to her own mounting passion. "Listen to me; think of making love in the spring!"

"By Christ, I have the most demandin' wife ever known to man, I swear it!"

She moaned lowly, becoming more and more appreciative of both the sensation of his hand caressing her peaked nipple and of him moving within her.

It was at this moment the captain arrived with the physician. He was about to unlock the door when he peeked inside the window of the large wooden portal. He looked once then looked away, but looked back again.

The physician wondered what had startled the other man so completely. "Are we not going to go in to take them the spring water and the ointments?"

"I think the woman is administering her own type of treatment at the moment. We'll not disturb them for a time!" Mac felt his cheeks flame and shook his head at the very consideration that Killian O'Brien was bedding his wife, or she him as it appeared to be. The lashes on the young man's back were as deep and laid open, as severe as Mac had ever seen. He'd been lashed once as a lad, about Killian's age, and he'd barely been able to move for days. Killian was either an extremely virile, young lad, or his wife was capable of making him forget anything but her.

The physician finally peeked inside the door himself to see what had the large Scot blushing and had left him speechless.

"I don't see anything!" He declared.

"Well, maybe they're through with it then!"

"No, Captain, I don't see anything or anyone. This chamber is entirely empty!"

"What in hell are you talking about, man? Are you blind, then?"

Mackenzie MacArthur turned and glanced inside the cell once more and he thought he'd lost his mind completely, for indeed, the room was vacant. Killian and his young bride were nowhere to be found, and Mac deemed he was going to be in an unenviable predicament if Hugh O'Brien learned of this unusual development!

KILLIAN WAS NOT yet vaguely aware that they were no longer in the dungeon. He'd felt Alainn move from him and now she was apparently attempting to remove his trews. The pain wracked his body and made him tremble involuntarily. He heard her weeping in earnest and he wanted to comfort her, but he was far too weak and weary. He wanted to feel her warm hands upon him, sense her healing him, but mostly he wanted to sleep. He needed to sleep and he knew she'd understand. His hand briefly managed to touch hers before he gave in to the nagging, overwhelming weariness.

Alainn struggled to remove the trews. And when she finally managed it she realized the disturbing reason for the difficulty. The lashes had gone through the fabric of the garment and pieces of the fabric were deeply imbedded in the wounds that covered Killian's buttocks as well as his back. She sobbed throughout the entire time she gently pulled him through the water and onto his side against the bank of the creek that fed the spring. She removed the remnants of his garments and then bathed his wounds with the healing waters. She'd returned their amulets to the place around their necks as soon as they had been transported to the glade. She watched as the wounds slowly begin to heal. It was taking longer than usual, but these wounds were not of a usual type. They were deep and lain open and she reasoned whoever had issued the lashings had not shown any mercy because Killian was the earl's nephew. In truth, he'd probably suffered a greater infliction of the whip.

She heard the many fairies and creatures whispering around her. Many came to see what they might do by way of magic to assist them. She attempted a smile at their sympathetic gazes but her tears continued to fall.

"Whomever amongst you who claims magical powers of healing please direct the healing to my husband and to the water. I would be much appreciative to all of you." she sobbed.

The many orbed fairies flew just above the water and Alainn saw the water begin to glow. The larger fairies lifted their enchanted wands and the water immediately grew warmer and Alainn inhaled the new scent of healing herbs.

The elves, sprites, and nymphs, gracefully skimmed along the water so quickly it appeared they were running upon it, and soon it began to bubble and churn. The gnomes who were unable to tolerate being too near the water and who could not fly, soon congregated toward Alainn and whispered many words of enchantment and their bright smiles warmed Alainn's heart. Soon the water began to swirl and tiny magical waterfalls poured gently upon Killian's back.

Then Alainn looked up to see a truly unusual sight, the one solitary creature they had seen previously, dressed in green and known for his mischievous tendencies and elusiveness, stood before her and the empathy in his deep-set eyes and crumpled face was obvious. His homely, little face smiled a sad smile at her as a lone tear rolled down his cheek when he looked at the many wounds upon Killian's back. He sniffed aloud and then formed a fist and Alainn was uncertain what the creature intended by that action, then he whistled loudly and surely a thousand tiny prisms appeared above the water like miniature rainbows that shone upon the water and made it twinkle and sparkle surely brighter than any starlit night.

Alainn smiled back at him for she knew his magic was of an unusually strong variety and that it would assist greatly in Killian's healing.

"Thank you, I thank all of you most sincerely!" she whispered to the mystical creatures. "My husband and I thank you for your many acts of kindness! It shall never be forgotten."

The little, solitary creature blushed deeply and then raced to hide behind the bushes once more as fast as his small legs would carry him. The other creatures replied in different manners. Some bowed, some sang, some spoke in their high squeaky voices, but it was evident that each of them needed no inducement to assist Alainn.

She realized her own ailments were beginning to ease in intensity and she prayed Killian was beginning to notice some relief from his anguish as well. When she felt she'd done all she could for her husband, she sensed she was on the verge of sleep herself. She employed her powers to move his head and shoulders to rest upon the soft grass, but his body remained within the warm magical waters. She removed her own soiled garments, lay beside him and placed her arms around him protectively and lovingly. Finally, she allowed herself to enter slumber as well.

⌘

WHEN KILLIAN AWOKE, he stretched and was astonished to find the movement caused little pain. He then became aware the sun shone brightly and magically upon him and he soon realized he was not within the dungeon. He had an unclear image of Alainn arousing him and them making love, and that was the last he recalled. He had still not opened his eyes and when he did he shook his head, thinking he was experiencing visions caused by possible fever.

Alainn lay beside him, naked, sleeping, and he knew at once where they were, but remained uncertain how they'd come to be there. He turned in attempt to look at his injuries on his lower back. The lash marks were visible, but they no longer gaped open and, for the most part, but for a couple of scabbed areas where the wounds had been the deepest, they appeared nearly healed. He knew her powers and the healing waters had accomplished this seemingly impossible task. The bruises on her back were faded almost entirely, and her wrist no longer looked bent unnaturally. He wasn't certain what time it was, but he reasoned they would need to get back to the dungeon before anyone learned they were gone. He gently shook Alainn to waken her and she awoke in a frantic state.

"Killian? Where are you Killian?" she cried out.

"I'm here, Lainna, right here with you, my only love!"

He put his arms around her as she turned to face him. Her eyes held a haunted quality, and he wanted to see them shine once more with love and contentment. She only allowed the embrace to last for but a moment and then she sat up needing to assess the damage that had been done to him and how effective the water had been.

"Move your arms, Killian! Show me you are mostly well!"

"Aye, I'm a good deal better than I was last night! In truth, I'm feelin' quite well!" he murmured as he gently pulled her down to the ground beside him. He attempted to nestle her in hope of a more amorous union. She swatted his hands away from her and she moved away and in an instant she stood and was attired in her tattered gown.

"By Christ, Alainn. You practically raped me last night, had your way with me when I wanted was to lie still and never move again, and now that I'm feeling well and healed and in need of an intimate time with you, you'll hear of none of it!"

"You will expend not a muscle to love me or do anything else that requires strength or endurance, not until that infernal challenge is concluded, and if you attempt to argue with me, I'll…"

"What exactly will you do to me, Alainn?" he whispered tauntingly as he stood beside her and tried to kiss her once more.

"Killian, I am most serious, and you should be, too. We must get back to the castle dungeon before Mac is punished for allowing us to be placed together."

She glanced at his muscular, impressive body and its present state of obvious arousal, sighed a deeply regretful sigh, and then reluctantly called upon her powers to see him clothed in his garments as well. He smiled a half-smile and that only proved to make tears to form in her lovely blue eyes.

"Please forgive me, Killian. I would never have wished for you to be forced to bear the pain that was meant for me. And I did not intend to cross the priest. How did you know to come to my rescue?"

He placed his strong arms around her and held her tight to him with his chin resting upon her head. "I place no blame on you, Alainn. The wee boys and their father came to me. They told me what had happened. Their father showed me their many brutal bruises, and I was horrified at what that despicable old man had done to them. When they told me he'd beaten you as well and that you'd been taken away, I imagined a hundred different punishments you might have been dealt. I was only thankful I made it to you in time to prevent you from receiving the lashes."

"Thank you, my only love." she whispered again.

"I'm your husband, Alainn. 'Tis my duty and my honor to protect you from any and all unpleasantness, and from whatever hardship I am able!"

"But how did they know to go to you, Killian?"

"They said when you were sleeping they heard you speak to them inside their heads! Their father was greatly disturbed by that notion, but he was wise to listen to them."

"I don't remember any of that, Killian, but I do know children are much more open to and highly attuned to the acceptance of supernatural abilities. I am most thankful for that!"

Killian glanced up toward the sky to determine what time it might be, but then looked at Alainn for he knew there was no way for him to be capable of judging the time here in the glade.

"Aye, 'tis time we must return!"

"And how do we manage it? Can't we go back in the same manner we came?" He suggested as he kissed her passionately.

"Not this time. We are of considerable sturdier health than we were last night, so now I think we can simply envision the dungeon and we'll be able to transport ourselves back. Hold tight to my hand and think hard of the darkness, the unpleasantness!"

"I'd really rather accomplish it the other way," he interrupted her.

"Killian, I am attempting to be serious."

"And so am I." He jested and playfully swatted her backside.

"Heed me, husband." She ordered and her eyes narrowed solemnly.

Chapter Twenty-Three

KILLIAN SIGHED, BUT took her hands in his and envisioned the setting she'd been describing. When nothing happened, she pulled her amulet from her neck, yet again. Slowly the area around them became blurry, the daylight turned to darkness and they found themselves back within the chamber they'd been the previous night. This time, however, they weren't alone for the captain stood there looking worried and displeased.

"Och, Lord Jesus Christ Almighty!" He spoke in a voice that was a combination of fright and exultation. "You're back!"

"We wouldn't have seen you pay for our absence." Alainn assured him.

"Aye, I appreciate you allowin' us time together last night, Mac. You're a good man and a valued friend. I only hope to find a man as loyal and trustworthy to be the Captain of the Guard at my castle." Killian voiced.

"Well, if you're offering me the position, I'd be inclined to accept, Killian, for I've no great desire to remain here any longer, not when the chieftain starts issuing lashings to women and his own kin. I believe it's time to move on."

"You're serious, Mac—you'd be willin' to move north with us?"

"Aye, but I'd need to take Pierce with me, too, of course, and the lad's asked the Cook's daughter to become his wife, so if they'd be welcome to live near your castle as well, I'd be greatly obliged to you."

"Molly and Pierce are betrothed?" Alainn squealed and began to move up and down on her toes. "Killian, Molly and Pierce will be wed and will one day soon live near us!" She jumped up and down and hugged him tightly.

"Aye, I heard." Killian chuckled. "My ears seem to be workin' adequately." He mockingly placed his hands over his ears and feigned deafness after her delighted squeals had assaulted them. He smiled warmly at her obvious delight.

Alainn giggled at that and then she looked out the window to see the sun had begun to rise and her recent joy was all too soon forgotten. " 'Tis nearly time for the challenges, Killian." Her face had grown pale and she closed her eyes.

"Nay, the challenges will not take place this day. In light of last night's dire events, the earl has postponed the bouts till the morrow." Mac informed them.

"That was certainly most generous of him!" Alainn sarcastically remarked.

"In truth, you seem to be in amazingly good condition all things considered, Killian."

"Aye, I'm much improved. I'm married to a most apt

healer, you'll know."

"Aye, she's unusual methods to be sure, but apparently she knows what she's doing!"

Alainn heard the captain's thoughts and her cheeks colored at realizing he had witnessed them together the night before. She cleared her throat and tried not to meet Mac's eyes.

"I've been ordered to bring the two of you directly to the chieftain."

"Should we not don clean garments then if we are to take audience with the chieftain? Alainn considered.

"I'm afraid we've not time for that, lass! The O'Brien is with Chieftain O'Rorke and your cousins, Killian. And your aunt, Lady O'Brien, has joined them now, as well. The menfolk have been up most of the night in lengthy discussion. And I'll tell you plain, it was not a pleasant discussion being held and not a night without many harsh words spoken."

⌘

As THE CAPTAIN led them to a sitting room just off the Great Hall, Killian took her hand and held tight to it as they walked in together. Lady Siobhan rushed to them from her seat at the table and Alainn noticed the unusually distraught look upon the other woman's face. Throughout all the time Alainn had known her, she had always been calm and distinguished, she'd always behaved in a controlled and dignified manner, but she appeared to be in a rare disposition this morning, for her rancor was clearly evident on her face and in her voice.

"Killian, are you well! I must see your wounds for myself to believe my husband would truly have his own nephew lashed!"

"You needn't fuss about it, Aunt Siobhan, for I am much improved!"

"You'll not dissuade me so easily!" She declared firmly as she attempted to lift the back of his tunic to look upon his wounds.

Killian, realizing she would not relent, unbuckled his belt and pulled up the garment. He knew there was of little use objecting for the woman appeared entirely intent on her purpose. He reasoned caring for loved ones and seeing to their mending was as important to a woman as keeping their loved ones protected was to a man. When she had apparently seen enough, she allowed his garment to fall back down and she stared at Alainn.

"You have aptly healed him?" she whispered so only Alainn and Killian could hear.

"As best I could, but the wounds were most severe… and the punishment was to be mine." She spoke softly as her tears began to fall.

The other woman's own eyes brimmed with tears and Killian felt the need to reassure the females who now each held tight to his arms.

" 'Tis not nearly as bad as it appears and I am scarcely aware of any ill effects now; it will soon be forgotten."

"It shall never be forgotten, Killian!" Alainn seethed as she spoke through tear-filled eyes.

"Never!" the other woman agreed whole-heartedly and threw her husband a caustic glare laced with unmistakable loathing.

"Do not become overly dismayed by this or look at me in that unbecoming manner, woman! There was little to be done about any of it. If the girl had not crossed my priest and our nephew had not rashly and unthinkingly married her, he'd not have felt the need to serve her punishment. And I could hardly make exception because he was my kin. He is not above reproach, clearly not above the law of this land, not without consequence for his actions, though stupid and half-witted those actions may well be!"

Killian barely acknowledged the presence of his uncle, but took Alainn's arm and went to sit in the chairs Niall O'Rorke had pulled out for them next to him. The elderly man touched Alainn's shoulder in a caring gesture and shook Killian's hand heartily.

"I thank you, Killian. You are a valiant man, an honorable man, to withstand such harsh and severe punishment for my granddaughter. I am well-pleased at your marriage even if my son-in-law and I differ greatly on that matter."

Hugh O'Brien voiced his opinion on the other man's statement. "Aye, well, her paternity has yet to be proven, and

I have not been persuaded on that count, but you've all accepted it so readily, I suppose it is useless to discuss that any further until more is learned on the subject. But, we must take sustenance together while we discuss other matters. You have heard the challenge has been postponed until tomorrow?" The chieftain directed the query to Killian.

"The captain has alerted me, but I assure you there is no need to delay it on my account!"

"Don't be foolish, lad!" Niall insisted as he glanced at the proud young man beside his granddaughter.

Several trays were brought in to them by servants and Alainn was thankful for the interruption for she wanted to scold Killian earnestly for his stubbornness.

"Aye, you'd best hold your tongue, Alainn!" He quietly warned her as she glowered at him.

Rory attempted to make small talk and directed the conversation to other matters in the chiefdom. The air was thick with tension, however, and the conversation soon waned.

Killian tried to avert his eyes from his uncle, but he found they both continued to look at one another with disparaging expressions.

The chieftain narrowed his eyes and finally directed a question to his nephew. "I suppose there is little hope the marriage was not yet consummated?"

"None!" Killian declared in a combination of pride and insult. "You'll not attempt to annul my union to Alainn. We are man and wife and I intend to remain so joined for as long as fate allows us!"

"And will your mother's clan be so eager to accept a woman not proven to be of noble blood?"

"They would have accepted her even without any possibility of her being of nobility!"

"Then the O'Donnel's are perhaps less intelligent than I believed. Have they no need for proper dowry? It is a requirement necessary to the O'Briens. How do you plan to deal with that, Killian?"

"Rest assured, Hugh, a most substantial dowry will be provided to the O'Brien and the O'Donnel clans. And if you chose to use your mind in a lucid manner as of late, you might come to know there are other assets to be considered in a union besides wealth or material possessions. There are strengths and abilities that cannot be measured by worldly assessment!" Niall O'Rorke informed his son-in-law.

"Ah, you speak of her unnatural abilities. Because of your druid association, you are clearly more accepting of such qualities. My priest has great suspicion regarding these powers and has suggested she be burned as a witch for possessing such black magic!"

" 'Tis not dark magic!" Lady Siobhan dared to declare. " 'Tis of a godly origin!"

"You border on blasphemy and heresy yourself, wife! Refrain from speaking in such a manner, or I will have you taken to your chambers!"

"Do not bully my daughter, Hugh, for your priest is a

fool and you right along with him if you allow him to color your thoughts and form your opinions based on his bias. The great druid Irish kings once recognized how valuable a seer is to the clans and to the welfare of this country. Druid seers were once employed by each king and lord to ensure this land remained strong and its people safe.

It was the Roman priests with their suspicion and ridicule of the old ways that caused the demise of the use of seers. They proclaimed the pagan ways to be wrongful and sinful, but how can centuries of such practices simply be obliterated because a new faith has been found? Druidism predates Christianity by numerous centuries. And most certainly not all men of Christian faith are pious or to be trusted so completely! And you, Hugh O'Brien, are more of a fool than I previously believed if you cannot see that!"

"You dare to insult me to my face, Niall O'Rorke!"

"I do! And were it not for my daughter and my grandsons, I promise you the insult would run much deeper, for I would dissolve the allegiance between our clans, without hesitation! Perhaps I would even be of a mind to wage war with the O'Briens."

"I ask that there be no violence or unrest between our clans because of my sons and the many people here that are dear to me, but you needn't consider me in your decision, Father," Lady Siobhan interrupted, "for when you make the journey back to your lands, I intend to accompany you. I will not remain in a union with a man who has become a cruel tyrant and a stranger to me." She glared at her husband as she spoke, but Rory stood and addressed her.

"Mother, you don't truly mean you intend to leave our father?" Rory's face clouded at the prospect.

"Do not attempt to dissuade me, Rory. I know how you dislike conflict and how admirably you strive to keep the peace in our family and, for that, I regret causing you discord, but I have thought long and hard on this profound decision. My mind is now made up. When I learned this morning of Killian's lashings that was the last in a vast series of many appalling events I will not abide or adhere to."

"Don't be ludicrous, woman, you could be hanged for treason for disobeying and humiliating your husband, the chieftain!" Hugh O'Brien raved.

"Then your son will be hanged beside her." It was Riley who stood now and stared in open contempt of his father. "For it is my intention to leave this castle, as well, to become chieftain of Grandfather's land. I told him of this just this morning, and it was your dealings with Alainn and Killian that prompted my final decision as well."

"Have you all lost your minds, entirely? Are you all so damnably bewitched by this woman whom you don't even know for certain is your kin, that you would risk being disowned, or worse, by the O'Brien?"

"I know without a sliver of doubt she is my granddaughter, Hugh. And if you actually possessed an ounce of intelligence at the moment or a hint of intuition you would know it as well!"

"You may be another chieftain and an important and respected one at that, but I will not allow you to insult me, Niall, not here in my own castle. I shall have you removed from this land before the nuptials of my sons."

"You could try!" The older authoritative man declared. "But you may find not even your captain or your own guards have the respect for you they once had. When a man has his very nephew lashed out of spite, it is truly a sad state. And you refuse to accept Alainn when, if you actually took a good long look at her, you could clearly not discredit the resemblances of her to your wife's kin, to my kin!"

"And even if I were to accept the fact that she may be your son's daughter, by the same token, I must accept her as the accursed glade witch's daughter. And a bastard child at that! I cannot condone my blood marrying that wicked creature's spawn!"

"Then the curse shall never be lifted!" Alainn spoke solemnly.

"If you and your abominable mother were put to death perhaps then, and only then, will the curse finally truly be ended once and for all."

Chapter Twenty-Four

KILLIAN STOOD AND glared at his uncle. "You lay a hand on Alainn or order the so doing by any other and I will see you dead, uncle. And you needn't threaten me with treason for it would be worth ending my life to see you sent to hell!"

"Killian, you must calm yourself, for I have located something that may be of assistance." It was Rory who placed his hand on his cousin's shoulder and attempted to diffuse the escalating unpleasant situation. He pulled a worn creased paper from within the pocket of his tunic. "I recently found this in the records in the village church. It is not entirely recognizable and it has clearly been hampered with, but it leaves little suspicion that a marriage took place on the date Mara spoke of. See for yourself, Father!"

The displeased expression on the chieftain's face grew more noticeable as he examined the document. "This surely proves nothing, Rory!"

"I beg to differ, Father! It leaves many questions unanswered. If your priest tried to conceal this, then he should be called to clarify what names once were inked upon this page." Rory insisted.

Killian asked to be allowed to view the document and Alainn studied it, as well. Niall O'Rorke beheld the decree and fairly tried to magically will the words to become more legible to all of them. It was to no avail!"

"Fetch my priest to me!" Hugh O'Brien finally ordered a guardsman who remained at the door. "Make haste!" He hollered as the man hurried to carry out his orders.

The short, round man was escorted in to the room wearing an expression of displeasure and annoyance as he hastened to the side of the chieftain as fast as his plump, stubby legs and newly acquired walking stick would allow.

"What matter demands such urgency, milord? I was in the confessional and do not take kindly to having such tasks interrupted." The chieftain passed the worn paper toward the man and he took it, but barely glanced at it. "What am I to make of this?" he asked, further irritated by being ordered to the earl's table with such disregard for his station or his duties.

"Did you deface this document to hide what was once written upon it, to conceal the names and annul the union of a couple joined some years back?"

"Years back; how am I to recall such details? I have wed surely hundreds of couples in the time I have served you and your father before you, and on a few occasions have had cause to annul such unions."

"Did you perform a marriage between Teige O'Rorke

and the glade witch, the woman once known by the name of Mara?" Hugh barked, losing patience with the holy man who clearly evaded his questions.

"Do not become fretful, milord. Take a drink of the wine I have provided you with. It will calm your nerves and your temper!"

"Answer me, Father!"

"I can recall no such union, but I must confess to you, my memory fades in my advancing years."

Alainn found herself growing as increasingly impatient as the chieftain himself. She called upon her powers and summoned the paper from the priest's hands and it gently floated to rest in her own. The man's eyes bulged and he was about to begin a lengthy speech of how her powers could only be a product of evil when she waved her hand over the paper and began to speak.

> *"As it once was, once more shall it be! Reveal the words in clarity,*
>
> *Remove the doubt that time has caused, Prove that two once wed before God,*
>
> *Lawfully, willfully joined in sanctity, As it was then, once more shall it be!"*

Killian looked down and saw the words truly magically appear. The names and the date were revealed in bold, dark handwriting as it would have appeared nearly twenty years earlier.

Killian smiled triumphantly and handed the paper to his uncle. He in turn passed it to the priest. "Does this jog your memory, perhaps, Father?"

"What trickery is this? This evil female has conjured the words and falsified this decree to suit her own means. Surely this only further proves to implicate her wickedness and unnatural powers!"

Niall O'Rorke took the paper from the stammering man and his eyes filled with tears as he looked upon his son's signature. If any doubt had remained in his mind that his son had been wedded to the woman known as Mara, it had been resolved. He glanced at Alainn and grinned, a pleased smile. He passed the paper to Riley, to Rory and then to his daughter.

"She is a legitimate child! As much a descendant of mine as your own sons, Hugh, and a child of my son, so perhaps first heir to my land, my castle, my wealth and position."

"This surely proves they were married, I'll give you that!" Hugh admitted.

"But, it was annulled soon thereafter!" The priest declared.

"Your memory has miraculously returned!" Killian directed the comment to the man. "Only moments ago you could not recall a wedding taking place and now you seem certain it was annulled. You are not to be trusted. And in truth, it should have been you lashed and sent to the dungeon for your unmerciful beating of the two small lads and my wife!"

The priest glanced at the chieftain to see what impression his nephew's words had on the earl, but it was the young healer that spoke.

"My mother admitted the marriage was annulled, but after nearly a month and a fortnight of union, after it had been consummated, and on grounds only falsified by you and the previous chieftain. So, in truth, it was the annulment that was entirely void!"

"I am of a mind to believe that they were wed, but this does nothing to prove that your new wife is a product of that union. The witch could have been with any number of men besides Teige O'Rorke, and even if the family crest is found it will not prove she is his daughter only that he gave his wife the crest. The fact that she may have hidden it away speaks nothing toward proving this woman is his child!"

"So in truth, uncle, you are admitting no manner of evidence will ever sway your way of thinking or make you believe Alainn is an O'Rorke, and therefore if you do not accept her as nobility, the curse will never be ended? The O'Briens shall never produce a child that will be allowed to live!" Killian accused.

"Don't allow it to weigh so heavily upon you, Killian! It is not even certain the child she carries within her is yours; surely she's as free with giving herself to many men as her mother was!"

Killian's face turned ashen and he looked at his uncle

with an abhorrence he'd never felt until this moment. He'd despised what his uncle tried to do to Alainn, he'd disagreed with much of what the man had done lately, but never before had his feelings toward him crossed the brink of violent hatred. They now did and with a mighty vengeance. He noticed the room had gone completely quiet as each person digested the information that had been divulged by the chieftain.

"How long have you known Alainn carries our child?"

The chieftain stuttered and stammered, apparently realizing he had misspoken while attempting to convince Killian.

"How long?" Killian asked yet again, his voice growing ominously quieter and not louder in his obvious rage.

"A week or so... perhaps a fortnight!" he finally admitted.

"Aye, so when you arranged for Alainn to be wed to the farmer you knew she carried my child, and last night when you ordered my wife lashed, you knew full well she was with child, yet you issued the order, just the same?"

The chieftain's eyes narrowed to match those of his nephew's.

"And by what means did you come by this information?" He continued with the interrogation as he glanced around at those in the room trying to interpret who might have known the secret and who would have told his uncle.

"It was me who confirmed his suspicions!" Alainn quietly spoke up.

"So he knew the truth of it even before you thought to tell me?" His voice had grown lower as he rebuked her, but she only nodded sadly when their eyes met. Killian's eyes were filled with such unquestionable ire and torment every person present wondered what he would do to either calm or avenge his temper. He chose the latter.

"I have proposed the challenge between you and I, uncle, and you have drawn up the conditions, but I will make an amendment to the conditions. Our bout will not simply be to first blood, but to the death!"

The room, already quiet, went deathly silent. Alainn attempted to take her husband's arm, but he pulled away from her. "Don't you even attempt to dissuade me on this count, Alainn! You'll keep your opinions to yourself regardin' this matter, and I'll thank the entire lot of you to do the same!"

"Killian, this is completely preposterous! I will not kill kin over a woman."

"No, indeed you will not, uncle, for 'tis you who will be dead at the end of our challenge. Mark my words, for it will be so!" He then directed his anger to the priest. "And you'd best keep away from me and my wife in the next days for I admit full well I'd take great pleasure in ending your life, as well!"

"Killian!" He heard both Rory and his aunt call after him as he marched angrily from the room. He turned, not to address them, but his wife.

"You will meet me in my, in *our* bedchamber, for we've a

matter to discuss!"

The expression on his face and the look in his eyes clearly indicated she would be wise not to oppose him on this, and she watched as he turned and left without another word.

Alainn slowly lowered herself once more to the chair where she'd been sitting. Riley wore an expression of dread as did his mother. Niall O'Rorke was staring at Alainn and his smile told her he was well pleased to learn of the child she carried, but his serious eyes revealed his concern regarding Killian's words. Hugh O'Brien or his priest had not said another word and the silence was deafening to Alainn. Her knees trembled precariously as she attempted to stand, but she knew she must obey Killian and go to his bedchamber. Rory stood as well and went to her.

He gently put his arms around her and held her close as he spoke. "I did not know of the babe, Alainn. Sure, the curse will be ended and you'll bear a fine healthy child!"

"I wish I could be so certain, Rory, for I think your father will never accept me. If he should die without accepting me I am uncertain what the outcome will be, and if Killian dies, I doubt anything will truly matter to me ever again!"

"I'm certain it won't actually come to that, Alainn!"

She appreciated him attempting to console her, but she recognized the doubt and the fear in his voice and in his eyes as well.

"I must go to him now!"

"Aye, I think it would be advisable!" Rory agreed.

Chapter Twenty-Five

WHEN SHE OPENED the door to Killian's immense bedchamber, she hesitantly peered inside, but he was nowhere to be found. Alainn located a chair and sat down to await his arrival. It was some time before he returned and when he did it was obvious he'd located the ale wife and clearly sampled her wares before he'd come to deal with his wife.

When he saw her sitting there uncharacteristically obedient, he almost wished she appeared combative or belligerent for that would have been preferable to the melancholia and uncertainty he noticed in her azure eyes.

He anxiously walked back the entire length of the chamber, hoping to calm his temper and decide how to best contend with his willful, young wife. He stared at her often, yet did not speak a word. Much time passed, and he continued to pace. He seemed unable to decide what must be done.

"Remove your garments and get into my bed this instant!" He finally ordered in an enraged tone.

Her eyes grew wide with startled disbelief at his unusually demanding request, but she did not move a muscle and remained seated.

"I am quite serious, Alainn! For when I'm beddin' you, sure 'tis the only time I truly know what is to be done with you."

He sighed and then looked at her once more in exasperation as she sat stock still.

Although he did not raise his voice, his temper was evident. "Perhaps I might begin to deal with you as most men are inclined to handle their wives? If I should order you about or mistreat you, oppress you and keep you under my thumb, would you then become more accommodating in our dealings? Clearly, I am at a loss as to how to contend with you!"

He stared at her with exasperation on his face and he took to pacing once more before he resumed his displeased lecture. "You oppose me often and, though I don't pretend to like it, I know how strongly you feel regarding husbands who are controlling and overbearing, so I attempt to not place harsh restrictions upon you in the hope you won't think I am unreasonable. But when you continue to keep things from me, things I have the right to know…when you insist on disallowing me to protect you, on handlin' things on your own and allowin' me absolutely no say in matters, it infuriates me more than you know and I'll not take kindly to that any longer."

He was quiet for a time, though he continued with his pacing.

Alainn remained frozen to the chair and for the first time since she'd met Killian, she felt a deep chasm forming between them.

He stopped and stood staring at her momentarily and then continued on with his fury. " 'Tis time you began to heed to me. You are my only love, and my truest friend! In truth, Alainn, you are my life, but you are now my wife as well, and I plan to have some say regarding what you do. And so…hither now… for I intend to have you, sure it is my right as your husband to take you when I please. Now you heard me, disrobe this instant and get into that bed, before I am made to tear off your clothes!"

She glanced down at Killian's overcoat that remained about her shoulders and the already torn gown. She was uncertain how to act or to respond to his peculiar unsettled mood, his rare harsh tone, and his willful request. Always when they had shared a bed it was of mutual desire and passion, and unquestionable loving respect. What Killian was requesting at this moment seemed void of any of those elements. She slowly stood.

She averted her eyes from him as she trembled and her bottom lip quivered as it often did when she fought to still her tears. He turned away from her and would not meet her eyes. She hesitantly approached him and placed her arms around his waist. She laid her head upon his back and softly wept. When he felt her warm tears soak through his tunic to his skin, he finally relented. He encircled her with his arms and rested his chin upon her head, though he sighed deeply and remained silent.

"If you desired a woman who possessed qualities of submissiveness and obedience, you have chosen very badly, Killian!"

He looked down at her, gently wiping the tears from her melancholy eyes.

"Aye, well, if that had been what I'd been looking for in a woman, I'd never have given you a second glance, for you've never been either, Alainn. But I think, even you are unaware how severely you rile me. Please explain to me how the man who tried to rape you, a man who you openly despise, came to know you carried my child before I was told!"

"I did not actually tell him of my condition. It was the night we returned from your castle when your uncle discovered us together in my chamber. When you lay unconscious on the floor, he threatened to have you hurt for attempting to harm him. I struck a bargain with him, in return for no ill befalling you. I told him I would do whatever was within my power to end the curse. He questioned my motives and then apparently came to know I had a personal vested interest in ending the curse, he drew his own accurate conclusion."

"He's known for that long?"

"Perhaps he truly believes the child is not yours, Killian. He doesn't trust me nor know how deep my feelings run for you, that I have and will always be faithful to only you!"

Killian remained disillusioned and questioned her further. "You have not yet flayed me for my manner in dealing with him. You've not mentioned the new condition to the challenge. I cannot believe you do not have many unkind and disagreeable thoughts on the subject."

"You have done what you felt you must! I am most fearful, but I will attempt to neither oppose nor disrespect you. Not on this, when I know what importance this holds for you! And I have great confidence in your abilities. But, Killian, will you truly be capable of ending your uncle's life when it comes to that?"

He did not respond for he'd wondered that himself ever since he had altered the conditions of the challenge. He chose to avoid the subject and broach another that would be perhaps even more difficult to discuss. "You must truly listen to me closely now, Alainn."

He'd taken her oval face in his hands and he looked down at her and into her eyes with an intensity and seriousness she did not care to see.

"Do not speak these unwelcomed and unnecessary words, Killian!" she whispered as she attempted to turn away.

"But, Lainna, you know these words are most necessary; we must discuss this now. If by some cruelty fate does not allow tomorrow to end as we hope…"

"Do not speak further on this, Killian, for sure I will not listen."

"But you must, Alainn. If tomorrow is to be my last, you

must promise me you'll stay ever distanced from my uncle. Do what you are able to end the curse, and I pray you will be capable of keeping our son safe. Go to live with your grand-father. Niall will treat you well and see to your best interests. Take advisement from him. Listen to him well!"

He continued to speak, though she did not respond. "Your grandfather will surely see to it Danhoul remains close by to provide guardianship and protection when it is needed. Niall knows much of druid ways and he and Danhoul will be capable of assisting you in magical matters as well. Sure your grandfather will take great consideration in helping to choose an adequate husband for you."

His eyes clouded and his voice cracked at these words. Killian searched her face for an indication she was truly listening to him for she had lowered her eyes and would not meet his gaze.

"Perhaps he may advise you to marry Danhoul, and sure the boy would not question that for he seems to like you most well, and you've much in common with your shared abilities."

"Marry Danhoul?" Her eyes flashed in displeasure as she looked up at him once more. "What absurdity is that? I'll marry no one bar you, not ever."

He did not push the issue of speaking further regarding her taking another husband for he felt a distinct jealousy in dwelling upon Alainn marrying another and curiously most especially the young druid.

"Tell me, you'd do as I say! Promise me, you will," he pleaded.

Alainn finally gazed into his eyes and offered her opinion. "If tomorrow is your last day, do you have any notion how soulfully grieved I shall be to live out my life without you? Do you have any indication how woefully angry and entirely displeased I will be with you, Killian O'Brien?"

"Aye, I've an inkling. You once told me you'd never let my soul find peace if I died before you, and I'm sure you'll remain true to your word on that count, but I think I would be at peace just knowing you and our child are safe. And I'd be well pleased for our souls to spend eternity together, my love."

"Aye, our souls shall be united always, Killian, my only love."

Tell me you'll heed me, Lainna! Promise me you will."

"I promise!" she finally whispered through her bitter tears.

He released her from his arms and his brow was furrowed with the weight of the undesired, yet necessary conversation. He glanced down at their unclean garments, the same ones they had worn while in the dungeon, and strode toward the door.

"Where are you off to, Killian?"

"I'm after finding servants who might assist me in finding a bath and some hot water for I feel we'd both benefit from a soak to ease our minds and our bodies. Though it won't be the same as the spring in the fairy glade sure we'll make the most of it, Lainna."

"Aye, 'twould be lovely, Killian."

ALAINN WAS MOST pleasantly surprised to see a large wooden bath being carried into the chamber followed by no less than a dozen servants hauling pails of steaming water with which to fill it. After a lengthy time and many trips, the tub, clearly big enough to accommodate the two of them, was filled. After the servants had left the room, Alainn smiled at Killian and his thoughtfulness.

They disrobed and climbed into the enormous bath where they lay together in the gloriously warm water and soaped each other with a pleasingly scented soap Alainn had procured from the herb chamber. They hoped to ease the anxiousness and distress of the past day and a half. Alainn hummed softly as she leaned back against her husband and felt his arms encircle her, each content to silently keep their thoughts to themselves. After they'd been there a time and the water had begun to cool, they stepped out and dried one another off, neither one breaking the silence.

Their eyes met and both revealed a knowing serious quality. He lowered his lips to hers and he kissed her deeply, thoroughly, and then carried her to the bed where they would spend this night together, and they both prayed that it would not be their last.

Chapter Twenty-Six

ALAINN STOOD ON the small open area outside the arched window of the east solar while Killian dressed and donned his armor in preparation for the approaching challenges. They'd remained in the bedchamber for the entire evening and through the night. Killian had a maidservant bring food for them after they'd made love, but bar that servant, they had seen and spoken with no one. Alainn inhaled deeply of the fresh morning air. The sun had just begun to rise and the hazy mist looked beautifully enchanting across the rolling green hills.

She trembled whenever she dwelled on what this day might bring. She was attempting to be courageous and confident for Killian's sake but, in truth, she felt like a hundred daggers were being driven into both her chest and her belly. Though she could not foresee what the day had in store, she felt a cold clamminess and a steadily increasing dread within her. Three consecutive challenges were entirely unheard of and the third was to be to the death.

She'd slept fitfully, dreaming of the morning star, pithaxe, and the broadsword, all weapons flying at her and

Killian as they attempted to flee from his uncle and from an ominous dark cloud that hung over them. And, as of the way of dreams, it was muddled and confusing and made little sense. One moment she was holding their child in her arms and the next the priest stole him away and threatened to sacrifice him. Soon after, their baby appeared to be a small child with the face of one of the boys the priest had beaten so severely only two days ago.

Alainn glanced over toward the far-off field where the battles would be held. The morning dew remained heavy and the air held a chill within it. She shivered and pulled her shawl more securely around her shoulders. She still wore only her nightdress for she'd barely felt she had the strength to manage even the menial task of dressing herself. She pulled apart her plait and raked her fingers through her long hair all the while trying to discern where she might spend this morning. She wanted to go back to bed and cover her head with the many quilts and sleep until day's end. She doubted sleep would come to her and through the open window she would be capable of hearing the many distinctly disturbing sounds of battle.

She turned when she heard Killian step out toward her. He was fully clad in battle gear and how strong, proud, and handsome he appeared to her. His green eyes compelled her to look into them. She flung herself at him in a most unlady-like manner and felt the coolness of the metal armor against her thin garment.

"Don't fret so entirely, Alainn! I will be cunning and skillful and use the many years of soldiering and battle training to compete this day. And in only days' time we will begin our journey to our land, to our castle."

"And we'll live happily ever after," she mumbled more to herself than to him.

"You utter the oddest phrases at times, Alainn, but aye, we'll be happy, I can sense it as surely as if I was a seer as well. We deserve a long life of happiness, you and me, aye?"

She nodded and then kissed him firmly and attempted not to let the thought enter her mind that this may be the last time they embraced, the very last time she ever felt his warm lips upon her own.

He stepped away from her and he gazed at her intently and lovingly as though memorizing every detail. He looked as the pink glow from the glorious sunrise framed her lustrously beautiful hair and shining blue eyes. He observed her full, rosy lips and her soft perfect skin. He took in the shape of her lovely body and slightly rounded belly where their child grew.

She realized all too well what he was doing and she held her head high, hoping to still the tears that threatened to fall. He was planning to hold this vision within his mind so if he should meet with death this day, he could summon this sight so she would be the last thought, the last memory he would take with him to the beyond. It made her heart ache with the possibility and soar with pride at the knowledge that he loved her so entirely he would desire her image to be the last he ever saw.

Alainn had sat at the deathbed of enough people to recognize the importance of a person's last images and their final thoughts as their soul left to go to the beyond. She swallowed hard and attempted a smile for Killian. Her eyes filled with love and adoration for this young man, her beloved husband whom she'd loved since she was only a child.

A loud pounding on the door to the bedchamber broke the silence and the tender moment, and Killian looked down at her with a pained expression surely knowing that would be a guard coming to escort him to the games field.

" 'Tis time. I must leave, Lainna."

"Keep you safe, Killian. Come back to me, husband, for you well know how much I need you, and our son will need his father!"

He kissed her once more, a thorough all-consuming kiss, knelt down and placed a soft kiss upon her slightly swollen stomach before he turned to go. As he was leaving, Rory met him at the door to the bedchamber.

"Rory will capably see to it you are kept safe this day should anyone think to cause you harm." Killian stated.

Before she'd had time to respond or disagree and without daring to look upon her again, he was gone. She felt her tears stinging her eyes and her heart aching as she listened as the footsteps grew faint and then could be heard no longer. She glanced up at Rory and she noticed the deep empathy in his eyes.

"I am not yet donned in day garments, Rory, and sure I'll be safe from harm here within Killian's chamber."

"Nay." He shook his head determinedly. "Killian has asked that I take you somewhere that it is unlikely anyone would think to search for you, and I've given my word on it; therefore I will do just that. Now get yourself dressed, Alainn. I'll wait outside the door."

She reasoned there was little use arguing with Rory, although he was of a much kinder disposition than his twin brother and perhaps not as strong-willed as Killian, he was honorable and trustworthy, and he would never break a promise made.

Alainn finally carried on with washing and dressing. It seemed to take an unusually long time to do any task for she had to fairly will herself to make her body move. In truth, she felt almost numb with fear and fretfulness. Her stomach was most unsettled and several times she was overcome with the need to retch. She managed to finish brushing her hair and tie it back. She'd barely finished when she heard a knock upon the door.

"Are you nearly ready then, Alainn? 'Tis time I took you to where you'll be safer."

She opened the door, nodded her head, and located her shawl. Rory took her arm, guiding her down the corridor toward the castle's steep, winding stairs. As they began the descent, they met two of the castle's guards.

"Under the chieftain's orders, we are to take the young healer to the dungeon where she shall be detained for the entirety of the challenges."

Alainn hadn't been startled by this announcement and in truth she had possibly expected it. She knew the chieftain and the priest believed she would summon her powers to assist Killian in the bouts. And, in actuality, they were perhaps correct. Even though she'd promised Killian she would not interfere, she wasn't certain that was truly within her capability. However, Rory sternly objected.

"My cousin's wife, Lady O'Brien, shall be accompanying me this day, there's no need to take her to the dungeon; I assure you."

"But the chieftain has insisted and we must abide his orders!"

"I will speak with my father regarding this matter so leave Alainn with me, I give you my word neither of you shall meet ill will because of this. I will inform my father you were admirably conducting your duties accordingly."

The pair seemed not willing to be dismissed so easily from their pledge to the chieftain.

"Rory, 'tis fine, I'll go with the guards, 'tis only for a short time."

"But there is no need of you to be held in such a despicable location. I won't have it!"

He regained Alainn's arm and was displeased to see the

two guards followed them, intent on carrying out their orders.

"She must be taken to the dungeon! Both your father and the priest have demanded it be so!"

"What does the priest have to do with any of this?" Rory demanded to know, his hackles now fully raised along with his suspicions.

The two guards glanced at each other as though they were keeping something concealed.

Alainn felt a sudden sharp pain in her head and a deep all-encompassing feeling of dread began to overcome her, filling her senses. These were telling signs of an ominous premonition.

"You go discuss the matter with the captain, or perhaps your father or our grandfather, Rory." She urgently suggested.

He looked at her with concern in his eyes, but she went on attempting to convince him.

"Sure if you talk to them it will all be sorted directly and I will be required to spend little time in the dungeon. Go now, Rory!"

She slowly lowered herself to the step and Rory, knowing of her condition surely recognized she suffered from an expectant woman's dilemma. He did not insist she accompany him to take audience with his father. Instead, he took her arm and slowly led her back to the corridor to a seat by an open window where she'd be allowed fresh air. The two guards followed close behind.

"Aye, I'll go now, and I'll make haste, but the two of you must wait here with Lady O'Brien until my return. If you dare to take her down into the dungeon, you'll have me to answer to as well as Killian, and Chieftain O'Rorke. They'll not take kindly to having her spend but even a moment in that damnable dungeon. Now stay put while I go get this matter sorted!" he ordered.

Alainn breathed a huge sigh of relief as Rory left them for she'd felt almost certain great harm would come to him if he remained here.

One guard held tight to her arm as if he believed she'd make a run for it, and they whispered to each other trying to keep their words from Alainn. They obviously decided against waiting for the chieftain's son's return, for they swiftly and purposefully started steering her back down toward the dungeon.

She did not resist for her dizziness and nausea did not allow for her to put up any fight. She was thankful this castle's dungeon had steps to the very bottom, for she had heard tell of many dungeons that had a very long drop to the bottom. The unfortunate souls who were forcefully thrown into those pits were surely never removed from them while they still lived.

The dungeon was considerably emptier than when last she'd been here. She reasoned either many of the prisoners had been freed to take part in or watch the games. Or perhaps they had been allowed freedom to act as entertain-ment for the nobles. Many times the prisoners were taken to a secluded area and made to fight each other for the pure enjoyment and entertainment of the lords. They would place bets on them and take much pleasure in seeing wretched destitute men inflict pain and suffering upon each other often for a mere crust of bread.

The thought made her shiver and she looked up at the one small window in the dungeon. The guards were about to place her in a cell with a handful of prisoners when she heard several displeased voices at the top of the winding stairs. She recognized Rory's voice once more and her heart lurched with fear. Her head ached and her mind was filled with an unimaginably tragic premonition. Like the one she'd experi-enced when she was only a child, Rory would soon meet his death from a fall. At that very moment there seemed to be many angry, heated words and much debate and then it was clear an altercation was taking place there on the steep stone steps.

She tried to pull from the guard's grasp, but he held tight. She attempted to employ her magic to prevent the misfortune as she'd done years earlier, to ensure the happen-ings in her dreaded premonition did not unfold. But Killian was not here this time to assist in saving Rory, and it was happening too fast. She felt the ground around her shake and reasoned that would be of no assistance in protecting Rory. She screamed out Rory's name and the two guards held her tight and roughly pushed her to the ground when she resisted them. She remained lying on the cold stone floor, feeling it quaking beneath her. Her head spun, and the pain within felt as though it were splitting wide open. She was horrified when she saw Rory being forcefully pushed from high above and come careening down hitting the floor with a sickening thud.

Chapter Twenty-Seven

E VEN IN THE dimly lit chamber, Alainn could see Rory's neck was bent at an unnatural angle and an immense pool of blood was forming by his head. She screamed in outraged terror and grief. Her stomach lurched and retched as she tried to crawl to him, even knowing no amount of healing or magic could undo a broken neck or a head wound that severe.

The guards appeared stunned and all stood there motionless, clearly uncertain what must be done. She cried out loudly and continued to try to reach her valued friend and cousin, the man she'd loved like a brother since they were children. The guards finally let go of her arm and allowed her to go to him. She gently placed her hand to his forehead and pushed his light blond hair from his open eyes. She tenderly closed them as she continued to sob.

She was momentarily pulled from her deep misery when she heard footsteps descending the stairs. She squinted to try to allow her eyes to become accustomed to the darkness. When she realized who the man was, she was disturbed and even more fearful. The small, squat figure of the priest in his dark hassock was followed by two more guards.

"You have killed the chieftain's son!" The guard still holding tight to Alainn's arm declared in an agitated tone.

"Father, what are we to do now?" one of the others asked nervously.

The priest seemed strangely calm about the entire situation. "We will tell the chieftain, it was the healer, that she placed a malevolent spell of madness upon his son and caused him to jump to his death straightaway. The chieftain rightly distrusts her. He will surely believe it to be truth, especially if the entire lot of you agrees to confirm my account of what transpired!"

Alainn felt as though she was in a wretched nightmare and as she was roughly pulled away from Rory's lifeless body, she felt the warm wetness of his blood upon her hand. Her stomach reeled and she felt it lurch yet again. The priest calmly ordered the guards to have Rory's body taken away and then he turned his attention to the guards with Alainn.

"I will reward you well if you place the woman where I desire," the priest said.

"Sure it makes no difference to me now where she's placed," the younger of the two guards admitted in an emotionless voice, indicating he remained greatly disturbed at what had just happened to the chieftain's son.

"The chieftain did not specify where she was to be placed; only that she was to be taken to the dungeon and kept bound until the last of the bouts are completed." The other guard managed to finally speak.

"I request she be placed in this cell then, if it is of no consequence to you. And, if I promise you both a gold coin, might you allow me the keys, and a time left alone with the woman."

The guards seemed somewhat startled at the request and were fairly certain what the priest had in mind, but one tightly bound the woman's hands and then they greedily held out their own hands as the priest rewarded them with a shiny gold coin he'd pulled from the pouch within his pocket. The older guard pushed her inside the cell for she had begun to fight him in earnest when she realized the priest would be accompanying her inside the dungeon cell. The guard was strong and with her hands secured he was able to easily push her inside. The priest hurriedly closed the door behind them and listened to be certain the guards had actually left them alone.

When Alainn turned to look around the dark room, she heard a movement behind her, and listened to the disturbing laugh beside her. She narrowed her eyes to make out the face of the man and was repulsed to learn it was Richard McGilvary.

She was alone in a dungeon with the two darkest souls she'd ever known, her dear friend and cousin, Rory, was dead and Killian was even now in battle and would not be coming to her aid this time. With difficulty, she put her bound hands to her amulet and tried to determine whether it would be an advantage or a detriment in this present situation. She'd always been told the amulet protected her from evil, but it also suppressed her own powers, so she was in a quandary and the two men wore satisfied sneers upon their faces as Alainn struggled with what was to be done.

She felt rather than saw a presence behind her and she turned to see a large, leering dark shadow upon the wall. A sensation of pure terror filled her heart and took her breath away. And when the shadow materialized into a figure she recognized it as one of the hideous creatures she'd seen that day so very long ago in boundaries of the fairy glade. This was surely the dark creature whose presence she had sensed when she'd attempted to enter the dungeon to locate her father's family crest. It was almost certainly a being from the Unseelie Court and his evil sinister smile raised the hackles on Alainn's neck. She placed her bound hands to her amulet once more and began chanting a spell to cast the creature back from where he'd come.

The priest also seemed fearful and he crossed himself, but the young man who had always been a demented soul, clearly reveled in the complete evil the being emitted. Alainn slowly stepped backward when she learned her words had no effect on the devilish creature. His lips curled back and revealed jagged fangs and when he drew nearer to her, she could smell the pungent rankness that permeated from the thing. His clawed hand grazed her face and she felt the cold clamminess of its scaly skin. She heard the scurrying of surely a hundred rodents and looked down to see the cell was overrun with vermin. On the walls, there appeared to be an infestation of crawling, squirming creatures. All things horrid and despicable were obviously drawn to the demon.

"What do you want of the woman?" It was the priest who spoke and his voice quaked with fear.

When the indescribably loathsome beast began speaking, his voice held an unusual raspy inhuman quality that frightened her to the very core. "To take her powers, her life, her soul." His eerie voice and the casual way he spoke of ending her life disturbed Alainn far more than his actual words.

"Might *I* be allowed to take her life, milord!" the young man leered at her as he spoke, "But might I be allowed a time alone with her to aptly torture her first?"

The evil demon laughed a far more sinister and malevolent laugh than the man, and he praised the younger man. "You have always been a worthwhile servant, Richard McGilvary. Your soul has always been filled with unmistakable darkness and is why you came to me so easily even as a child. Because of your loyalty, you will be rewarded this time with her. But only a short time, for there remains further deeds you must do for me. I shall soon return to instruct you further. Keep her hands bound." He warned.

The demon left as quickly as he'd come through a now visible glowing portal on the wall, but before he disappeared completely she briefly saw him transform into a figure of a man. A man with dark hair, and an appealing form, and when he spoke again, this time she detected a charming velvety voice that spoke in a distinctly aristocratic English accent, though his face was entirely hidden from her view.

He called back as he entered the portal. "Be cautious, McGilvary, for she possesses a rare level of power and ability. Here, in the darkness, her capabilities will be lessened. Keep her within the shadows, surrounded by the darkness!"

When he was finally gone, all the loathsome crawling creatures apparently accompanied him. He left behind such an offensive odor that Alainn found her stomach grow queasy. She turned and retched, but nothing was emitted. She'd been unable to eat this morning, fearing for Killian as she did, and now she was equally fearful for herself and her child, for she was uncertain she knew how to deal with this measure of evil. Her thoughts returned to dear, sweet Rory and of his mother and what grief she would feel at the loss of her son. Alainn held her hands to her queasy stomach attempting to settle it and saw the two men watched her every movement.

Niall O'Rorke had told her the powers she had displayed during the drawing of the circle might have attracted dark forces. And when she'd removed both hers and Killian's amulet, she had possibly allowed the demon to alert others in the Unseelie Court, which surely was a portal to hell. She had needed to get Killian to the glade to heal him and allow him a fair chance during the challenge, but now she was desperate to know what to do about the being and her present dire situation.

"Would you care to have a turn with her, Father, when I'm through with her?" The horrid young man's voice brought her back to her present unenviable dilemma. "I'd be willing to share her with you, but only if you ensure me you'll cause her great torment and pain!"

"What? No, I think not," the priest stammered nervously obviously understanding only too well what the other was suggesting.

"Have you ever had woman, Father?"

The priest did not respond, for he appeared nearly as disturbed by the happenings as Alainn. She decided to take advantage of his doubtfulness in the hope he did claim some faith or possess any level of decency.

"You must release me, Father. You do not want these sins upon your head. Killian will reward you, I am certain of it. If you allow me to be freed, sure you will not be sorry."

"Don't try to bribe me, woman. I have thought you evil ever since you were a child. You should be dealt with and destroyed before your child is born and another demon is allowed to enter our world."

"You truly believe that I am evil? You think *I* am a demon when you have just looked upon an actual demon?"

The man appeared to be assessing her words and their situation. The younger man apparently did not care for the fact she might actually be altering the priest's mind to her way of thinking, for he grabbed her roughly and threw her to the ground. She managed with some difficulty to get back up again and placing her secured arms in front of her she was able to prevent him from coming nearer.

"Don't you see, Father, she has unnatural abilities that surely stem from Satan!"

"Though I admit full well I am uncertain where my powers have originated, Father, I assure you I have never used them in an evil capacity." Alainn pleaded with the man to believe her though she doubted he had any conscience to speak of when he remained so calm even after he'd caused or at the very least contributed to Rory's death.

The young man remained unable to move any nearer to her so he settled on attempting to convince the priest to band with him against the woman.

"Father, I believe she fears fire. Get the candle sconce from the wall. Surely she must be cleansed by fire."

The priest appeared filled with uncertainty and Alainn chose to allow his thoughts to come to her. Even he was left reeling at the thought of the horrific creature he had just witnessed. He believed there was a hell, without question, and he was reasonably sure the being he'd just seen had surely come from the darkest depths of hell. But, though this girl was beautiful in appearance she could be a shape-shifter, able to mold herself into whatever vessel she needed to suit her purpose.

"Father!" The younger man's voice pulled him out of his trance. "Get the candle and bring it to me!"

"And what do you fear, Richard McGilvary, besides me and the chieftain's dogs?" Alainn hoped to distract the young man while the priest wrestled with what to do and whom to believe.

The young man heard a low snarl behind him and saw the old dog he had once tortured so many years ago. It appeared as young and strong as it had ten years earlier before he'd harmed it. Its lips curled back to reveal its teeth, and Alainn noticed the deep unhidden fear in the other man's eyes.

"Look at her, Father, she must be a daughter of the devil for she has summoned her demon-dog to do her bidding."

"I have brought him here to protect me, 'tis true, but he is no demon, only a loyal canine. He remembers it was me who saved his life and prevented you from causing him further torment."

The priest's eyes bulged widely again when he saw the animal simply appear out of nowhere. He felt himself in the middle of a hellish nightmare and he knew not what or whom to believe. He looked at the dog and the woman and then glanced at the candelabra on the wall.

She thought the dog might be able to deal justly with Richard McGilvary, but then the priest would only insist her evil powers had caused another death. And she had little time to consider this for as quickly as the dog had appeared, he disappeared. Somehow the nearby demon must have some control over her ability to employ her powers. The priest started to walk toward the candle and Alainn felt herself growing ever frightened. The fire would partially lighten the darkness, but she knew the two of them with the aid of fire would be able to harm her greatly, and, if that horrid demon returned, she reasoned she and her unborn child were as good as dead, and surely their souls would be lost as well.

She thought of Killian and how he would respond if she were found assaulted and murdered in the dungeon. He would feel the need for vengeance and he would have no notion who to blame for her demise. She thought of attempting to summon Danhoul, but if he were unable to assist her, she would be greatly saddened if, like Rory and Ramla, his young life was lost while attempting to aid her. Then she recalled Aine's words, she'd said Lugh would be her guardian when Killian or Danhoul could not. She envisioned him and although he did not appear before her she was certain she could hear his voice within her mind.

"You have the power over time, woman, use it!"

She immediately held out her hands again and momentarily the other two men were frozen where they stood. But, this was only a temporary solution, for she surely could not hold time still for long, certainly not until someone could come to assist her. Surely by then the demon would return and then she would be done for. She weighed her options. She could possibly steal the keys from the priest and hopefully get away from the two men, but where would she run to? And would the demon not be capable of locating her wherever she went? Or did he need the power of darkness?

Again she heard the Celtic god's voice. *"You have a greater power over time than simply stopping it. You are able to move through it, backward and forward, but take heed, for if this unusual ability is not perfected you could possibly end up in an entirely different century. Dwell upon a time in only recent memory for that would undoubtedly be the safest path."*

Alainn felt herself growing weak and dizzy when she even attempted to deal with moving through time. She heard unusual voices she'd never heard, saw faces she'd never seen. The face of a beautiful young woman with brilliant green eyes and lovely red hair kept flashing before her eyes and another with large, dark eyes and soft, dark hair. Alainn sensed a powerfully strong connection to both of them, but was hesitant to go to that point in time for she believed it was not to be, not yet. And another voice kept coming to her, a voice she did not recognize and this one was filled with deep contempt for her.

She heard her whispering. "Did you truly think you were the only one of your kind; that yours was the only line of witches?"

She snapped back to her present, precarious situation and was startled to find the two men had begun to move once more. The priest had snatched up the candelabra and passed it to the other man. He smiled nastily at her and almost gleefully jabbed it in her direction. She moved backward as the flame nearly touched her skin. Her long hair swished near the flame and she saw the ends of it had caught on fire. She screamed loudly and awkwardly smothered them between her sleeve and the stone wall. She could smell the putrid odor of singed hair. The man was clearly delighted by her terror, and purposely came at her again.

She felt the darkness consuming her as the horrid young man walked toward her with the flame outstretched once more. Then she heard enchanting gentle music from the other side of the chamber. As she dared to glance toward it, she noticed a soft light that began to grow in size and in brightness. And within the center, radiating light, was the figure of a lovely young woman. A fairy, perhaps… or maybe even an angel. She had long, light hair, so fair, it was surely nearly white and the light radiated from her and swirled around her. Maybe she truly was an angel coming to take Alainn to heaven.

Perhaps Richard McGilvary had already violently taken her life and having no memory of it was a simply a final gift, a last act of kindness granted to her. Yet, something about the female figure seemed familiar. She did indeed possess an angelic glow, but also a hazy otherworldly tinge as well… a quality that often accompanied a specter. Alainn finally reasoned this young woman was a spirit. And when she looked directly at her, Alainn noticed her eyes were very similar to her own.

"You needn't fear me dear, Alainn, I would never harm you!"

"You know who I am?" Alainn's voice quavered.

"Aye, Aine and Morag have sent me to assist you for both remain unable to come to aid you. Aine wishes to protect you and Morag loves you well, as she loves me and your mother, my daughter, Mara.

"You are Ainna, my grandmother, daughter of Aine?"

"Aye, my kin. I regret I was not strong enough to live to raise my child, and perhaps to see you born as well. But, alas, nothing can be done about the past and regrets are of little use to any of us. I had hoped to assist your husband with searching for the amulet as Morag wished, but the dark forces are not a few. For now, I will do what I can to aid you at this time of great peril, my kin."

With that, the glow that surrounded her spread widely throughout the chamber and filled it with an almost blinding brightness. She smiled appreciatively at the spectral female.

Alainn looked at the two men who wore matching expressions of fear and disbelief. She took advantage of this momentary distraction and concentrated fully on stilling time again…and of Lugh's words. She thought of this morning, when she and Killian lay together in each other's arms, she remembered even in her fear and concern for him, how warm and safe and protected she'd felt. She envisioned that again. She closed her eyes tightly and wished herself back to him. Ainna smiled at her as she felt her surroundings becoming blurry and her reality began slipping away. She was vaguely aware of the glowing portal that housed the dreaded demon. The specter's brightness appeared to ensure the portal remained closed.

The dizziness nearly left her sickened, and the sound was as loud a humming as when she crossed over to the fairy glade. She felt herself falling dizzyingly as she sometimes did in her dreams. When she finally landed, she dared to open her eyes and it was as she'd imagined as though none of the horridly disturbing events of this morning had happened. She was lying unclothed in Killian's arms. He was startled when she sat up in a panicked state.

"What is it, Lainna? You look as though you've had a terrible fright! Did you have an unpleasant dream? I didn't realize you'd fallen back to sleep."

She did not respond and tried to sort out if what she'd just seen and experienced could have been a vivid and terrifying dream. Could it all have been imagined, Rory's death, the demon, the whole of it?

Chapter Twenty-Eight

A LAINN PRAYED IT was so, that she had dreamed or imagined all of it, but her hopes were short-lived when she heard Killian's next words.

"What's happened to your hair, Alainn? Sure, you've edged too close to the candle's flame. I've never known you to be careless with fire, knowing your distaste for flames. Best you be more cautious, Lainna," he said as he placed his fingers to the singed ends. "The smell is most unpleasant. When did this happen? It must have been only recently for such a strong odor to remain."

She glanced down at her hand and saw the repulsive sight of Rory's dried blood upon her palm. Her heart both leapt and sank with the knowledge that Rory was still alive, and that she would now need to find a way to ensure that he remained so.

Alainn could think of no words to explain any of this to Killian and she wasn't sure she'd care to elaborate even if it was just an ordinary day, one when he did not have to prepare for battle in a short time. She did the only action she could think of that would ease her mind and prevent further questioning on his part. She passionately kissed him and initiated a much needed time of lovemaking.

"Again?" he whispered as his voice grew raspy with arousal, and his smile told her he was pleased to accommodate her need. "Didn't you only yesterday tell me I wasn't to expend any strength even to love you?"

"Aye, again," she murmured as she tried to diffuse the fear in her heart and warm the chill in her soul. "And I'll see to it you needn't use up too much of your strength!" she promised as she pushed him back upon the bed and capably mounted him.

WHEN KILLIAN LEFT once more after they'd said good-bye again, precisely as they had earlier, she was exceedingly joyful to see Rory alive and well and waiting for her to accompany him this day. She embraced him tightly and didn't want to let go. He gave her a curious look as she left him in the corridor waiting for her to join him. This time Alainn dressed as quickly as she was able, and hurriedly tied back her hair without attempting to brush it. She'd felt an uneasiness within her belly ever since she'd passed through time. A slight pain made her fear for the child. As she went to the tiny private chamber that housed the chamber pot, upon inspection she was relieved to find no hint of blood. She struggled with what to do.

In only a few short moments the guards would come to

take her to the dungeon, Rory would end up fated to die once more. She determined what she might do and where she should go. She thought of going to her grandfather or to her aunt for surely they would attempt to shelter and protect her, but clearly that would put both of them in danger as well. She felt within her they and anyone who assisted her would meet with peril if the demon sensed they protected her. She decided she must do this on her own.

She glanced out the castle window to the ground below. It was far too high for her to jump, or even attempt to climb down. She leaned over the small arched window and looked to the windows below. They led to the Great Hall. If she could simply get down to the lower balcony below, she could enter the Great Hall and then decide what was to be done. She thought of using her powers to send herself to that location, but she thought it might be best not to attempt using her powers for the slight pain within her midsection had not ebbed. And the demon may be alerted to her if she continued to use her powers again for her Grandfather had told her as much.

She wasn't clear how long the spirit of Ainna could hold the demon at bay behind the portal in the dungeon. She tried to keep her concern from the young apparition as well. Perhaps Ainna would be made to pay dearly for assisting her. Alainn reasoned she couldn't be fretful any longer of what she could not control, for surely she would need whatever strength her powers allowed to deal with the dark demon.

She heard Rory calling out to her somewhat impatiently and she opened the door a crack to peer out at him.

"Rory, 'tis sorry I am, but at the moment I'm sorely plagued with the weak morning stomach due to the babe." She only partially lied for indeed her stomach was wretched with all the quandaries she was facing. He gave her a sympathetic, knowing gaze and closed the door as she hung her head above the basin. She hurried to lock it as quietly as she could and formed a plan that would ensure Rory O'Brien did not die this day.

⌘

ALAINN QUICKLY TIED the bed sheets together and then to a heavy post of the massive bed all the while making loud exaggerated retching sounds to assure Rory she was indeed unwell and spewing in earnest.

She slowly lowered herself downward, thankful Killian's bedchamber was not directly across from the grounds where the challenge was being held. As she felt her feet touch the window that led to the Great Hall, she heard a loud and excited cheer from the crowds who watched the bouts. Killian must surely have won his first match for the cheers and exuberance continued for some time. One more to go, she thought, and this time the morning star, she calculated and prayed he would not be too tired and weakened from wielding the pith-axe for such a lengthy time. And then there remained the challenge with his uncle to be considered.

Before she entered the hall, she peered inside to see only a few servants clearing the tables from the morning meal. No one even seemed to notice her so she made her way into the stairwell where she planned to hide until later. She realized how dark the winding stairs were and therefore she raced up the steps until she came into the lighted room...the priest's room. She was grateful he wasn't there and she felt certain he was either still standing in the dungeon, wondering where she'd gone, or he had given up trying to search for her and perhaps gone to watch the challenges with the rest of the castle residents and the villagers.

She looked around the small room the priest occupied and noted it was not much larger or more adorned than the one she had shared with Morag for many years. He did possess a large writing desk and volumes of richly bound books. Her powers of perception made her sense she should look through the desk though ordinarily she would never think to be so guileful or intrusive. She hesitantly opened a small drawer and saw several beaded rosaries. Another drawer contained the vial that once held the elixir that served the purpose of deadening his physical male urges. Alainn noticed it was empty and reasoned the priest would not have come to her for the potion. Now that Morag was not here to issue the conncoction to him, she wondered if the physician had done so or if the man had simply decided to deal in his own way with whatever desires he felt.

Another larger drawer contained papers scrawled in Latin

and in the priest's scratchy handwriting. When she heard footsteps on the stairs, she quickly pushed the papers back in the drawer, but in doing so another smaller paper fell loose from the pile and floated down to the floor. She quickly picked it up. This was entirely different paper of a finer quality, and the handwriting varied markedly as well. She stuffed it in her pocket and regrettably squeezed beneath the small wooden bed frame. It was dusty and dark, and she immediately thought of how she was to avoid the darkness. When she heard someone straightening the bedcovers and tidying the room, she dared to glance out from beneath the bed and saw a woman's slippers. She breathed a heavy sigh of relief and pulled herself out from under the bed. The woman nearly fainted in her fright but, when she saw it was Alainn, her expression turned to only one of curiosity.

"Did you wish to see the priest?" the woman asked meekly.

"No, I was actually trying to hide from the man!" Alainn admitted.

" 'Tis a strange place to hide from the man, beneath his very own bed!"

"Aye, entirely odd!" Alainn agreed and then picked up her skirts and continued up the winding stairwell. She would go to the east solar. The sun was bright there, and the arched window would provide a view of the field below. She needed to know Killian remained safe. The guards would surely not look for her here although she was certain if the chieftain had been alerted to her disappearance they would begin searching the entire castle. If she could remain hidden until the bouts were concluded then she could go to Killian and explain to him…she wasn't even certain what she could explain to him. If she told him about the demon, he would only worry for her and surely there was nothing he could do to avert the demon, and then he would be at great risk.

She found a bright spot near the edge of the castle that allowed her a partial view to the field below. The second bout had not yet started and she wondered what the delay was for the chieftain had made it plain the bouts were to be consecutive to ensure he would have a better chance at defeating Killian.

She turned herself around so she could see the field clearer and she noticed the physician was attending to Killian. Her heart caught in her throat. Killian had won the match, but apparently not gone entirely unscathed. She could barely see them through the crowds, but she noticed the physician attending to a wound above Killian's left eye. She cursed under her breath and dearly wished she could be there with him to heal him. She prayed the surgeon had used the spring water and the healing ointments she had charmed. How could Killian be expected to fight in two more matches with his vision surely hindered? And why if the match had only been to first blood and Killian had won, was he bleeding also?

From her vantage point she could see the chieftain as

well. He sat upon a raised chair overlooking the challenge. He surely thought himself as regal and important as any king overlooking the bouts. She saw the two guards who had earlier taken her to the dungeon heading toward the chieftain. They spoke to him for a time and then she noticed he appeared displeased. He got up from his perch and went to speak to his captain and to two other guards.

As the second challenge was about to begin, Alainn saw Killian swinging the heavy dangerous weapon that he would next do battle with. His opponent, a man nearly as tall as Killian and of obvious strength and sturdy condition, the man she'd danced with at the banquet, was doing the same type of preparation when the chieftain walked across the field to speak with Killian. Alainn felt certain Killian was being questioned about her whereabouts.

⌘

"WHERE IS THE young healer, nephew?"

Killian's face clouded at the sight of his uncle approaching and his questions further enraged him. "Why would you need to know the whereabouts of my wife?"

"She is to be detained in the dungeon for the duration of the challenges, and she is nowhere to be found."

"Alainn was in our bedchamber when I left this morning." He snarled, choosing not to implicate Rory in any way. "I am not certain where she may be, but I am thankful she has avoided the unpleasantness of being taken off to your dungeon for no good reason!"

"You know I have a justified reason to keep her imprisoned. She will surely aid you in the bout and I will be at a very unfair position."

"Alainn has promised she will not interfere." Killian insisted as he continued to swing the weapon faster and with more fury. The chieftain jumped out of the way as his nephew purposely swung it closer to him than was safe.

"And do you truly believe she would allow me to kill you without calling her powers to stack the odds more in your favor?"

"She has promised me and her word means far more to me than yours at the moment, uncle."

The piper stood ready to signal the beginning of the match, but he waited for the chieftain to leave the area and for him to give the nod to begin.

"If she crosses me again, or attempts to intervene or impede my way in the bout, she will be punished. And you'll not be taking that punishment for her, for sure you'll lie dead on the field and then she'll meet with a noose if she causes me any ill will!"

The loathing for his once beloved uncle was clearly evident in Killian's eyes, but he did not respond. He walked to the center of the court and stood near the man who he would rally against in mere moments. He tried to keep his thoughts only on the challenge and not on the dilemma Alainn surely faced at the moment. He prayed she would either call Danhoul to assist her or use her clear thought to keep her safe, and if that was not enough to ensure she remained safe, he hoped her powers would see to it she was not harmed. If the guards could not find her then Killian reasoned she knew what she was doing, and that she was protecting herself and their unborn child.

ALAINN GLANCED DOWN and saw the chieftain walk away from Killian. Their words had not been clear in her mind, but she'd heard some of the chieftain's thoughts. She placed her hand against her belly as she often did lately. The child had been quiet this morning. Ever since she'd moved through time, she'd barely felt movement within her. She attempted to nudge him, and was rewarded with a small quickening, but she remained fearful, for the pain had not left her entirely even now while she sat here quietly. Perhaps altering time, by traveling through it, was perilous for the child. She must not attempt that again, therefore she needed to keep safely hidden. But how could she truly attempt to remain hidden when that hideous, dark demon had intentions of taking her powers and her soul. Would Ainna be able to help her again or should she attempt to summon Aine?

She attempted to push these dilemmas and consistently disturbing thoughts to the back of her mind and she once more thought of her unborn child. As she moved her hand over her belly she noted it was beginning to grow. It was not nearly as flat as it had been only days ago. As she touched the tiny swelling, she felt the folded paper within her pocket. She was curious to read it and retrieved it immediately.

I write this to you this dismal night, for I have been ordered to leave this castle on the morrow. I am consumed by a pain within my heart, a dark emptiness within my soul that no man should ever know. My darling wife met with grievous injustice and now I have been informed that she no longer lives. I was not even permitted to view the remains of my beloved for I was told she met with a most violent misfortune and has therefore already been laid to rest.

Your chieftain is elderly and bitter so I might attempt to understand his cruel actions, though I will never forgive his misdeeds.

Although I have not been raised in the Christian faith, I always believed a man of God would not be driven to such lengths simply because his chieftain demanded it. I was clearly mistaken to think you had morals or conscience simply because you wear a cross.

You officiated the wedding between my lovely Mara and myself. You know full well our union was lawful and binding. What God has joined, let no man separate! You spoke those words only more than a moon ago. You even were recently made aware she carried our child and yet you declared our marriage annulled, sided with your earl. Though it may have been him who ordered her death, you had a part in it as well.

You are young and supposedly a pious, important man, but I pity you! You may be loyal to your chieftain, but not to your God. I hope every day of your life you know that you have helped to destroy a love that was strong and pure and right. You married us in the name of your Father. How ironic this is, for you claimed Mara must be evil to possess her unnatural abilities, but it was Mara who insisted upon a Christian wedding, for she was raised in your beliefs and she wanted to be certain it was binding in the eyes of her God.

The only solace I am able to find in all of this is in the knowledge you will surely one day find yourself within the hell you so aptly describe to your parish. And if there is truly a just God of Christianity, he will see to it! I also rest assured the gods of my faith will never see you at peace!

I had promised to avenge my wife's death, but your earl threatened the life of my sweet sister, his own son's wife and mother to his grandsons, so therefore I have no choice but to be gone from here as I have been ordered. I shall leave you and your chieftain to a harshly dealt, just punishment by your God and by mine.

Teige O'Rorke

Alainn had reread the letter numerous times. Though her eyes were blurred with tears, and she could no longer make out the words, she held the paper close to her heart and felt consoled even through her father's grief. This letter was a testament to his great love for her mother. It left no doubt that she was conceived of love. It was also proof he knew she carried their child…he knew about her. And he believed she and her mother were both dead… he could not know they'd lived, that she'd been born. But why would the priest keep such an incriminating letter? Had he truly a hint of conscience hidden somewhere deep within him? Did he keep this paper as a reminder of his part in the injustices that had befallen the young couple he had once united?

She was pulled from all other thoughts when she heard the pipes below and glanced down at the field. The second bout had begun.

Chapter Twenty-Nine

KILLIAN APPEARED STRONG and focused. He splayed the weapon with mastery and he dodged and avoided the other man's morning star with agility and skill. She watched as Killian's weapon grazed the shoulder of the other man, but it glanced off his armor and he stepped back to allow himself a time to recover from the brunt of the blow. Killian swung once more showing no mercy, which was how he had been trained since he was a young boy. The man stepped backward again and nearly lost his footing. He pulled his weapon through the air and it met with Killian's shield.

The men fought on for what seemed like an eternity to Alainn. The clashing of weapon against weapon, and weapon against shield, was nearly continual and she knew they would both be tiring. She could not see Killian's face for he had his back to her, but she fretted much regarding the cut above his eye. She noticed the other man stagger backward and when Killian swung at him, the man kicked out and though Killian had expected it and jumped back with dexterity, the other man tossed his heavy shield at Killian and sent him falling backward.

He still maintained hold of both his weapon and shield, and the other man was now without benefit of his own shield. If he went to retrieve it, he would lose the advantage of having Killian down. He began waving the weapon wildly and aimed it straight for Killian's chest. He moved his shield to stop the blow, and then rolled out of the way of the next one. Killian managed to grab hold of the handle of the other man's weapon and pulled him down to the ground as well. He'd needed to drop his shield to accomplish it, and now both men were on the ground, both held tight to their weapons, but neither had their shield.

Killian was the first to jump up to a standing position and Alainn noticed he favored his right leg when he stood. The other man obviously noticed as well, for he came at Killian fiercely and with a heavy backhand blow. Killian caught the blow with his own weapon and both men felt the jar of the weighty weapons meeting. The other clansman must have injured his shoulder for he now seemed unable to lift the weapon to its full extent. He eyed Killian carefully and this time was about to swing it upward from his waist, but Killian must have anticipated that move, for he brought his morning star down hard upon the other man's weapon with a mighty blow, and it actually split the weapon. Alainn saw the jagged splinters pierce the opponents forearm and heard him cry out in pain. The bout was finished. Killian had won again, for that she was of course grateful, but now he had an injured leg and an abrasion near his eye. And he was surely tired to the point of exhaustion, for the match had been unusually long and fast-paced, especially considering the weight of their weapons.

Alainn saw Killian's uncle had already stepped upon the field donned in his armor and waving his sword to proclaim he was ready for the oncoming match.

Killian glanced up in her direction surely sensing her location and she tried to mentally send him a wish of luck and love. But she feared for him so entirely she wanted to scream at the injustice of him fighting again now, injured, tired, and in a bout to the death. She could see Riley had brought Killian a cup of water and that a servant boy had also handed him a wet cloth to wipe his brow. When he pulled it away from his face, Alainn saw the dark red blood had stained the cloth. His cut was open and his vision would surely be severely impaired.

Alainn glanced around at the crowds of people and she was startled to see the priest standing in the crowd and even more stunned to see who stood beside him. It was Richard McGilvary. Clearly the priest had allowed him to be released from the dungeon and in his hand she could see he held a weapon. Were they hoping to find her and have McGilvary take her life as he'd wanted to do earlier that morning? She had little time to dwell upon that for the piper had begun his loud announcement of the commencement of the battle.

Killian held his sword as capably as always. His arms appeared to remain strong though she could nearly feel the ache in his strained muscles. He stood trying to bear most of his weight on his good leg. And he swiped at his eye often. And the chieftain remained standing, waving his sword at the crowd looking pleased and pompous and well-rested. How could he appear so joyous about the prospect of killing his own nephew? Alainn thought she would never truly understand the ways of men if she lived a thousand millenniums.

She was disturbed to see that the McGilvary man had slowly made his way closer to the edge of the crowd nearest Killian and his uncle. The nod was finally given for the bout to begin and the chieftain came at Killian with a series of brutal and well-aimed blows. Killian managed to deflect each blow and the sound of metal upon metal seemed to go on forever.

Alainn turned away more times than she could calculate, but each time there was a second's lull in the banter, she would quickly turn her head back to make certain Killian remained well and whole. Killian managed to nick his uncle's sword hand, just a tiny cut, but it was first blood. She turned once to see the chieftain's sword graze Killian's forearm and she saw the trickle of red that spilled from the cut. The chieftain looked toward the crowd for applause and approval and he was soon rewarded, but when Killian deeply sliced his uncle's shield hand, the zealous crowd cheered just as loudly.

Noticing how winded the chieftain had become, Alainn dared to hope Killian might be capable of enduring the remainder of the bout even though his movements, too, had begun to slow. The chieftain looked furiously at his recent injury and he threw a nasty glare at his nephew and started with an intense barrage of hand movements that ended up meeting Killian's sword or shield each time. But now, Alainn saw how badly Killian was limping and his sleeve was soaked with his blood. When she was growing ever fearful, Killian landed a blow to his uncle's shoulder just above his armor and he stumbled backward trying to get his bearings again. Killian pursued him, sensing he would need to keep the older man under constant attack or he would surely get the better of Killian.

The battle would have been over long ago, Alainn reasoned if it had only been to first blood. She felt herself growing tired even watching Killian and looking upon all his many injuries. But he continued on valiantly and determinedly. Surely the chieftain would soon tire. He was of greater years and of heavier set. The swords continued to clash and bang. One blow finally sent Killian's shield to the ground, too far for him to retrieve it. His uncle came at him with not a hint of mercy on his face.

Killian now held his broadsword with both hands and this allowed him even greater strength and longer range, but it left him unprotected as well. When he stepped back after a series of heavy blows, Alainn saw his leg buckle and he fell to the ground, hard upon his back. She looked at Killian's handsome face and saw the blood and the sweat that poured down his forehead. She heard the rumble of thunder in the distance and saw the lightning bolts that zigzagged across the sky. She inhaled deeply trying to calm her powers for she'd promised Killian she would not use her magic in any way to determine the outcome of the bout.

A steady rain had begun to fall and she tried to will it to stop for though it would serve as a detriment to the chieftain, it would adversely affect Killian as well. As the rain washed down upon them, Killian looked up at the tower again, as if scolding her for her interference. His uncle had approached him as he lay upon the ground still holding tight to his sword. The older man jabbed at him with the blade and Alainn saw the slash that was so close to her husband's throat. He used his own sword to knock the other man's shield from his hands, which seemed to take the man back for he'd clearly though the last injury would keep Killian down.

He threw himself at his nephew his sword outstretched, but Killian managed to roll out of the way on the muddy ground. His uncle lunged at him just as he was attempting to stand. This time the sword caught in the back of his leg and Killian went down again. Alainn felt the sob in her throat and turned away again. She whispered to Killian in her mind trying to send her thoughts to him.

"You are not done for, Killian. You are as strong and brave and able as any man who ever lived. You must live to teach your son such talents. You must live to love me for all of our days!"

She saw him smile. He had heard her words. She knew it! She'd been able to send her thoughts to him. He stood again, though he was not entirely steady, the look of complete determination on his face plainly distracted his uncle. Killian managed to hobble over to his uncle and the two men looked at each other with equal pride and stubbornness on their faces.

The older man tried not to envision the young boy, his brother's son who had come to live with them so many years ago—the boy whom he'd thought of as his own son for nearly as long, the boy he'd been so very proud to call his kin. And Killian attempted to forget momentarily this was the man who'd saved him on the battlefield all those years ago, who'd taken him in his arms and consoled him, the man he'd greatly respected and wanted to aspire to since his own father had been taken from him.

They came at each other again, both exhausted, both wounded, both wanting this to be ended, but neither entirely sure they could end it if it meant seeing the other die. Killian fell down to his knees this time and though he held his sword up to protect himself his uncle brought his own sword down sharply and knocked Killian's sword from his hand. The earl glanced at the crowd and knew what must be done, he closed his eyes and drove the sword downward toward his nephew feeling he had no choice but to end this by taking his life, for it had not been him who'd made this a battle to the death.

Killian saw the blade coming toward him, and thought this would be the last moment of his life, but somehow he summoned the strength and the dexterity to capably twist quickly enough to dodge the blade. It stuck in the ground beside him with the great force behind it. The suddenness of the weapon striking the ground sent the heavier man to the ground with a forceful thud. Killian painstakingly managed to retrieve his own sword and to pull himself beside his uncle. With difficulty, he rose to his knees and he weakly lifted his weapon over his head intending to drive it into him, to run him through and end his life for all that he had done to Alainn. But he found himself hesitant even knowing he had little choice when it was he who had declared how the bout must end. He clearly heard her sweet voice inside his head, yet again.

"You needn't do this for me, Killian. You have fought for my honor and I know you have won, the entire land knows you have won, but let not his death be on my hands or your own. Let this never be a wedge between us, my love!"

Killian stared down into the dark eyes that reminded him so much of his own father's eyes. He slowly began to lower his sword, but he spoke determinedly as he looked into the eyes that at the moment were fearful and filled with the knowledge he would soon surely die.

"I cannot take your life, uncle. I want to, in truth, I want it more than you could ever know, but it does not seem to be within me to take the life of my kin. And I pray Alainn truly understands I mean her no dishonor by allowing you to live. But, you must apologize to her for all that you have done and said to demean and abuse her. And you must think long and hard on accepting her, the curse must be ended for I want my son to live! I want my father's grandson to live, and begin a new generation of O'Briens!"

The man nodded respectfully as Killian spoke. Killian leaned over to assist his uncle in rising, and then he painfully began to limp away. Alainn had watched the exchange and known that what Killian had done had been right, and perhaps the only decision he could live with. She glanced at Killian's face and then she saw the figure heading toward him. She screamed out, but he could not hear her. She tried to force the warning to him in her mind, but he did not appear to hear her this time.

She tore the amulet from her neck and envisioned herself standing down on the ground. When she opened her eyes she was in the crowd of people and she screamed out his name. He turned abruptly to look, half expecting to see his uncle with his sword ready to run him through. He saw the man was indeed holding his sword, but he had a look of terror on his face and he called out in warning to his nephew, as well.

Killian saw out of the corner of his eyes, Richard McGilvary was coming at him with a dagger in his hand. He attempted to move out of the way, but in his gravely injured state his movements were unusually slow. The man was nearly upon him when he saw his uncle's sword being hurled through the air and finding its target, it landed in the man's belly. He fell to the ground clearly wounded and in agonizing pain, but he still lived.

Killian watched on as Richard McGilvary heard, and clearly recognized the terrifying sounds of barking and snarling. He glanced up to see Alainn heading toward him from amongst the sea of people, and behind her the entire pack of his uncle's wolfhounds followed and purposefully lunged upon the despicable young man. They tore at his flesh and ripped him apart in a horribly brutal fashion. Even people with the strongest of constitutions had to avert their eyes from the disturbingly gruesome sight.

Killian turned to greet Alainn who ran toward him with such a relieved expression on her lovely face he felt tears in his eyes, and when she was nearly in his arms he saw her own beautiful blue eyes fill with a knowing, pained expression, and she fell into his injured arms in a crumpled manner. He grabbed her and lifted her into his arms, perplexed at what could have caused her to fall unconscious, when he saw the dart that protruded from her back. He pulled it from her straightaway and noticed the acridly pungent smell that came from it. He felt his heart sink. It had been poisoned. She'd been struck by a poisoned dart. He felt her grow entirely limp and he sensed a deep, shattered hopelessness overcoming him. He was at a loss to know what to do. Morag knew much of poisons, but she could no longer help, and he was unsure at how skilled the physician was at the knowledge of poisons. Perhaps Mara... or Danhoul, he frantically wondered. He felt himself growing weak and dizzy with exhaustion and deep emotion.

Rory and Riley were at his side almost immediately and Niall as well.

"Get the physician!" Killian weakly managed as he felt himself stumble and he dropped to his knees still holding tight to Alainn. "And the young druid, Danhoul Calhoun."

"Find the witch as well!" Hugh O'Brien hollered himself.

Killian looked at him with disbelief in his eyes.

"Aye, you heard me, someone fetch the glade witch. She may be the only one capable of saving her daughter, and ending the curse!"

Killian was aware that Riley had taken Alainn from his shaking arms and lain her upon the ground. He felt himself fall over as well, but as he sensed the darkness overtaking him the last memory he had was the sweet scent of his face upon her beautiful hair and the knowledge they would be together, perhaps in death, but undoubtedly together, and he was at peace with that.

Chapter Thirty

S HE SENSED THE sharp pain in her back between her shoulders, but it was the pain within her belly that frightened her most. And then she'd felt a warm, wet rush of fluid between her thighs so that even in her fading consciousness she had realized her unborn child was in great peril. Though she was relieved to fall into the protective arms of her husband, she felt paralyzed by whatever object had struck her back and by the knowledge she would surely lose their child. Her body immediately became unnaturally cold and so still, and she felt her heartbeat first race wildly and then beat slower and slower.

She barely heard the whispered voices around her and she could no longer see, though she strained to open her unwilling eyes. She had grown steadily numb and cold as she felt the poison seeping throughout her entire body. And her last thoughts were of Killian, lying beside her and knowing no one knew how to deal with the poison that now flowed through her veins. And then she could think no more.

KILLIAN AWOKE AS if from a hellishly bad dream and moaned lowly as he tried to move. Every part of him ached, from head to toe. He opened one eye and it dawned on him the other was obviously completely swollen shut. He glanced down at his unclad body. A cloth was draped over his manhood, but the rest of him was unclothed and he reasoned there was scarcely any part of him that was not badly bruised, cut, or battered. The physician attended to his many slices that needed to be mended with needle and thread. He was lying upon the table in the physician's chamber and he noticed Riley stood beside him and he came to Killian when he saw his cousin had come to. His uncle, too, remained there, clearly awaiting his nephew's rousing.

Killian laid his head back down for even the small movement had sent pain searing through his body, and he felt as weak as a small child. He noticed his uncle still remained unattended to, for the many wounds that had been inflicted by Killian in their challenge were still gaping and bleeding. How odd the physician had tended to Killian's wounds before that of the chieftain. Suddenly, with great clarity, he remembered and he began to sit up without consideration of the pain that would cause.

"Where is Alainn?"

"Lie down!" the physician demanded. "You have lost a great quantity of blood, perhaps a mortal amount, and I've yet to close the many wounds. They are numerous!" he stated.

"Where the hell is my wife," he asked in a ragged voice, entirely ignoring the other man as he continued his pitiful attempt to sit up.

"Killian, listen to my physician, he knows what he's doing!" His uncle ordered.

"Riley, where is she?" Killian looked toward his cousin obviously believing he would not hold back telling him what he needed to know.

"She is with her mother!" Riley said, and Killian did not miss the anxious tone in his cousin's voice. He heard quick-paced footsteps and saw Rory had now joined them.

"What news have you, son?" The chieftain barked.

Rory glanced at Killian, and upon seeing he was awake, he did not speak.

"Rory, you must tell me straight what you know!" Killian's voice shook as he tried to force Rory to reveal the truth.

Rory took a slow breath and regrettably looked down into the fearful eyes of his cousin. "Alainn's condition is undoubtedly most grave, Killian. She has not yet woken, and her mother fears she will not. The poison has slowed her body, her heart barely beats. Mara and Danhoul are uncertain what can be done. They have attempted to heal her, administered an antidote Mara thought would counteract the poison, but she has witnessed no improvement."

"And what of the child?" It was the chieftain who dared to pose this inquiry.

Rory once more looked at Killian with dread on his face

as he revealed what he knew. "She threatens to lose the child; her mother says she cannot impede the bleeding and that the babe is surely ill-fated."

Killian's ashen face grew even paler and he grasped the cloth that covered him as he finally managed to stand. The physician had been in the process of suturing a large slash on the back of his leg, and he quickly sliced the thread though the wound remained unclosed.

"Find me my trews, for I must go to Alainn!" he called out to the men that surrounded him.

The physician knew he would not be swayed, so he passed him the badly torn trews he had worn in battle. Killian saw they were soaked in blood and so ragged he doubted he would be able to pull then on without them falling apart entirely. He saw Riley who was much the same size as himself, pull off his own trews and pass them to him.

"Aye, you must go to her!" he agreed.

Riley didn't even bother with the fact that he only wore his long tunic for he knew he must help Killian get to Alainn. Killian leaned on both his cousins' shoulders as he made his way up the stairwell to where Alainn had been taken.

⌘

SHE LAY IN the bed in his bedchamber, in the bed where they'd made love this very morning. She looked so tiny and helpless as she lay upon the large structure she was pallid, so unnaturally pale! Mara sat beside her on the bed, and his aunt was there as well. Danhoul looked at Killian with an expression of mingled regret and exasperation.

Killian had briefly noticed Niall outside the door, but had barely acknowledged his presence for he'd felt such desperation to get to Alainn. Mara moved and allowed Killian to sit beside her. He noticed Mara observed his unclothed chest and the numerous slashes and bruises that covered his upper body. He grimaced as he painfully sat beside her daughter.

Killian took her slender hand in his and tried not to think of how unnaturally cold it felt. Had she already left him? Did her heart truly still beat as her mother had assured him?

"What poison was it?" he asked Mara, though he did not take his eyes from her daughter.

"Henbane, I believe!" she said in a small voice that quivered.

"And the antidote has had no affect?"

"Not as yet, and sure it should have diminished the poison by now. I have attempted to heal her by way of my magic, I have chanted many healing spells, tried to draw the poison from her by way of alchemy. I have used all the herbal remedies I am aware of, but to no avail. She has responded to nothing."

"Is she in pain?" he asked, though he wasn't certain he wanted to know the answer.

"I believe she is incapable of feeling anything any longer, Killian. I fear she is near the end now. Death is almost certain to soon follow!" Her voice broke as she spoke.

"What can I do, there must be something I can do to help her, Mara?" the man pleaded to the woman who stood beside him, the woman he had despised most of his life because of the wretchedly devastating curse she'd placed on the O'Briens.

"Hold tight to her hand for if she is able to feel any sensation, if she is capable of any thought, then sure she will know you are with her! And if she is to leave this world then let your presence be the last certainty she knows, for she loves you well and dearly!"

Killian not only took her hand, but gently lifted her head to rest upon his arm as he leaned on the bed. He kissed her cheek and let his lips graze hers, then put his cheek against her forehead.

"You must awaken, my sweet, Lainna! I love you more than mere words or simple gestures could ever demonstrate, and I need you to return to me!" How am I to go on if you are not here beside me, my only love? You have always been so unusually strong, Alainn, since you were a wee child you have possessed great strength and tenacity. You must fight this damnable poison. Return to me, my Lainna!"

The others in the room had all gone, knowing this time was for Killian to be with his wife. Even Danhoul cast a remorseful and completely defeated glance toward the young couple and left the chamber.

Mara had remained, but rose to leave the chamber as well.

Killian stopped her. "You have been denied a life with the man you loved, and with your daughter; you will not be denied this time if it is to be when her life ends!"

The appreciation in the woman's blue eyes presented itself in the form of large tears and Killian noticed now, how like Alainn's her eyes were. The woman sat down on the chair beside the bed and held her daughter's hand in her own while her husband still held her slender body close to him. Killian tried to avert his eyes from the large dark red stain upon the bed clothes. If she truly died, his grief would be two-fold for their child would be gone as well. He thought of his uncles and their wives who had lost so many children. His thoughts went to his own father who lost his wife and his daughter within hours of each other. How could he have managed it, he wondered? How had he lived through it? If he lost Alainn, Killian believed it would be a tragedy far too tragic to bear!

Killian heard a knocking at the door and wondered who would dare to disturb them at this grievous time. A servant girl hesitantly poked her head in the door.

"Milord, there are two women who insist on entering. I have tried to dissuade them, but they seem unwilling to leave without seeing your lady."

Killian turned toward the door and saw Mary and Molly

standing outside. Mary wore a dismal expression and stoic teardrops rolled silently down her cheeks, but it was the cook's daughter that sobbed openly and pushed against the door to be allowed within. The fretful servant girl looked toward Lady Siobhan who now stood at the doorway, for a sign of what she should do, and Lady Siobhan in turn, glanced at Killian.

"Aye, come in then, sure she'd want you here beside her now."

Mary slowly, cautiously entered the chamber, but Molly raced across the room and swiftly dropped to her knees by the bed, grasping Alainn's hand.

"She cannot die. Your cousins have said she will surely die! That is not possible, she is young and strong and she has an unequivocal will to live!"

Killian did not answer the girl, but simply laid his forehead against his wife's hair once more and he felt his own tears stinging his eyes. Molly only then seemed to notice the bright red spot upon the bed where Alainn had been lying.

"I hadn't thought of the child, as well!" Molly's face crumpled further.

Mary dared to ask the question Killian had not even allowed himself to dwell upon. "Who has done this to her?"

Killian shook his head and shrugged as if it mattered not to him, for at the moment nothing truly mattered to him.

"What has been done to her?" Mary asked further.

"She has been poisoned." Mara spoke quietly as Killian

seemed deep in thought and apparently had not even heard or acknowledged the question.

"But Alainn said she was immune to poison; she told me that herself."

"Immune?" her mother asked, startled by the girl's declaration.

"Aye, she told me so. She said, from handling the poisons so consistently through her life and in dealing with them in the balms and ointments, that she is unaffected by poisons."

"Perhaps to some poisons… in small quantities; but not when directly, violently driven into her body!"

"But she said you must use poison to fight poison!" The girl would not relent.

"Aye, I've tried with the safe amounts, and the lesser poisons that I dare use."

"Who did this to her?" Molly asked through tear-filled eyes, the question Mary had already asked, but no one had answered. "Who would hurt dear Alainn, when she has healed and helped so many?"

"The assailant has apparently not been found!" Mara said, her tone regretful tone.

Killian had closed his eyes and he held Alainn so tightly the sight made Mary's tears begin again. And it was clearly too much for the other young girl to take. She burst into heart-wrenching sobs that startled Mary.

"You simply cannot die, Alainn. You are, and have always been, my dearest friend for all my life. I am resolute that I shall never find a friend as true as you. And I have not yet told you of my joyous news. Pierce has asked me to marry him! You must awaken so I can tell you how happy I am!" Molly continued to weep as she pled with her friend.

"She knows, Molly. Mac told us and she was most happy for you and extremely excited as well." Killian assured the young girl. "And she was so very pleased to hear you will be living..." Killian stopped mid-sentence for when he looked down at the unnatural paleness of his wife's pretty young face, he felt a deep pain in his chest for he believed she looked as though she surely no longer lived. He placed his hand to the softness of her throat fearing he would find no heartbeat, but finally he found it, weak and infrequent, but it remained present nonetheless.

He heaved a huge sigh of relief and the two young women realized they now must go and leave Killian alone with her. Mary glanced at Alainn once more and then looked upward with her eyes closed obviously sending a desperate, heartfelt prayer for her young friend. Molly was less quiet about it, for she placed a tender farewell kiss upon Alainn's cheek and then the typically shy, reserved girl wailed loudly and mournfully as she ran sobbing from the room.

The silence after they left was most disturbing. Mara looked at Killian. There was desperation upon his young, handsome face that at the moment looked severely beaten and marred. She thought of another young man whose face had appeared just that way for been beaten as severely after he'd crossed this young man's grandfather. That had been the last time she'd seen her own beloved, Teige. He'd been taken to the dungeon while the chieftain dealt with her. And then apparently he'd been told she'd been killed. And he'd evidently believed it for he'd gone away and she'd been left alone to contend with the wrathful chieftain and months later the child who now lay so near death herself. Had Teige O'Rorke met with death? Mara had wondered that every day for the past ten and eight years. And if he had died, in death would he finally be allowed to meet his daughter in the beyond?

She felt her own hopeless tears sliding down her cheeks. She'd allowed herself to weep so seldom throughout the years. She'd always felt it was a sign of weakness, and a useless frailty to allow hers tears to flow, but now it seemed pointless to try to conceal her deep fear and heartache. The young man beside her took her hand in his at their shared grief and this profoundly moved her.

"You are a good man, Killian O'Brien. My daughter was wise beyond her years to give her heart to you. Even if she and the child are taken, I sense the curse will now be broken. No more O'Brien babies shall be taken because of my horridly unforgivable curse. Alainn has been accepted by you, and by your cousins. I think deep within your uncle's darkened soul, he, too, knows the truth."

Chapter Thirty-One

DANHOUL'S EYES SKIRTED the bushes behind the stone ruins, hoping to locate the priest. He knew through his abilities that he was surely the one who had shot the poisoned dart at Alainn. Through all his attempts at healing Alainn, he had been unable to render any improvement, and so feeling entirely ineffective and at wit's end, he deducted he would use his abilities to discover the whereabouts of her assailant.

He had enlisted the Captain of the Guard, Mackenzie MacArthur to accompany him and the man seemed to agree with his conclusion it was quite possibly the priest who was to blame for Alainn's grave malady.

They had gone to the castle's abbey and to the priest's chambers, but to no avail. The man seemed nowhere to be found. The captain had sent out many men to search for the priest, but there was no evident sign of the man. They had searched the dungeon as well, for it was learned through a castle guard it was the priest who had freed the prisoner, Richard McGilvary.

Danhoul finally had been able to conjure a vision of the

priest hidden amongst the ruins of the nearby ancient abbey, and Mac believed him without question. Together with a dozen guards, they began searching the ruins for the man. To everyone's disbelief the man simply came out from where he had been concealed behind the stones. He was carrying the bundle of poisoned darts and made no effort to keep them hidden.

"Drop the weapons and surrender yourself to us immediately!" the captain demanded.

The priest, whose eyes were wide and filled with fear and torment, did as instructed but seemed to be intent on looking behind him, clearly far more concerned with the unseen terror than the captain and his guards.

"I purposely killed the man with the dark skin and unusual abilities and the young healer as well. I killed them both and now you must kill me! I beseech you, take my life now!" the priest begged the captain.

"You'll not be getting off that easily, Father. You'll be judged by the chieftain and the just punishment will be issued in due course!"

"No, I beg of you, you must end my life now, for death must be preferential to this loathsome darkness that surrounds me, I'd risk eternal fire and damnation in the pits of hell if it will mean the darkness that surrounds me and from within me is no more!"

The guards all appeared hesitant to capture the priest who had wielded much power and issued so many threats of what would befall them in hell. Now that he was surely driven to unquestionable madness, they backed away from the stricken man.

Mac started toward the priest and the holy man's eyes registered great relief. Just as the captain detained the man, Danhoul noticed the immense shadow of a demon beast enshrouded the priest.

He issued a swift warning to the captain. "Back away, Captain and don't look back! Leave him where he stands!"

Although Mac was uncertain of the young druid's meaning, he had witnessed enough of Alainn's unusual abilities to realize this young man also had the gift of second sight. He let go of the priest and jumped back out of the way. As the ruins of the stone abbey began to quake and rumble, the dark sinister shadow began to completely cover the priest. Danhoul aimed his dagger directly toward the priest's heart. At precisely the same moment he saw from within the clouds above him that Aine had come to avenge her youngest kin and she, too, hurled a dagger at the priest. Both daggers simultaneously pierced his heart and he crumpled to the ground. The dying man smiled gratefully at Danhoul as his terrified eyes grew blank and then closed. Danhoul shivered as the demon's ghastly silhouette shrank back into the shadows. When he glanced skyward he saw Aine was no longer present.

Not one of the guards or the captain seemed to question the fact the young druid had taken the priest's life without judgment by the chieftain. Though they had not witnessed the sight of the demon as Danhoul had, each and every one of them had become filled with such a palpable dread of inexplicable evil, they all had feared for their own lives.

Danhoul and Mac exchanged a knowing glance and then Danhoul looked toward the skies and knew well he could sense the presence of another Celtic god nearby. When the captain and his guards had removed the body of the priest and made their way back to the castle, Danhoul waited until they were gone from sight. He sensed the demon still rested in the darkened shadows of the ruins where he'd last seen the hellish beast.

The priest had been wise and learned enough to know the creature was following him and using him to do his bidding. He must have known he was incapable of ridding himself of the beast so he had led him to the ruins of an abbey, a holy place in bright daylight. Now that the priest had been killed, the creature would surely need another dark soul to latch onto while daylight remained. Only in darkness could he move about freely on his own. As daylight slowly dwindled Danhoul knew he would soon have little choice but to leave before it became too perilous to remain. He glanced upward and silently called to the gods.

"Do you mean to assist me with this matter? Now your fireballs would actually be of some use, Lugh!"

He recognized the scent as he heard the whizzing and popping in response to his request.

As flames engulfed the trees that surrounded the abbey, it formed a circle of blazing light in the holy place that capably imprisoned the dark beast. Danhoul heard a distinctly familiar shriek and a pathetic howling. Then he watched as the sky above the abbey grew ablaze with the flames and the creatures tortured screams grew louder. He waited until the sounds stopped and the flames died down.

Danhoul dared to walk within the charred stones and viewed the grotesque blackened corpse of the hideous creature. Although he was well pleased that the demon had been killed, there was something about the death that did not leave him completely relieved or certain that the threat had been entirely extinguished. Was this actually the demon who had pursued Alainn or just another of his dark legions who had joined forces with the dark one and assisted him in threatening and harming Alainn? Then he stepped back as he saw the spirit of Ainna appear before him and encircle him in a welcomed white light.

"You have killed the dark demon." She smiled appreciatively at the young druid.

"Aye, well one of the dark demons," he answered in a forlorn and disillusioned voice. But I am not certain he is the actual beast who has been pursuing Alainn for so long. He was perhaps only another being recently released from the Unseelie Court when the portal opened. And I can feel not a hint of joy or relief at the moment as I cannot for all my attempts cause even the slightest improvement in Alainn's condition. I fear she will not live."

"It is not certain! Have you spoken with my mother, with the Council of the Gods?"

"Not yet, I suspect I will be summoned soon."

"Aye, you are to come with me now!" The booming voice of Lugh called to them from the clouds.

Danhoul felt himself being transported away as he saw Ainna's spectral presence fade as well.

⌘

"WHY ARE WE not permitted to interfere in this matter?" Lugh declared, ready to stand his ground. "If I am assigned to be her guardian why have they deemed we should do nothing at this time?"

"I am uncertain, Lugh. What I do know is if she is not pulled from this deep sleep straightaway, she will never waken, and there are many tasks she must fulfill. The council was clear on that, so I cannot say why they allow us to simply stand by and do nothing at this critical time." Aine fretted.

The young druid stood listening to the two others, but did not speak. He doubted he would have any say in any of it. He never had, and sure he never would.

"If we could send her forward now, the future remedies may save her and ensure her safety from the dark ones, but then it will be necessary for you to bring her back to her time again!" The woman directed her comments to Danhoul. "And in my very bones I sense events will be changed much too drastically if she was to do so now, for she is not to venture forward for some time. The others have not arrived yet."

"Then someone must do something to assist in changing events or allow my magic to be heightened so that I may do so." The young man finally spoke.

"Lugh cannot enter the human world, and I, too, have now been forbidden to interfere at this time. I am no longer allowed to return to earth. Because of the unrest between the gods and the recent battles with the dragons and the Fomorians, it has been a time of chaos and unrest in our realm. The Council of the Gods has placed unwavering restrictions on all of us.

I secretly enlisted Ainna's spirit to assist me and she was able to thwart the evildoers' attempts to harm Alainn in the dungeon. She ensured the demon and the two men with the dark souls did not do her harm there. The gods thought Alainn's powers should be tested by going against the dark demon. I was disinclined to believe she was ready.

I also assisted Danhoul in killing the priest of my own accord to avenge the great harm he has caused Alainn, but the gods do not take kindly to me going against their decisions."

Aine's stern expression grew even more solemn as she continued with her explanation to the other two.

"They had apparently hoped to lure more of the dark creatures to that location by using the priest as bait, for it is said that those who are of a holy association are often sought after by demons. As are those such as Alainn and you, Danhoul, who possess magical abilities. The Council of the Gods now believes because of my blood connection I should not be allowed to cast vote on any further matters pertaining to Alainn. Because of my interference, I regrettably was unable to return to earth to prevent the poison from getting to her."

"As it is now, I seem unable to heal her for all my magical attempts so you must, at the very least, assist her in regaining enough strength to remember what she must before it is too late!" Danhoul pleaded.

They wore dismal expressions as the conversation continued.

"And what of the child?" Lugh asked Aine.

"It has not been clearly decided although perhaps it would be a kindness if she were to lose…" Aine mused more to herself than the others, but did not complete the grim consideration.

"So you mean to simply stand by and allow her to die?" Danhoul's tone was pained at these words.

"It may be so destined," Aine answered.

"As so many times before." Lugh reflected.

"To what end?" Danhoul angrily questioned in a voice that shook.

"To relive it over and over again until the desired outcome is achieved. Until she manages to survive once again, so that both of you are taken to the future, with the other two witches and their guardians. As searchers and guardians you will then right the wrongs and bring back the lost ones." Aine reasoned.

Danhoul's tone was that of utter defeat when he responded and he dared to openly reveal all within his mind. "One day Alainn will remember all that you have done, all that each of the gods have done. Though you have repeatedly assured me she will have no memories, she has begun to recognize me and soon the other memories will follow. Each time she relives this life, she gains more knowledge of the previous times and each time more powers and stronger abilities present themselves. The outcomes may be different each time but, as you've seen, never before has she found the dragons or the hellhounds. Even you and the whole Council of the Gods did not anticipate that... and what ramifications are being felt in this realm because of it!"

Aine and Lugh exchanged knowing glances at the druid's frustration and the truths he spoke.

"If each time Alainn gains more magical strength and power and memory, one day she will remember everything and I would not desire to be any one of you if that day should come! Sure you'll rue the day you do battle with Alainn in all her glory! You intend to employ her in the ultimate battle between good and evil, but should she remember all, she might be angry enough to thwart you in the end!"

They seemed unwilling to heed the young druid and Aine lifted her chin in stubborn defiance as Danhoul had seen her do so many times before, another trait Alainn had inherited.

"You have been a part of this as well, young Danhoul!" Aine accused.

"Not by choice, only by destiny as you have stated and by affiliation and loyalty to Alainn, but never because I agreed with how you control me or the lives of the many people I care for."

"The end will justify the means, Danhoul, there are always difficult decisions and losses we must incur in the fight of good and evil. I much regret my young descendant must endure this pain and misfortune indefinitely and, because you care deeply for her, I see how it wears on you, but at any rate there is little use dwelling upon any of this. We must rejoice in the triumphs we do accomplish. We were finally able cast away the dark demons who search for the powers of the witches of my line." Aine stated.

"One of the darkest demons has been dealt with, Aine. Perhaps if your young descendant should live, for a time she shall be free of the threat of those with dark alliances wishing to take her powers. But it is believed the darkest demon has managed to escape and there are sure to be others lurking in the shadows, especially now if they sense she is near death." Lugh warned.

"They will not accomplish it; even in her deathlike state

no creature of the darkness has ever been able to take her alone. The priest and the young man with the dark associations are now dead. Even the strongest of the dark demons will always need a human accomplice to aid him, and he will employ many in attempts to take her powers for his own." Aine insisted.

"There will always be humans willing to assist the dark ones." Lugh countered.

"But there will always be people with magical powers drawn to assist Alainn and her kind as well. Perhaps the spirit of Morag who has always had a strong connection to Alainn will be capable of making her hear and heed her words now that one of the dark creatures has perished." Danhoul hoped aloud.

"Perhaps," Aine agreed but her tone lacked conviction.

He stood staring impatiently at the other two as they argued and discussed the young witch. Danhoul had long ago, in truth, several lifetimes ago, become deeply attached to Alainn and he was in much despair knowing how short her time in this life would be, yet again, if someone did not swiftly come to her aid. He continued to purposely will his thoughts to Alainn's mind and to the old healer's spirit.

Chapter Thirty-Two

KILLIAN AND MARA heard the sound behind them and turned to find Hugh O'Brien, staring in at them from the doorway, a look of confusion upon his face. He slowly limped into the bedchamber and with great hesitation drew nearer to them. He stared at the bruised and broken lad who leaned upon the bed and at the woman who sat beside him…the glade witch—the terrifying sorceress who had been the source of great pain and tragedy to him and his line. She did not appear to be evil or strong. At the moment, she was likened to any mother whose heart grieved at the knowledge her child would soon die.

He allowed himself to look upon the young woman who seemed lifeless in his nephew's arms. Her ashen face was beautiful even in her present state. Her long, dark eyelashes rested upon her perfect skin and he recalled a similar image of his own son. Once, when Rory had been a young boy he'd been ill and Morag, the old healer, had been uncertain if he would live through the night. His face had been as deathly pale as this girl's now was, and his eyelashes had looked just as hers did now. He put his hand to her cheek, but Killian would not allow it and pushed it away.

The man sighed deeply. "She does look so like my, Rory. I suppose I was a fool not to see that before now. I believe she is an O'Rorke, perhaps I have always known, but was too proud and bullheaded to admit it."

"And do you simply declare that now because Alainn is near death, in hopes to make amends and to end the curse, or do you actually believe it within your heart?" Killian cynically quizzed.

"No, Killian I do believe it, without question."

"And if she dies, how can you possibly prove you have accepted her as nobility?" The girl's mother posed.

The man's face, already serious, became more solemn as he considered it.

"She will be laid in our family graveyard. She shall have a high-cross as grand as that of my father or any other noble chieftain, and shall rest near the graves of my own children."

"And do you think your priest would truly allow her to be lain on sacred ground when he believes her to be evil?" Killian's tone still held unmasked contempt for his uncle.

"My priest is dead."

The two people looked at him with identical expressions of disbelief.

"He was duly killed by my captain and the young druid for they learned it was he who shot the poison dart at your wife, Killian!"

"How would a priest know of such poisons?" Mara

snapped.

"I am not certain; it is supposed he did not act alone! He was found with the poisoned darts in his possession and he fully admitted he committed the act toward your daughter."

"I hope he did not die a swift or painless death!" Killian commented in voice that seethed with the bitter agony he felt at the moment.

The chieftain did not respond, but turned to leave. Mara called after him. He stopped and she held a paper toward him. He did not seem to understand the meaning.

"I found it within my daughter's pocket. I cannot read, save a few words, but I recognize my husband's handwriting for he had begun to teach me to read and write. I believe it is a letter written to your priest by my husband. Though why my daughter had it in her possession or why your priest would keep it for such a lengthy time, I cannot say. You must tell me what it says."

The man looked doubtful about reading it to the woman as he scanned the words.

"Do as she says uncle, but before you do you must tell me what plans you have for Mara...after...after this day?" Killian needed to know.

"She will be safe, I assure you, no harm will befall her and she will be forgiven and allowed to stay here in the village if she so desires. The old farrier has apparently told the village priest he wishes for Mara to claim his cottage when he is gone. He said it would be in appreciation for

Mara raising his son and keeping her part of their bargain when he could not. By all accounts the farrier's time is apparently not long. My physician met with him only yesterday and his condition has become most serious. He is not expected to live but days at the longest. But Mara will have a home in which to dwell. I will not challenge the old farrier in his wish to bequeath his cottage and what worldly possessions he owns to your wife's mother."

Seemingly satisfied with the man's answer, he nodded toward the paper and for the man to read it to the woman. He did as instructed and when he was done, Mara's eyes had filled with tears again.

"Oh, Teige, what happiness we might have known if we'd been allowed a life together. What happiness all here might have known!"

"I will speak to my brothers, though I well know they will side with me, they shall come to know your daughter is of noble blood, and a descendant to the O'Rorke."

"Then the curse will be no more!" she whispered to herself in a voice filled with bittersweet finality.

Killian felt the weight of his sorrow and of the day's events upon him. His arms ached with even Alainn's slight weight. He gently lay her back down upon the pillow and covered her with the many bedclothes. Then even in plain view of the others, he painfully pulled himself upon the bed and lie down next to her. He took her in his arms and soon fell into a sleep born of exhaustion.

The chieftain looked down upon the sorrowful sight and felt an immense lump form in his throat. He was as much to blame for these young people's woes as his priest. If he'd not attempted to harm her, not kept the two of them apart and been so adamant they would never be together, the challenge would never have been forced. The two of them would surely be together by now, off to Killian's castle, living out their lives in contented happiness. He turned and sadly left them alone, but for the witch.

Mara watched him leave and for the first time in nearly two decades, she felt no intense hatred for the man, or even for his father who had caused such anguish for her. She looked morosely down upon her daughter and her young husband and left the two alone.

Alone, she had brought the child into this world, but her husband would have the honor of being with Alainn when she left it. Mara wasn't certain she could watch her only child take her last breath. She slowly walked across the room with the intent of looking one more time through what potions Alainn had stored within her cupboard, and to dwell on what else might be done to ensure she did not die, though Mara held little hope.

THE TWO SLEPT, both presented with unusual dreams. Alainn felt herself floating amongst the clouds, as she stared toward the brightly lit tunnel before her and listened to the angelic music that peacefully surrounded her. It called to her and she felt her weightless body drifting to the beyond. She longed to enter. She saw the spirit of Morag hovering near the entrance to the tunnel, but she was not welcoming her, she was clearly demanding Alainn steer clear of the light. And she heard Danhoul's voice insisting she fight to live and to remember. She felt Killian's warmth beside her and heard his heartbeat. She resisted the temptation of the heavenly light and suddenly remained intent on a distant memory.

She could clearly see a vision of Morag sitting with her when she was a very young child, so young she still possessed fine, baby-soft pale golden hair. They sat together in the herb garden, and Morag dug a deep hole and placed an object within. The child with bright blue eyes crawled toward the small opening and watched on intently as she touched the herbs that so abundantly grew in that location.

"One day this memory will come back to you when you need it most, caileag leanabh," Morag whispered.... "Remember this day, remember... the belladonna...never entirely forget the belladonna!"

Still in her dreamlike state, Alainn's memories darted to the many times she and Morag were in the herb garden together and Morag seemed to often make it a habit to mention belladonna. Alainn recalled the latest time another day perhaps only two years previous when she and Morag had once more been in the herb garden together. She remembered the conversation they'd had.

"The herbs have wintered well, caileag. Most especially the belladonna, it has flourished most assuredly."

"Why do you choose to refer to it by belladonna, I much prefer to call it by evening nightshade, it has a much more romantic sound to it, don't you think, Morag?"

"Sure, there's nothin' romantic or fanciful about a deadly poison, caileag, and you know it well enough."

"Aye," she'd agreed, yet she clearly remembered feeling wounded by Morag's harsh words. Although the old healer had never been a gentle sort, she'd not often spoke to Alainn in such a cutting tone.

"Remember the belladonna, caileag!" She'd repeated and Alainn could hear the old healer saying it over and over in her mind, repeating it so often, Alainn felt displeased by the very sound of it.

Alainn thought to waken and alert someone to what Morag had told her for she sensed it was clearly of great importance, but she was far too weary, and much too cold. The pain in her belly had waned and she felt the warmth of Killian lying beside her, she felt his arms holding her. She would continue to sleep now... just for awhile longer!

⌘

KILLIAN'S OWN DREAMS were filled with much confusion. He dreamt of Aine and Lugh, the two gods he had seen in the fairy glade, but the young druid, Danhoul, had been there as well. Throughout this peculiarly distorted dream, even without being capable of actually hearing the words of their discussion and in knowing it must be a dream, he sensed most assuredly that this unusual young druid appeared to harbor deep feelings for Alainn, or eventually would, and that somehow he was an intricate part of ensuring Alainn did not meet with death. It was all entirely muddled and nearly nonsensical, as if he saw and heard them through the thickness of a suffocating fog.

He felt himself being pulled from the dream like state to a sound beside him. He was almost certain he had heard Alainn speak, only softly in her sleep, but he was sure she had spoken. He listened for any sound that might prove him correct. When he had begun to believe he had only imagined it, he heard her soft voice barely more than a whisper.

"Morag, why did you place it beneath the evening nightshade; why ever did you choose the belladonna? 'Sure, 'tis a most powerful poison if you've not developed a magical immunity to it!"

Killian sat straight up in bed. Alainn truly had uttered words. Surely she couldn't be near death if she was able to speak. His eyes skirted the room in attempt to locate Mara. She was no longer there. He must find her and tell her the words, Alainn had revealed, but he wouldn't leave her here alone. He painfully attempted to drag himself from the bed, all the while wishing he had Alainn's power of telepathy so he might send a message to someone.

In his weakened and painful condition, he wasn't certain

he could make it to the corridor. He mustered what strength he could and called out raspily. The door opened almost immediately and Niall O'Rorke and Lady Siobhan entered the chamber with both Rory and Riley close behind, and Mary as well. All wore a look of dread, for clearly they believed Killian needed to convey the message that Alainn had succumbed to the poison and died. Yet, the urgency in his voice seemed to imply otherwise.

"Where is Mara?" Killian asked hurriedly.

"She is off to the herb chamber." Mary offered.

"You must find her and tell her this message. I am not remotely certain what significance it holds, but you must tell her something lies beneath the belladonna. The belladonna is important somehow as is magical immunity!"

"What are you talking about, Killian?" Riley asked.

"Did Alainn speak?" Rory questioned disbelievingly.

"Is she awake?" Niall asked with a hint of hope seeping into his weary voice.

Lady Siobhan approached Alainn to see for herself, but was further saddened to see the girl seemed to have not stirred from when last she'd looked in on her.

Killian's remained in a weakened condition himself and he felt himself growing ever frustrated and angry that no one seemed to be complying with what he'd asked, but then he noticed Mary met his eyes knowingly and she hurried down the corridor. He believed somehow she would find Mara. Riley followed her, and Killian once more succumbed to his exhaustion and weakness and lay back upon the bed.

Chapter Thirty-Three

KILLIAN FELT SOMEONE gruffly shaking him and he could scarcely pull himself from his deep sleep. He reasoned a part of him truly never wanted to wake up. He finally forced himself to be roused and he saw it was Mara who shook him roughly.

"Killian, you must awaken, for you have a most grave decision to make?"

"What is it?" Killian asked and he glanced down at Alainn, guilt-ridden that he had fallen asleep again when he wanted to spend every moment he could with her. He looked at her pale complexion and could not clearly comprehend Mara's words.

"Killian!" She shook him again, this time even more roughly and less patiently.

Niall stood beside the bed as well and he stared down at Killian and Alainn.

His voice was gentle as he spoke. "As my granddaughter's husband, it shall be left up to you to make this enormous decision, Killian. Her mother and the young druid have done all they can to heal her. Your Aunt Siobhan and I have called upon our own druid abilities in hope of a desirable outcome, but to no avail, now it is your decision to make."

"What decision?" Killian finally seemed to understand and his eyes registered clarity.

"Mary told me the message regarding the belladonna." Mara elaborated.

"What is belladonna; Alainn mentioned something about a poison?"

"Aye, it is a deadly poison and is usually referred to as evening nightshade, but Morag always called it belladonna, as it is another name for it. Usually only a tiny amount of it can cause death, or worse."

"Worse?" Killian asked.

"Aye, irreversible madness!"

"What are you askin' me, then?"

"Mary insists that Alainn is immune to it. She says she handles it without benefit of covering. If that be truth then perhaps we can use it to fight back the henbane. It is probably the only poison stronger than the one that already has pulsed through her body."

"Then surely you must give it to her, Mara. If she has no hope without it then, aye, you must give it to her!"

"All my attempts to heal Alainn by way of my magic have failed so I fear it is the course that must be taken!"

"I concur!" Niall nodded his head at Killian.

"Then do it, Mara, and make haste!"

Mara stood with the elixir in her hand, but looked at

Killian with a morose seriousness.

"If Alainn lives through this; if this poison truly aids her, it will most certainly kill the child!"

"By God's nails!" Killian loudly exclaimed at the enormity of all they were facing. "But if Alainn dies our child is lost at any rate... so we've truly no choice. You must do whatever you can to save her."

"And will you tell her of this if she lives and the child is lost?"

"I suspect she will know!"

"Aye!" the woman simply said as she slowly began trickling small amounts of the concoction onto her daughter's lips as she gently opened her mouth. All the while she spoke in words that Killian did not comprehend, but he knew without question Mara was employing her magic along with her potion. At that very moment an unusual wind blew through the arched window. The candles flickered and rose, the bed shook ever so slightly and a soft glow filled the room.

"How do you know when she has had enough?" Killian asked, knowing full well something supernatural was happening surely by way of Mara's magic. He dared to allow himself to feel a degree of hope.

"I don't!" Mara admitted truthfully. "I am only hoping it is enough, but not too much!"

"And did you find something of noteworthiness hidden beneath the belladonna?" Killian finally remembered the words Alainn had spoken.

Mara placed her hand within the pocket of her frock and pulled out a round silver adornment.

" 'Tis the missing portion of my husband's amulet. Morag must have buried it there to ensure no one would be capable of locating it. I suppose she didn't trust my protection spell would hold until Alainn found it in the dungeon. She buried it beneath the belladonna knowing no one could touch it and live to tell of it, and she must have had Alainn handle the belladonna through the years. There is now no doubt Alainn is an O'Rorke for it fits perfectly with the other half of the amulet. I placed it around Alainn's neck when she was but two days old, the day I left her to be raised by the farrier and his wife."

The tears fell slowly slid down her cheeks and the memory clearly still brought pain to her heart.

"Even if Alainn cannot live through this, the curse will finally be forever ended for she has been accepted as nobility without question or doubt!"

"Aye, she is indeed an O'Rorke, daughter to my son, Teige," Niall said with combined pride and sadness.

Killian and Niall both watched as the woman finally moved the bottle from Alainn's lips. None present were certain how much she had been able to swallow in her present condition, but they all remained stock-still anxiously waiting to see if there would be any change. Mara claimed if it did not prove to be a cure, the poison would quickly end Alainn's life. So Mara kept her hand on Alainn's weakened heart, waiting. And Killian watched for any indication of change. Niall stood by the bed and stared at the young girl.

Alainn did not waken as they'd hoped, but neither did she die hastily as Mara had warned. Mara's eyes seemed to slowly dim and lose all hope. Niall once more joined his daughter and grandsons in the corridor.

Killian found himself down on his knees beside Alainn, with hands clasped and, for the first time in almost a decade, he prayed. He had attended church all these years as was demanded and expected, and outwardly he claimed to possess a strong faith. But, in truth, since his entire family had died and his father remained missing, he'd found it difficult to maintain his strong beliefs. When he was a youngster after Alainn had told him she believed his father still lived, he had done nothing but pray for weeks on end, but when that had never proven to be true, he'd felt abandoned by God, and so he had abandoned him as well.

Now as he looked down at Alainn, he realized though God had not answered his prayers of allowing him to be reunited with his father, instead he had given him someone who had come to be his entire world. He had sent Alainn, for he would never believe she was evil and in truth maybe she was an actual angel sent to be with him even if for only a short while. But now, he prayed. He prayed with all his heart as he determinedly held tight to Alainn's hand. He prayed all the rest of that day and well into the night.

⌘

MARA NOTICED IT first, for Killian's eyes remained tightly closed. She saw Alainn's finger twitch ever so slightly and she hoped it was not simply her body's involuntary response. But when it continued, she poked Killian and he opened his eyes. He, too, saw Alainn's fingers begin to move. Slowly she uncurled her fingers and then she moaned weakly. She began to cough and Killian assisted Mara in sitting her upright. And then Killian's greatest prayers were answered, his most desirous wish came true, her beautiful eyes slowly opened. He had thought he would never again be given the chance to gaze into her unusual azure eyes again.

She glanced at both of them with a curious expression almost as if she didn't recognize them, and Mara appeared fretful that perhaps Alainn was experiencing the madness she'd spoken of. But then she took one very long look at Killian, and her undying love for him was evident. She smiled and she reached out to him. She gently placed her hand to his eye still so severely bruised and swollen shut.

"Oh, my only love, what a dreadfully battered state you are in, but what a valiant battle you fought, my champion! You must allow me to heal you. Come here, come closer to me!"

Killian tried to smile to show her how greatly relieved he was that she was truly alive and seemingly well, but he felt the tears falling down his cheeks. All the fear, pain, and fatigue of the last days seemed to overcome him completely and he openly began to sob as he rested his head upon her heart. Alainn soothed him tenderly as she hummed softly to him and gently caressed his dark hair.

Mara once more intended to leave them alone, her own relief so overwhelming she felt her heart would explode with utter joy. Though the fate of the child was yet to be determined, her daughter was back and apparently with all her wits about her.

"Do not kiss him!" She warned as she turned her back to them from the doorway.

"What? Why?" Alainn couldn't understand why her mother would try to keep her from kissing her own husband.

"You have belladonna on your lips!" She warned.

"To render the henbane harmless." Alainn realized, but then a look of complete horror crossed her face. "Tell me of our son, Killian! Mother, what of the child?"

"You have not lost him, yet." Mara assured her as she came back to her daughter's side and touched the top of her head in reassurance. "But indeed, there has been much bleeding."

"And the evening nightshade will make the bleeding increase!" Alainn exclaimed worriedly. She looked down at the bedsheets and then pulled her nightdress up so that she might assess the situation closer. No fresh blood seemed apparent. She placed her hands to her stomach and closed her eyes. The child still lived; she sensed it though she could feel no movement. She slowly lay back down again, taking Killian's hand and squeezing it tightly. Killian had managed to compose himself admirably and knew he must now console her.

"I pray he will survive, Alainn. But, if it is not to be so...if it is the cruel hand we are dealt, then we will have many other children. As long as we are together, my sweet Lainna, we will surely be blessed with other children."

Alainn nodded sadly and tried to believe their son would be strong enough and have received enough of her immunity to live through this.

Chapter Thirty-Four

A MOON AND a fortnight had passed since Alainn had nearly succumbed to the poisoning. And for the first month she had barely been allowed to move from the bed. She'd slowly regained her strength and to nearly everyone's surprise and elation, she'd not lost the child. With each day he seemed to grow stronger and more active within her. Killian had been fiercely protective of her and would scarcely leave her side, the entire time. Ten days previous, when she'd finally asked to be allowed to at least stand at the window of the east solar, he'd nervously relented though insisted on carrying her even that short distance.

Each day since then, she'd moved a little more, and re-gained more freedom along with her strength. Today, she'd bathed again in the round washtub Killian had hauled up for her. He'd also carried the pails of hot water up the many stairs himself. She knew he would do anything for her and he showed her several times a day, and in many ways, how grateful he was that she was still here with him when he believed he had lost her forever.

After she'd enjoyed the lovely sensation of soaking in the

warm, scented water and washed her hair, she'd brushed out her long tresses and dressed in her most appealing gown. Now she stood at the small open area outside the window, looking out upon the bright midsummer's day. The day was warm, the flowers and trees full and beautiful, the river and everything in nature appeared so entirely enchanting to her. A soft, fragrant breeze tousled her hair. She breathed in the freshness and reveled in the glory of the warm summer afternoon. Though she had missed the outdoors, she could not think of it as a hardship to remain indoors or even confined to her bed even for her entire term, if it meant it had kept her unborn child safe.

She pondered all the many happenings of the past weeks.

The O'Brien weddings had taken place. Riley and Mary, Rory and Brigid, and Sean and Iona had all been married the same day in a joint ceremony. Though she'd not been able to attend, Killian had been present for the nuptials, but not the celebration afterwards. Although Molly had sat by her side so she'd not be left alone, Killian was adamant he would not be parted from her for that length of time.

Alainn had insisted on hearing everything about the weddings. Killian had told her some, but he'd explained it only in a vague manner typical of how men were often inclined, leaving much to be imagined. She'd finally been told every detail, by Mary, who had visited often in the days following Alainn's grave mishap. Alainn had been curious to ask Mary how she'd found her wedding night, when she'd expected it to be such an unpleasant ordeal, but they'd not had much time alone. Alainn judged by Mary's happiness and radiance, she'd not found it nearly as objectionable as she'd been led to believe she might.

Molly had come to see her often, so her days were not spent entirely in boredom, and only occasionally when she was not alone, did Killian dare to venture away further than the castle walls. She had encouraged him and insisted she would be quite well, but he seemed to need the reassurance that being close at hand had given him.

Alainn had grown closer to her aunt, Lady Siobhan O'Brien, as well. Though they'd always been connected more than any lady and a commoner should be, now that they knew they were blood kin, they continued to strengthen the connection. To Alainn's utter delight, her aunt had ensured her cherished Irish harp be brought to Alainn's bedchamber.

At first knowing how Alainn was drawn to music, her aunt simply soothed and entertained her niece during her time of rest and healing, but soon Alainn showed an interest and aptitude toward music as with so many ancient druid talents. Her aunt instructed her in learning how to play the lovely harp and in little time her aunt claimed Alainn was playing as well as she did. Though she doubted that, noting how gifted Lady Siobhan was at bringing the music to life with a beautiful and poignant clarity, Alainn reveled in the fact she was now also capable of playing the harp. She knew the gift would be a treasure and a solace to her throughout her entire life. Killian adored sitting with her and listening to the lovely, melodic Celtic pieces she loved so well and produced so effortlessly.

Hugh O'Brien and his captain, Mackenzie MacArthur, and his entire army had made a valiant effort to discover who might have aided the priest in his attack on Alainn, but no conclusive clues had ever been found. Alainn knew no other trace would be found, for she knew his accomplice had not been human. The dark demon that had come to her in the dungeon was surely responsible for the priest's actions. He had gotten to him and to Richard McGilvary for both had possessed dark souls and been willing to aid him in his misdeeds.

Alainn shuddered when she thought of the hideously evil being and it frightened her more than she would care to admit, knowing he or perhaps any other dark creature of evil origin could surely take human form. She was nearly certain she had not seen the last of such abhorrent devils.

Ramla's spirit had come to Alainn and he explained to her that not long before his death he had seen someone he believed was a demon. He had come to him in attempt to employ him to concoct a strong poison. He had refused and cast him away from him with a magical distancing spell. But, he'd known it was only a temporary spell. And apparently the demon had found someone who aided him in creating a potion and then gotten it to the priest. Alainn couldn't, in all her dwelling upon the matter, determine who that might be.

What disturbed Alainn most about all of this was not even the fact that the Ramla described him as she'd seen him in human form, dressed entirely in dark clothes, with dark black hair and eyes, and that he'd spoken in an English accent as she'd heard herself. It was that when Ramla saw him he was in human form and he'd seen him in daylight. Surely only the most powerful and darkest demons must possess powers that allowed them to present themselves in human form in the light of day.

She had not told Killian about what had occurred in the dungeon or of what Ramla had told her regarding the demon. She was ruefully hesitant to keep another secret from him, but she saw no benefit to him being fretful about an enemy he could not fight. He had already suffered greatly trying to protect her, both her honor and her life. She remembered when she'd woken and seen him wounded, his face and body a mass of cuts and abrasions, she'd wanted to heal him. But, it had been the desperate state of a breaking heart and his woeful soul in seeing her so close to death that had caused him the worst pain. She was not eager to have any type of discord between them or unpleasantness for them anytime soon. She felt they'd both been through quite enough for a very long while. But through all of this, Alainn believed Killian's once strong faith had been renewed.

Alainn had been saddened and disappointed to learn that Danhoul had left Castle O'Brien without so much as a brief word to her. Killian justified his sudden departure, explaining his intent to immediately return to his duties in the kern, the Irish army. Alainn felt that didn't excuse him leaving without a word of farewell or Godspeed. She wasn't certain if it was because of his deep guilt or regret at being unable to assist in healing her, or if in truth he'd simply been called away, perhaps by the gods who had once insisted he was to be her guardian.

Occasionally, she sensed him nearby and in her dreams she was certain she could sometimes hear his voice reaching her through telepathy, but mostly he seemed incapable or unwilling to speak with her at this time. She would respect this, though she was almost certain that she and the young druid, Danhoul Calhoun, would one day cross paths again.

Chapter Thirty-Five

THE CASTLE HAD finally returned to common everyday life, for all the guests who had come to attend the games and celebrations had returned to their own lands and their chiefdoms. The McDonnels of Glynn had left their daughters and their niece to begin their lives with their new husbands, and headed back to the far north. Alainn's grandfather had gone home as well. She'd become emotional when he'd come to say his farewell to her. Though they'd only known each other a short time, she felt close to him and was thankful she would soon be allowed to become better acquainted with him when she and Killian journeyed to their home.

Riley and Mary had gone as well. Although Riley had mostly patched up his differences with his father, he had decided it would be advantageous to become chieftain of the O'Rorke clan, with assistance from his grandfather, of course. Though Alainn wondered how Riley and their grandfather might manage their relationship and their chiefdom when they claimed such vast differences of opinions in religious matters, she felt Riley had matured much in the last months, and that her grandfather's calming nature would be a good influence on the younger man.

She and Mary had shed many tears when they'd said their parting words as well. They had become close friends and Alainn was pleased she would soon only live a short distance from them. How peculiar fate was for the woman who was to have been Killian's wife, Alainn now thought of as a valued friend.

Lady Siobhan had remained here at Castle O'Brien for the time being. Although she had spoken of ending her relationship with her husband, she had chosen not to leave with her father and Riley and Mary when they'd gone on to Castle O'Rorke. Alainn knew the decision was weighing heavy on her mind. She recalled their recent conversation regarding the situation.

"Ahh, dear Alainn, with all these magical abilities you possess, would you be capable of telling me what path is best for me? Might you look into my future and tell me what I should do?"

"Nay, 'tis certainly not a decision that should be made by way of magic, and I have attempted to calm all my powers and abstain from using magic at least until my child is born. Sure this harrowing decision can't be made by anyone bar you, Aunt Siobhan."

Her aunt's lovely face appeared drawn and weary with the weight of her worry and her eyes held an uncommon sadness and the puffiness of having shed many tears regarding her future, and the difficult choice she had before her.

"Well, if not by use of your abilities might you give me any female advice simply as my niece and my friend, another woman whose opinion I highly value?"

"Well, firstly you must tell me how you feel regarding your husband; do you maintain feelings for him? Do you love the man?"

She seemed to contemplate this for a time before she spoke. "I did not love Hugh when we were married; I admit full well that truth. It was an arranged marriage and of course, I had the usual reservations and concerns when we were wed. I thought he was a handsome sort, and I was attracted to him. He did not mistreat me. He could be harsh and demanding as a chieftain, but as a husband he was not unkind. In truth, I did grow to love him. We created our two fine boys and we shared in the love and pride of being parents.

All was well for a time, we were happy, I suppose, and then the curse was upon us. After we lost our babies, five times we went through the unimaginable grief and despair of losing five wee newborn babes, Hugh changed markedly, and so did I. We no longer shared a bed, by my request for I couldn't bear the thought of carrying another child all those months to full term knowing it would be lost as well.

He did not force himself upon me of which I suppose I am thankful. I knew he had taken other women to still his desires. I accepted it for I was unwilling to go to his bed. Of course it pained me knowing I was his wife and he bedded any number of other women, but I was resigned to the fact. And so we lived out our lives in such a manner for so many years. I knew when he looked at me that he desired me still; that he did care for me in his own way."

Alainn looked at her aunt with much empathy as she spoke on.

"I did not think of him as a bad man, of course as a chieftain he needed to make harsh decisions that were not always easy and perform tasks that I'm certain he did not relish, but it was only recently that I felt his temperament and characteristics changed so drastically. He became a stranger that I did not know and I most certainly did not care for."

"Aye, I never thought of your husband as an unreasonable man. I considered him to be a fair chieftain. It is clear the combinations and amounts of the remedies and elixirs he was ingesting severely altered his temperament and affected his mind."

"Aye, I know he committed some terrible deeds and I am well aware I know not all of what he did. I see how Killian despises his uncle and that was long before he was issued the lashes in your stead. I understand Killian's anger when at the time Hugh ordered the lashings he knew you were with child. That in itself is surely unforgivable. I am certain the information I do not possess has much to do with Hugh attempting to keep you apart. Killian is a wise man for his young age and I feel inclined to agree with him, if he cannot forgive Hugh then I am uncertain if I can either."

Alainn turned away at these words for there were, indeed, many events her aunt was unaware of, one being that Hugh had attempted to rape Alainn and that he had also ordered the two vile, untrustworthy McGilvary brothers to have their wicked way with her as well. Even still, Alainn did accredit much of his instability and bad judgment to the use of mixing herbal remedies. An alchemist and a healer had great responsibility in handing out remedies and the alchemist in Galway had given Hugh elixirs that most certainly affected his mind. In truth, a vast many people were driven to madness because of such misdeeds.

If Alainn ever thought of actually attempting to speak in explanation of Hugh O'Brien's unsavory state and grave misdeeds, Killian refused to listen to her insistent reasoning. Even with the challenge ended, with Killian sparing his uncle's life and Hugh saving Killian's life, Alainn believed they would never truly be close again. Killian could never forgive the man for all he'd done to her and to keep them apart. Her continued attempts in deducting how gravely detrimental the herbal potions had ill affected him did nothing to ease Killian's disdain for his uncle, and she knew he felt a sense of betrayal when she attempted to ease the differences between them. Alainn believed she actually harbored fewer ill feelings toward the man than Killian did.

She surmised her husband's pride and loyalty were a

force to be reckoned with and, when crossed, he would not be inclined to forgive. Yet deep within her heart, Alainn felt there was a distinct possibility the chieftain had been plagued and pursued by the dark demon, and that in his mad condition and darkened state, the demon had perhaps nearly won him over.

Alainn would never be able to loathe Hugh O'Brien completely for he *had* saved Killian's life and because of that, part of her would always be thankful to the man. Now that the chieftain had refrained from taking the herbal remedies he appeared to be returning to the man Alainn had once trusted and defended. She did not envy her aunt in her difficult decision for past mistakes and wrongdoings held much weight, yet without forgiveness future peace would surely be impossible.

"Sure it must be you who decides what must be done, Aunt Siobhan. And whatever decision you come to, you know I shall respect it and forever support you."

The other woman warmly embraced her and smiled gratefully. "I am most appreciative of you, Alainn. I have always been, since long before you were known to be my kin. You saved the life of my dear, precious son, Rory, and I am thankful every day for that.

In truth, it may not be Hugh I consider in this decision as much as Rory. He is a dear son to me and a good, kind, sensitive man. I know he will miss his twin most assuredly and being apart will weigh heavy on his gentle heart. They have spent their entire lives together, barely ever been apart. Before Riley journeyed with his new bride to live with father, surely my twin boys had never been parted longer than a day at most. I cannot imagine that I could leave Rory, as well, and to be apart indefinitely and far distanced from him, not when I have nearly lost him twice before, to the fever and the fall from the tower.

Riley will have my patient and loving father to see him safe, and you and Killian will be nearby also, and so I will not worry for him as readily. And perhaps if I remain here, I might serve as a voice of reason when Rory and his father are surely at odds with the joint chieftainship for Rory has already begun to join in many of the duties of a chieftain."

"I believe you may have made the decision after all." Alainn smiled, and the other woman nodded.

"I believe I have at that!"

Alainn recalled the relieved expression on her aunt's face as she'd taken leave from the chamber in a much lighter disposition as though a great weight had been lifted from her.

Chapter Thirty-Six

A S ALAINN RESTED upon the settee and brushed her
lengthy hair, she continued to dwell on the events of
the past weeks. The old farrier had died. Alainn had felt
deeply affected by his passing. She had not expected to
experience such sadness. Although they'd never been close
and she hadn't lived with him since a very young age, she
had always thought of him as her father. And though it had
proven to be incorrect, a part of her would always feel like
the farrier's daughter.

Now Mara had title to his cottage and was living there.
Hugh O'Brien had greatly surprised Alainn by allowing
Mara to take over her duties as healer once more. And the
physician seemed most accepting of her. In fact, Alainn
noticed how Thomas O'Donaugh had been looking at her
mother most appraisingly as of late. She believed he might
well be quite smitten with her. She was, in truth, a very
beautiful woman, and even the residents of the castle and the
villagers seemed to no longer fear her and were accepting her
now that the chieftain and his family had so clearly done so.

Rory had stopped by to visit Alainn often in the past

weeks. Rory was one of her most treasured people. He was warm and caring and they shared an unusual sense of humor. Ever since they'd been children she'd thought of him as a friend, but perhaps nearly as close as a brother. She'd been undoubtedly pleased to learn they were cousins and she was very much relieved she'd been able to go back in time and prevent his death. She seldom allowed herself to think of that day for each time it made her heartsick.

Rory had come to see her again just yesterday and Alainn recalled their pleasant conversation.

"You look most jubilant and mirthful, Rory! I am well pleased you and Brigid are happily wed."

"Aye, she's turned out to be a lovely girl, Alainn. We get along splendidly and she's quite humorous as well, when she's kept away from her sister for a time!" he added in confidence.

"I'm well pleased, Rory, to know you will live a happy, wedded life."

"And I you, Alainn. I was beyond despair when we thought you would not live, and now you are radiant once more and I see the love that shines in your eyes for Killian and he for you."

"Aye, we shall both live happy lives, Rory!" She beamed.

He'd held her tight for a moment, smiled at her, and kissed her cheek as he'd left. Though she'd always despised the notion of having someone choose a husband for her, with seeing Rory so well matched with Brigid, she'd been forced to admit, occasionally, arranged marriages worked out remarkably well.

So seldom had she been left on her own in all these weeks, she hadn't realized how much she'd needed this time to collect her thoughts and sort out her feelings. As she'd told her aunt, she'd allowed her powers to become almost entirely dormant. Other than the witchcraft required to assist in healing Killian, herself, and their unborn son, she had used no magic. And she was content with that... for now.

Maybe the dark ones would not be so interested in her if she allowed her powers to simply be kept hidden. She doubted that and, as always, she wrestled with the ever-present notion that leaving them hidden and allowing them to become less than perfected might well be a detriment when dealing with a being of such evil origins. It was a conundrum best left to dwell upon another day and perhaps it was something that would never be clear to her.

She touched her amulet and felt the raised ridge on the back. On both her mother's and grandfather's insistence, the O'Rorke crest that had belonged to her father, Teige, had been forged to her own amulet. And when she touched it, she felt close to him. One day when she felt stronger, she would employ her powers in attempt to search for him, for she sensed he still lived. When their child had been born, she would use her abilities to see what she could see.

The English had once more become a force within Ireland. More and more often messengers brought reports of

English soldiers being spotted in many areas. Once mostly restricted to The Pale in Dublin in the east of Ireland, they had slowly begun to penetrate many areas and Alainn knew minor battles had already been fought, and she did not need to possess the gift of second sight to know there would be many more. They had begun to place and enforce strict laws once more and Alainn had heard once again they had taken to controlling much of everyday life of the Irish. They were apparently strictly forbidding the spoken Gaelic language and the manner of dress as they had done in the past. She signed and wondered if the Irish would ever be entirely free of the rule of the English.

She'd had the disturbing vision more and more often, the one she had first witnessed in Galway, and it was the exact image of what she'd seen then. And, once again, Killian, Riley, and Rory had been killed at the hands of the English. She'd been wide awake so she knew well enough it had not been a dream, and she'd broken into a cold sweat, and as before it had seemed so real she'd been relieved to see Killian walk into the room, well and unharmed.

When Riley had left to go to their grandfather's castle, she had breathed a heavy sigh of relief, for if the three were not together, they could not die together as the vision had implied. Before he left, she'd called the three of them to her bedside and warned all of them, that much to their displeasure, they could not all three be together, perhaps never again! She remembered the reaction she'd gotten from the often stubborn Riley, by making that suggestion.

"You can't truly mean to tell me you believe Rory and Killian and I cannot ever be together again?" Riley had scoffed at her insistence.

"Aye, that is precisely what I'm indicating. I have seen the three of you dead on a bloodied moor after doing battle with the English. I cannot say where it is to happen or even when it will take place. I am not remotely certain how to prevent it. The only solution I can now render is this manner of separation. If the three of you are apart then surely you cannot die together. I do not mean to suggest you cannot see Rory again or Killian, or that Rory and Killian cannot be together, just not the three of you, not at the same time."

"Well I'll not have it, Alainn! You'll not dictate what time I spend with my brother or my cousin!" Riley had stormed out of the bedchamber.

But Killian and Rory had taken her completely seriously and agreed without question.

"Don't pay attention to my unruly brother, Alainn. You know well he doesn't take kindly to be bein' told what to do. But I'll do what I can to see to it we all do as you've instructed. As I've told you many times, your powers saved my life once before when you experienced that telling vision so long ago and because of that I have been allowed to live these past ten years. If you believe this is the way to ensure we remain safe then I'll do what I must to abide by your wishes."

"As will I, Alainn," Killian had agreed.

She knew how difficult it would be for them, for they'd been together and the closest of kin for so long. But with Riley to the central area of Ireland, even though Killian would be close by, Rory would be at least a hard day's ride from them. She felt better knowing that. And she'd stressed again to all of them they must never enter into battle with the English if all three could end up on the same battlefield.

She'd made her grandfather and Hugh O'Brien listen intently to the portent warnings as well. And, much like Riley, she didn't believe Hugh was entirely confident in her prophetic visions. However, her grandfather had worn such a look of certain dread at the possibility of losing his grandsons and Killian in battle, he had sworn he, too, would do all in his power to make certain her vision could never come to fruition.

Killian had been displeased that she had wanted to speak with his uncle even on this topic, for things had not been mended between them. Alainn had decided she would soon convince Killian they must make the journey to their own home. She knew he wanted to be distanced from his uncle, to begin their life together, and that he was eager to become chieftain as he was destined to be.

She felt the sturdy movement within her and smiled. She would be thankful always that she had not lost their son. She prayed all was well with him and that the poison had caused no ill effects that would be presented upon his birth. She felt a persistent needling within her whenever she dwelled upon the time of his birth, an uneasiness that she pushed far back within her mind and would not allow herself to think upon it.

Surely, within the week, she would be able to persuade Killian to take her to their home, to their impressive castle on the lovely land near the sea. She remembered the night they'd spent there and she felt a heat within her. She'd missed being with her husband in an intimate manner. How she longed once more to have him love her and for them to reclaim the passion they once shared.

Killian had agreed he would share their bed for he did not want to be apart from her, but he'd kept his distance save a quick kiss or a short loving embrace. Persuading him it would be safe for them to make love would be perhaps a difficult feat. As it stood now, he would barely allow her to brush her lips to his, even though she recognized the fact he had begun to look at her with desire in his eyes once more. She would not have him seeking out a servant girl or making a trip to Galway City to find a harlot to ease his needs. No, they would resume their physical intimacy, and soon, she thought, for she could hardly go for months without him loving her.

Alainn slowly made her way back into the bedchamber and glanced at her reflection in the mirror. She was still pale, but surely a pleasant walk in the sunshine would remedy that. Her hair remained shiny and healthy-looking. She glanced at her figure in the large, oval looking glass that hung upon the wall, as she turned to the side she saw the tiny swelling in her belly. She smiled at that. She was pleased her blessed condition was becoming outwardly evident.

As she glanced at the shiny reflection in the mirror, she thought of the fairy glade. She often thought of the fairy glade. When she thought of the glade, she thought of the time they'd spent there after they'd been wed and it reminded her yet again of their passion, and once again she felt herself wanting Killian in that manner. It seemed no matter what subject she'd brought to mind in the past few days, she ended up feeling in need of a time between the bedsheets with her husband.

When she thought of the glade it also made her dwell on the disturbing vision she had seen when she'd glanced into the portal that led to the future. It had foretold of a time when she would be there, in a future she did not desire. She disliked pondering that and decided there was little use fretting about it. Fate had a way of dealing its blows or blessings and sometimes she thought it best to leave it to its will.

She stood on the open area once more and glanced down at the ground below. She gazed at the garden. She would miss the herb garden, but Killian had already promised her she could develop as big a garden as she'd like at their castle, and she would take many of the herbs from this garden to begin her own.

She knew she would miss the castle itself, for she did

adore Castle O'Brien, although there had been undeniable unpleasantness, she had spent her childhood here and it housed many happy memories. It was where she'd met Killian, spent so much time with him, and where they'd fallen in love.

She would also miss the herb chamber and the kitchen as well as the people here at the castle; the people who had always been an intricate part of her life. She would miss Cook and Margaret, Molly, and their family. Molly and Pierce would be wed next spring and both were noticeably unhappy about the prospect of Pierce moving with his father to Killian's castle, while Molly stayed behind with her family. But Cook would not allow them to be wed until his daughter turned six and ten. He was firm on that point and would not be swayed.

Mac and Cook and Margaret had assured them time would pass quickly and if their affection toward one another was truly strong and meant to be it would withstand a time of separation. They had agreed they would allow Molly and Pierce to visit a time or two in the next year. Alainn was certain their love would span the time and the distance, but she was most empathetic of how the two young people must be feeling for she knew a year apart from Killian would seem an insufferably long time.

Alainn had been most pleased to learn that Cookson would be journeying to their castle as well, for Killian had employed him as head cook. The young man had been hesitant at first and somewhat disbelieving that Killian wanted him when Castle O'Donnel surely already boasted a cook, but Killian explained the man was elderly and had expressed his desire to leave once Killian had found another to replace him. So Cookson had agreed wholeheartedly.

And in contemplating all she would miss here, Alainn thought of her mother. She believed she would miss Mara. Although she'd felt angered and bitter when she'd first learned Mara had kept the secret of her parentage for so long, she'd grown to understand the reasoning. And perhaps, more importantly now that she carried a child, she understood what an extreme sacrifice Mara had made to allow her to have a chance at a normal life. She felt sad in knowing that now that she'd begun to care for and become closer to her mother, they would soon be parted again. But they would not be such an insurmountable distance apart they would never see each other.

Alainn knew she would miss many of her friends, but she was grateful Riley and Mary would be living nearby and Mac, Pierce, and Cookson would all be there living in the castle, and sure she would make many new friends at Castle O'Donnel. She suspected she would surely make a few enemies as well. She always seemed to manage that!

She would miss the fairy glade here, but she knew there were many other glades. In truth, the fairies had once told her she would only ever have to imagine and look and there would be a glade, or tree, or hill inhabited by fairies somewhere nearby, so numerous were they in Ireland. Sure there'd be many close to Killian's castle as well.

She decided she'd had quite enough on dwelling upon what she would miss here, at what she would be leaving behind, for she would be starting an exciting new life with her husband, and soon their son and that was all that really mattered to her. She would from now on simply choose to look forward for she and Killian would make many new happy memories of their own at Castle O'Donnel.

She was suddenly overcome by the distinct scent of thyme. As she heard a soft sound behind her she turned to see Morag's spirit beside her. She was elated to see the spirit of the old healer. She hadn't been able to come to her in a long while, and they'd not actually spoken since Alainn had journeyed to the spirit world. Morag had insistently urged Alainn to go back, to return to her life with her husband, and Alainn believed this woman who had been so influential to her in life had been equally so when she hovered between life and death. For although Mara believed it was the evening nightshade potion that had counteracted the initial poisoning, Alainn believed it was surely God's will and Morag's strong pleading that had greatly affected the outcome.

"You look well, caileag leanabh! Though I see well enough, you are clearly no longer a child, my dear, Alainn." The old woman stared at the young woman's slightly swollen middle.

Alainn felt the tears threatening to fall for the old woman

had never ever referred to her by her given name, not in all the years that she had lived with the old healer. She went to the woman and to both their surprise, she was able to actually embrace Morag's spirit. She held on tightly until the old woman finally moved away.

"Your powers grow more diverse and ever stronger, my darlin' girl. You must be cautious in using them."

"I know, Morag, you have always warned me of such, and perhaps I would have been wise to listen more closely."

"But, sure you were given them for a reason."

"Aye, but will I ever really know the reason entirely, Morag? Do you suppose?"

"I wonder that myself. I always have since you were a wee girl, even before you came to live with me."

"I'd somehow forgotten the time you spent with me when I was still a young infant. You cared for me even long before it was your duty."

"Aye, well I cared for your mother and her mother as well. Three generations of the fairy line of Aine."

"You knew all those years we descended from Aine?"

"Aye, she came to me one night when your grandmother was only a wee babe, only days old, to ensure I was carryin' out my part of the bargain."

"You bargained with Aine?"

"Aye, she asked me to care for her child the night after she left her here in the castle's courtyard. I would have done so anyway, for she was a beautiful wee baby, as you all were.

But she insisted I be given a wish. I was given the gift of healing, and it allowed a life of reasonable health and safety for me and you girls as well."

"But sure it cost you so very much, Morag. You never married, never had children of your own. You spent your entire life dedicated to healing others and raising us."

"But I was of an advanced age by most standards even when Ainna came to live with me, and I tell you now it was well worth it all, caileag. I was a healer since I was a young girl for I learned all that I knew from my father. My path was chosen long before any of you came to be my charges; in fact, when I was but a young woman not yet your own age, my entire family was stricken by an unrelenting plague. They were one by one taken from me in a matter of days. Then and there I decided I would continue to be a healer and do what I could to ensure no one else I cared for would be taken without a mighty fight from me.

So when Aine enlisted me with the task of raising her tweenling child, I bargained for the ability to magically heal others so I might ensure the dear girl I was instructed to raise was kept safe and well. Alas, even so, I was not able to save her for she died brokenhearted only days after her she birthed your mother, I suppose you areas much aware as anyone even magic does not always hold the solution of ensuring all will be well. I do pray your line will now be free of unrest for your female kin have had their share of misfortune and now you as well, caileag leanabh!"

Alainn nodded solemnly, and both felt it was unlikely herself or any of her descendants would be entirely free of tribulations and woes. But who, human, witch, or any other species, truly was, Alainn wondered? Even the fairies had their burdens to bear, which was not often a consideration. Morag's voice pulled her from her deep thoughts.

"And you have now mended the soreness between yourself and Mara. That pleases me, also. She was once so dear to me, as well, though I never truly showed any of you—Ainna, Mara or you, caileag, how truly blessed I was to have each of you in my life. I seldom showed any form of affection or warmth. I never told you how very precious you were to me, how much you enriched my life. I never dared to speak the words aloud. I thought it would make you soft, unable to deal with all life's difficulties if I did not harden you. Perhaps I was wrong in that."

"We knew how much you cared, Morag, through all your gruffness on the exterior, we knew your heart was full of love for us. You may not have birthed us, but you raised three of us and we could not have loved you any more if we'd been born of your body."

"I know you will leave this location soon, caileag. Listen well to your husband, and allow him to guide you if not rule you. He loves you entirely and will always have your best interest at heart, though I'm certain there will be times you will question that. I will miss you, caileag, but I'll watch over you when I can. Though I sense I won't come to you again.

Alainn glanced at her, a brief hint of sadness in her eyes, but she did not disagree knowing the woman had lived her life and that her place was now beyond, in the spirit world.

"Be happy always, caileag! That will gladden an old woman's heart."

"I am happy, Morag. Though I shall miss you, I will think of you often and be grateful to you till the end of my days when it is my time to join you in the beyond."

The woman nodded, squeezed her hand one more time and then before she left, the spectral image of Ainna appeared. The two spirits smiled at one another and then at Alainn as they faded away together.

Alainn felt strangely content after Morag left as if she simply knew that was how it was meant to be, and she would not pine for the old woman who had lived a life that was long and full. She was also most pleased that Ainna and Morag would remain together eternally.

She heard the door open behind her and saw Killian walking toward her. When their eyes locked, he beamed.

"You're mirthful, Alainn, and you appear much improved. Your eyes and your cheeks are beginning to glow with health and radiance again! You've not overdone it though, standing for so long, have you?"

"Stop doting on me, Killian O'Brien, sure you sound like an aged, old crone." She smiled as she spoke.

"Back to barraging me; that must be a good omen. Sure you're nearly mended." He grinned.

"I am mended, Killian. My health is entirely restored!" She exclaimed exuberantly.

Killian raised his eyebrow as he gently took her in his arms. "Do I have reason to be concerned?" he asked suspiciously.

"Concerned, about what?" She seemed genuinely uncertain of his meaning.

"Of what you're about to attempt to make me do, or what you are about to request of me?"

"What makes you believe I am to ask something of you?"

"Your eyes hold that mischievous glint, the one I noticed the first day you came to me, and have seen perhaps a thousand times since. And your lovely, full lips twitch ever so slightly when you wish to ask me or convince me of something that you know full well I'll not be in favor of doin'."

She smiled up at him. "You know me far too well, milord."

"Aye, and I revel in that, Lainna!"

"I wish to finally make the long overdue journey to your castle."

" 'Tis a difficult ride. Even by coach, it is a long way and the road is not smooth."

"The road to what our hearts' desire is never smooth, Killian. And do you intend for us to wait here the remainder of my term, and for our son to be born here at Castle O'Brien?"

"If that is what is necessary for the two of you to remain

safe and well, then we shall stay here, aye!"

"I am well…we are well. I promise you, Killian. We can employ a coach and not travel on horseback if that is what you wish. We can go slowly, take a week to make the journey if you will simply agree to it. I am a gifted healer; surely I know when I am well, and our son, also."

He glanced down into her eyes and saw the excitement and eagerness within the lovely blue pools.

"My plight is greater!" he began.

"And why is it greater?" She smiled happily, playing along with the familiar game they'd begun so long ago.

"Because I do, indeed, desperately long to leave this place behind us, to begin our new life together, perhaps even more so than you, Alainn, but I must know with no uncertainty that you are well and that it will be entirely safe for you to make the journey."

"I am well! Trust me, Killian. I shall make the journey without incident and, in two days' time, we will be at your castle."

"*Our* castle, Alainn, all that is mine is yours, and you just told me we would take a week to make the journey!" He teased.

"Only if it is necessary, and that is what you desire, my love!"

She stepped closer to him and placed her arms around his neck, allowing her body to rest against his. He attempted to move from her, but she pulled his head down to hers so that she could kiss him deeply and passionately.

"Alainn!" He scolded her when he finally managed to break from the ardent kiss.

" 'Tis my plight that is surely greater." She pouted. "For clearly my husband now thinks of me as a matronly old, married woman, ripening with child and no longer desirable in his eyes!"

"You're a nasty, wee imp and you well know it! You're as lovely a creature ever created, and as beguiling as any woman who ever lived. And the fact you carry my child has surely only made you more radiantly beautiful! You fairly glow, Lainna! You know very well how badly I want you, and that it is not a possibility for me to bed you, yet still you insist on temptin' me."

"But, Killian, why do you believe it is not possible for us to be together?"

"You nearly died, Alainn. And you very nearly lost the child, sure there's no safe way to be with you in a physically intimate manner and not jeopardize the babe!"

"We are both well; I'm entirely recovered, Killian. And I need you. I miss being with you so very much. Tell me you don't miss making love to me."

"Aye, you know well enough I miss bein' with you, surely more than I could possibly begin to express to you, but I won't let my desires rule me and endanger the child, or you."

"It will be a very long few months, Killian. I am only just passed the middle of my term. 'Tis now only late summer and the babe is not expected till early winter."

"I know well enough when he is to be expected, and I am aware it is a goodly long time to be without you, but I suspect I am not the first man who has been made to wait so long, for others have faced the same set of circumstances."

"You will most certainly be the first that will not simply be permitted to stray, or be forgiven should you take a mistress, a servant, or a whore to ease your desires!" she said, this time her voice had become filled with jealousy.

"I'll take no other woman, Alainn, not ever! You were not to question my faithfulness ever again, you'll recall. You told me you would not. How can you think so little of me, to suggest I would want another woman when I have been given the greatest gift imaginable in having you come back to me from the brink of death?"

"A man's desires are great. Your desires are great, Killian," she continued, "and there are temptations all around you. Women practically throw themselves at you, and are willin' to lift their skirts at even a sideways glance from you." She had slowly made her way to his side again and was presently caressing his broad chest, but only momentarily for he effortlessly picked her up and carried her to the bed. When she'd barely begun to believe he was finally going to make love to her, he gently settled her and began walking toward the door.

"Killian O'Brien, get yourself back here this instant and make love to me, or I swear I'll find someone else who will, for clearly my desires are great as well."

"But you're so entirely old, married, and matronly, how could you possibly accomplish the task of finding anyone who might care to bed you?" He taunted.

She began furiously tossing the many pillows at him as she continued to pout prettily. "I suspect I might find some elderly man whose eyesight is not keen, or some young man who has never had a woman and is so desperate he won't care what I look like, only that I'm needing someone to ravage me!"

"You're not rilin' me, Alainn. I know you're set on doing so and only hopin' to make me come to you and accomplish what you've set out to do."

"And am I to be at all hopeful it might eventually occur?" she asked as she lay upon the bed in a most seductive manner.

"Use your good sense, Alainn. We can't be together. You might just as well become accustomed to the notion for I won't be swayed."

"I'll bewitch you!" She threatened. "Give you a love potion so unfailingly potent, you'll be filled with such complete lasciviousness you'll not be capable of resisting me."

"I'm barely capable of resistin' you now, you wee vixen; you've no need to create any damnable potion!"

"Then come here to me, Killian. I am most serious. All is well, and I need you, and I love you. And it can be slow and gentle and tender, if you wish, but please just come love me before I go mad with desire for you."

"Jesus, Mary, and Joseph, you have a way about you, Alainn. You'd be capable of talkin' a starvin' man out of his very last morsel of food, you would!"

" 'Tis not food, I am hungry for!" She cooed as she began to sensually remove the fastenings of her gown and let it slowly slide down her shoulders and breasts, to reveal she had no chemise beneath the garment. A look of complete surrender crossed his handsome face, and there was resolve in his green eyes, mingled with evident passion.

He drew nearer to her, took her face in his hands and looked deep into her eyes. "I will not see you hurt in any way, Lainna!"

"I'll not be hurt, Killian, unless I am made to be without you till winter and beyond for often a time without physical love is required after the birth of a babe. You must come love me now. I promise you as a healer and a seer, our bein' together will be good for both of us."

"Oh, I've no doubt, but it would be good." He felt himself drowning in her sensuality, and he finally relented and kissed her, a thorough, deep, and dizzying kiss. She moaned and pulled at his tunic and tugged his trews impatiently.

"Oh no, Alainn, you said you'd be willin' to have it slow and gentle, and that my sweet, Lainna, is what you'll get."

⌘

LATER AS THEY lay together beneath the bedcovers, tenderly

holding and caressing each other, she smiled up at him in contentment and in elated satisfaction, she sighed appreciatively. He chuckled.

"Well, Alainn McCreary O'Rorke O'Brien, since apparently you appear to get your way so entirely, sure you must tell me, would the day after tomorrow suit you well to be off to our castle, to begin our new life together, then?"

"Aye, Killian O'Brien." She smiled sweetly at her husband. "It would suit me most well, sure 'tis time we begin this next chapter in our lives and that I truly begin to experience life and new adventures as a chieftain's wife.

THE END

Don't miss any of Leigh Ann Edwards' books in…

THE IRISH WITCH SERIES

Book 1: *The Farrier's Daughter*

Book 2: *The Witch's Daughter*

Book 3: *The Chieftain's Daughter*

ABOUT THE AUTHOR

Since she was a child, Leigh Ann Edwards has always had a vivid imagination and lots of stories to tell. An enthusiastic traveler and author for over twenty years, her adventures in Massachusetts, Ireland, and the UK inspired The Farrier's Daughter and its sequel novels in the Irish Witch series. Edwards adores animals, history, genealogy, and magical places—and Ireland is filled with many magical places. She lives with her husband and two cats in the lovely city of Edmonton, Alberta.

Visit Leigh Ann at www.leighannedwards.com

Thank you for reading

The Chieftain's Daughter

If you enjoyed this book, you can find more from all our great authors at TulePublishing.com, or from your favorite online retailer.

TULE
PUBLISHING

Made in the USA
Middletown, DE
19 January 2022

59153752R00229